Everyone loves Angel's Bay!

AT HIDDEN FALLS

"Angel's Bay shines in Freethy's talented hands as she updates the lives of continuing characters, adds several memorable new ones, and dusts it all with magic and hope."

—*Library Journal*

"Reading *At Hidden Falls* is like learning more about personal friends and close relatives, as they continue to reside in your thoughts long after the book is finished."

—Single Titles

"A compelling, magical story of love, heartbreak, happiness, community, and courage . . . fast paced."

—My Book Addiction and More

"Truly a work of art . . . a very satisfying read."

—Joyfully Reviewed

"A lovely romance. . . . It is always fun to visit the little town on the bay."

—*Romantic Times*

IN SHELTER COVE

"A compelling story of intrigue, along with a romantic story of love, forgiveness, and faithfulness."

—Fresh Fiction

"A good solid romance and a spine-tingling mystery all in a tidy package.... Freethy does a fine job of keeping us guessing [and she] continues several ongoing stories to keep things fresh. I can't wait to see where they will lead as the series continues."

—A Romance Review

ON SHADOW BEACH

"A lovely contemporary romance."

—*Romantic Times*

"*On Shadow Beach* teems with action, drama and compelling situations.... A fast-paced page-turner that unravels small-town scandals and secrets."

—*BookPage*

"*On Shadow Beach* has a fascinating touch of magic plus an abundance of genuinely heartfelt emotions, where everything is wrapped around an intriguing mystery."

—Single Titles

"This compelling story is fast-paced, filled with renewed acquaintances, complicated relationships and plenty of mystery. You will love the story and be surprised on several accounts by the ending."

—Fresh Fiction

"An excellent, easy-to-read novel. It flows beautifully with intriguing and appealing characters. It will grab you within the first few pages and just keeps getting better."

—Romance Reviews Today

SUDDENLY ONE SUMMER

"*Suddenly One Summer* delivers a double whammy to the heart. Ms. Freethy cuts to the core with her depiction of a woman in jeopardy and a man who no longer believes that life has anything to offer. . . . A story that will keep you spellbound."

—*Winter Haven News Chief* (FL)

"Intriguing, suspenseful."

—*Library Journal*

"*Suddenly One Summer* transported me to be a beautiful place and drew me into a story of family secrets, passion, betrayal and redemption."

—*New York Times* bestselling author Susan Wiggs

"Angel's Bay . . . promises many poignant and heartwarming stories."

—Fresh Fiction

"Freethy has written a suspenseful and captivating story, weaving in human frailty along with true compassion, making every page a delight."

—Reader to Reader Reviews

"Angel's Bay is a place I'll want to visit time and again. . . . Freethy has done a beautiful job of weaving a compelling story."

—Romance Novel TV

"A well-written, captivating story, with good pacing that will leave you satisfied as it unfolds . . . fascinating story."

—Romance Reviews Today

The Angel's Bay novels are also available as eBooks

ALSO BY BARBARA FREETHY

At Hidden Falls
In Shelter Cove
On Shadow Beach
Suddenly One Summer

Now Available from Pocket Star

BARBARA
FREETHY

Garden of Secrets

POCKET **STAR** BOOKS

New York   London   Toronto   Sydney   New Delhi

Pocket Star Books
A Division of Simon & Schuster, Inc.
1230 Avenue of the Americas
New York, NY 10020

This book is a work of fiction. Names, characters, places, and incidents either are products of the author's imagination or are used fictitiously. Any resemblance to actual events or locales or persons, living or dead, is entirely coincidental.

First Pocket Star Books paperback edition October 2011

POCKET STAR BOOKS and colophon are registered trademarks of Simon & Schuster, Inc.

For information about special discounts for bulk purchases, please contact Simon & Schuster Special Sales at 1-866-506-1949 or business@simonandschuster.com.

The Simon & Schuster Speakers Bureau can bring authors to your live event. For more information or to book an event, contact the Simon & Schuster Speakers Bureau at 1-866-248-3049 or visit our website at www.simonspeakers.com.

Cover illustration copyright © by Thomas Szadziuk/ Trevillion Images

Manufactured in the United States of America

10 9 8 7 6 5 4 3 2 1

ISBN 978-1-4516-3651-2
ISBN 978-1-4516-3653-6 (ebook)

To Terry for always being there!

ACKNOWLEDGMENTS

I'd like to thank my writing friends who provided wisdom and support during the writing of the Angel's Bay series: Bella Andre, Jami Alden, Anne Mallory, Carol Culver, Lynn Hanna, Diana Dempsey, Kate Moore, Barbara McMahon, Monica McCarty, Tracy Grant, Candice Hern, and Veronica Wolff. And special thanks to Christie Ridgway for always answering the phone when I needed her. I'd also like to thank my family for participating in research field trips as I brought Angel's Bay to life. And to the readers who fell in love with Angel's Bay in the first book, *Suddenly One Summer*, and have read every one since then, I hope you enjoy reading *Garden of Secrets* as much as I enjoyed writing it!

Garden
of Secrets

ONE

New Year's Eve

It was a night for new possibilities, a night for dreaming. But would her dreams last past the stroke of midnight?

They never have before.

Normally an optimist, Charlotte Adams didn't usually worry about the future or think about the past. She'd deliberately lived in the present for more than a decade. But the past few weeks of hectic holidays, family changes, and now the flipping of the calendar made her feel ... restless. She glanced around the crowded room, wondering if she could make an escape.

The mayor, Robert Monroe, and his wife, Theresa, had invited half the town to their New Year's Eve party so they could show off their new home, the stately Sandstone Manor. Sitting on a bluff on the north end of Angel's Bay, the grand old estate had fallen into disrepair over the past thirty years at the hands of a wealthy, eccentric recluse. The hundred-year-old, seven-bedroom, five-bath house with the castlelike turrets, dramatic bay windows, and alleged ghosts had always fascinated the town, and when it had come up for sale two months ago, the Monroes had snapped it up. Everyone who'd been lucky enough to get an invitation to tonight's party had accepted, dying to get a look inside.

Charlotte made her way through the living room, past the dining-room buffet tables laden with shrimp and crab, and into the kitchen, where a busy catering staff didn't give her a second look. She slipped out a side door onto a patio overlooking the sea and reveled in the blessed quiet.

It was a dark night, the moon and stars hidden behind the fog that had rolled in after dusk. The cold, misty breeze felt good against her face. Maybe she could stay out here until the party died down. There would be questions if she tried to ditch before midnight. Most of her friends were inside, and they wanted her to be as happy as they were.

Sighing, she rested her arms on the wood railing, thinking about how many changes they'd all gone through in the last year. Colin had recovered from his shooting, and he and Kara were a family now, their baby getting bigger each day. Jason and Brianna were about to start the new year no longer enemies but lovers. And Lauren and Shane were getting married in two weeks.

Everyone was settling down, and this party was

making her wonder what the hell she was doing with her own life. She had a good career and loved being an ob/gyn, but her personal life was another story. She'd always had great friendships with men, but relationships . . . She had trouble letting anyone get too close to her heart. She never wanted to get hurt again.

The door opened behind her, followed by Kara's cheerful voice. "Charlotte, I've been looking all over for you. It's almost midnight. What are you doing out here?"

"Getting some air," she said with a smile, hoping her friend wouldn't see past it.

"It's freezing," Kara said with a shiver as she wrapped her arms around herself, her dark red hair blowing in the breeze.

"It feels good," Charlotte replied, although her short black party dress was no better defense against the winter wind than Kara's turquoise mini.

"Okay, what's wrong?" Kara asked, giving her a speculative look.

She shrugged. "I don't like New Year's Eve. Everyone makes such a big deal about it, and the night never lives up to its hype. I'd just as soon skip the whole thing."

"Would your cynical mood have something to do with a man?"

"No."

Kara raised an eyebrow. "Really? Because I thought you were coming with Andrew, and he's nowhere in sight."

"Something came up. He said he'd try to get here before midnight, but who knows?" Having grown up with a minister for a father, she knew the demands of Andrew's job. Her father had missed many important occasions in her life. She'd learned early on to lower her expectations.

"I'm sure Andrew won't miss a chance to kiss you at midnight," Kara said.

Charlotte smiled, Kara's words triggering an old memory. "Actually, he missed a New Year's Eve kiss once before. Senior year in high school, I was so excited to finally have a boyfriend on New Year's that I spent all my money on an incredibly hot dress. But Andrew got the flu and spent the night hurling his guts, and I wound up sitting home alone. Just another example of New Year's Eve not living up to its promise."

Kara's eyes sparkled with amusement. "That is a sad story, but you were never a loser." She paused, her expression growing more concerned. "I hope someone isn't in trouble and that's why Andrew isn't here."

"He didn't give me any details when he called." When he'd suggested meeting here tonight, she'd been relieved. Coming to the party together in front of the entire town would have been quite a statement, and she wasn't ready for that yet. Andrew Schilling was a big part of her past, but their future was still to be decided.

"You're going to freeze out here," Kara said. "You should have picked somewhere warmer to hide out."

"It's invigorating—the cold wind, the sound of

the waves crashing against the rocks below. It gets your blood pumping."

"The fog is frizzing my hair."

"So go inside."

"Not without you. I'm worried about you."

"Don't worry, I'll be fine tomorrow," Charlotte reassured her.

"Will you be? Or will you just have your guard back up?"

They'd known each other since they were kids, and Kara was very good at reading between the lines and seeing the truth behind a lie.

"If you don't go back in, your husband will send out a search party," she teased.

"He'd need one in this huge place. It's even more spectacular than I imagined," Kara said. "Theresa certainly got everything she ever wanted."

Charlotte nodded. "I knew Robert came from money, but I didn't realize the Monroes were this wealthy. This house must have cost a fortune."

"One of Robert's uncles recently passed away and left him a bundle. Did you see the diamond necklace Theresa's wearing? It originally belonged to Edward Worthington's wife; it was still around her neck when she washed up dead onshore after the shipwreck."

Charlotte made a face. "Thanks for the visual."

Kara grinned. "Sorry. But I just think it's interesting that Theresa bought herself a link to the shipwreck. She always hated that her family wasn't connected to the survivors who founded Angel's Bay."

"Whatever it takes, I guess."

"I'd feel happier for her good fortune if she'd been a little nicer to us in high school."

Charlotte nodded in agreement. Theresa and her beautiful band of cheerleaders had been a year older than Charlotte, and they'd ruled the school with their own brand of meanness. But Theresa's younger sister, Pamela, had been Charlotte's personal nemesis.

"So can we go in now?" Kara pleaded.

"Sure," she said. "But I'm going to leave. If anyone asks, just say I had a patient to check on."

Kara sighed. "Fine, but I wish you would wait. You could miss out on an awesome kiss."

"I'll take my chances."

When they returned to the party, Kara was swept into conversation with Colin and another couple, so Charlotte slipped through the crowd.

As she turned into the hallway, the front door opened, and Andrew walked in wearing gray slacks and a white button-down shirt under a dark sports coat. Her heart skipped a beat as she took in the tall, lean, golden man with bright blue eyes and an irresistible smile. The first time she'd talked to him, she was sixteen; he'd asked her for a pencil in math class. From that moment on, she'd spent hours doodling their names together and trying to run into him accidentally on purpose.

Andrew had been one of the most popular guys

in high school, and dating him had seemed like an impossible dream. She wasn't one of the cheerleaders or the wild girls who seemed to surround him. But somehow, on one of those "accidental" meetings, they'd started talking, and he'd asked her to hang out after a football game. From there, they'd become inseparable. With Andrew, she'd felt prettier, smarter, more self-confident, and wildly in love. Then the rug had been pulled out from under her. Sixteen and on top of the world turned into eighteen and as sad as could be.

She watched as Andrew made his way down the hall, hampered by the effusive Kelleher sisters, who smothered him with hugs and kisses and high-pitched conversation. The sisters were both divorced, in their late thirties, and they hung out in the local bars on Saturday nights trolling for eligible men. Apparently, they had Andrew in their sights.

Before she could make a move to rescue him, the front door opened again. Joe Silveira entered with a purposeful step, dressed in black slacks, a dark gray shirt, and a black leather jacket. The sexy chief of police was night to Andrew's day. Joe had thick dark brown hair, olive skin, intense eyes, and a rough edge that had been sharpened by his career as a cop. He was more rugged and less polished than Andrew. And where Andrew was talkative and outgoing, Joe kept most of his thoughts to himself.

Living in Angel's Bay almost a year now, Joe was well respected but kept most people at a distance. He rarely let down his guard, but on occasion she had

seen the simmering passion just beneath the surface
and wondered what he'd be like if he ever let go of
the tight control he exercised over his life and his
emotions.

It had been weeks since she'd seen him. He'd
gone to L.A. just after Thanksgiving, when his father suffered a stroke. She'd almost forgotten how
attractive he was, how her stomach flipped every
time she saw him, how his smoking-hot body made
her face flush and her heart race. Definite heart-
breaking potential.

She should have left the party sooner—both
men's gazes were in search of someone, and she
knew that someone was her.

A man in the crowd suddenly shouted, "One
minute to midnight."

She felt an overwhelming desire to run for her
life.

"Thirty seconds!"

Andrew and Joe were moving down the hall,
drawing closer. What was she going to do? Kiss one,
then the other? She'd been caught between the two
men before, and it was not a happy place to be.

She turned and fled. The grand staircase was the
only open path, so she ran up the stairs, ignoring the
surprised look of a passing maid. She could find refuge in some bathroom, she hoped.

"Ten, nine, eight . . ." The chant from the crowd
grew louder.

She turned one corner, then another. The huge
house was perfect for hiding out. She moved far-

ther down the hall, stopping abruptly as the lights went out.

Surprised cries and nervous screams echoed through the house, along with shouts of "Happy New Year." What the hell happened?

Someone brushed against her shoulder, knocking her slightly off balance, then the shadowy figure was gone. How could they move so quickly through the darkness?

Turning around, she put her hand on the wall to find her way back to the staircase. A chorus of "Auld Lang Syne" rang out from below. The blackout hadn't dimmed the party's champagne-fueled spirits. She followed the noise, glad when small flickering lights appeared. Someone had lit some candles. She reached the staircase with relief, her hand hitting the banister as the lights came back on. She blinked, then moved quickly down the stairs.

She had just reached the bottom step when she heard shrill screams from above. It took a moment for them to register over the party chatter, but as the screams continued, the crowd hushed.

Then the housekeeper appeared at the top of the staircase. "Mrs. Monroe!" she cried. "I think she's dead!"

Joe Silveira pushed through the shocked hush of the crowded hallway. He'd had a bad feeling when the lights went out, and now he knew why. Charlotte gave him a shocked look as he passed her, and she started to follow, but he waved her back. He needed to find out what was going on first. One of his officers, Colin Lynch, jogged up the stairs behind him.

When they reached the landing, the housekeeper burst into an agitated mix of Spanish and English as she led them down the hallway and waved them toward an open door.

The master bedroom was a picture of luxury: thick carpet, a huge king-size bed with an ornately carved frame, and a sitting area with a fireplace and a big-screen television. He registered the details with efficiency. The room was too messy for a party night; the drawers in the dresser were half open, and there was a scent of perfume in the air. As he moved further inside, his pulse jumped at the sight of the beautiful, skinny blonde sprawled on the floor between the bedroom and the bathroom.

Theresa Monroe was on her back, her skin pale against her bright red cocktail dress. Her short blond hair was streaked with blood, a pool appearing under the back of her head, which rested on the marble floor.

He squatted down next to her and put a hand to her neck. Her pulse was faint but present, and he could hear the whisper of her breath.

"She's alive," he told Colin, who was already calling for an ambulance.

"I'll get Charlotte." Colin jogged out of the room.

Joe grabbed two thick towels off the rack and covered Theresa. The mayor rushed into the room a moment later. He was a tall, balding man with a bit of gut stretching the buttons on his white silk shirt. His eyes widened in shock when he saw his wife. His mouth opened, but no words came. It was the first time Joe had ever seen him speechless.

"Oh, my God," Monroe finally got out, dropping to his knees.

"She's breathing," Joe quickly reassured him. "Paramedics are on the way. Colin went downstairs to find a doctor."

Robert touched his wife's bare shoulder. "She's so cold." His gaze moved to the pool of blood, and he drew in a shaky breath. "What—what happened?"

"I don't know yet. Your housekeeper found her like this a few minutes ago."

"I was just outside checking the lights. Do you think she slipped in the dark?"

"It's possible," he replied, his mind racing through a few other scenarios. He glanced down at Theresa, noting the red scratch marks on her neck. "Was your wife wearing a necklace?"

Robert's jaw dropped. "Yes. Oh, my God! It was a diamond necklace dating back to the shipwreck. It's quite valuable." His gaze dropped to his wife's hand. "Her wedding ring is gone, too." He stared at Joe in confusion and disbelief. "Someone robbed her, right here in our home, in the middle of a party. Who would do that?"

Just then, Colin returned with Charlotte and Ray Bennington, an ER doctor at the clinic. Joe stood up and moved out of the doorway, allowing the doctors a closer look.

"Jason just arrived," Colin informed him. "Davidson is on his way to handle forensics."

"Good. Because it looks like Mrs. Monroe's diamonds are missing—at least, the ones she was wearing."

"Damn. The blackout was planned?"

"I've never believed in coincidences. Get Sheila over here, too. We're going to need her to search the female guests while Davidson takes prints."

"I'm on it." Colin passed the paramedics on his way out of the room.

Charlotte stepped out of the bathroom as the paramedics joined Dr. Bennington. Her blue eyes were worried as her gaze met Joe's. "She's in bad shape."

"At least she's still alive."

Charlotte nodded, but there was doubt written all over her pretty face. He'd come to the party for one reason—to see her, and maybe use midnight as as an opportunity to kiss her. He'd been thinking about her for weeks, missing her warm smile, her light blue eyes, her silky golden-blond hair and sun-kissed skin. In a short black dress that showed off her slender legs and sexy body, she was even more beautiful than he remembered. He just wished their reunion wasn't in the middle of a crime scene.

"This is crazy," she muttered. "What do you think happened?"

"Too soon to tell."

"Who would rob her in the middle of a party? It's so bold."

"And personal," he said, thinking about what kind of thief he was dealing with.

"Like a friend?"

"Obviously not a very good one." He tilted his head to the side, giving her a thoughtful look. "Did you see anything? I saw you come down the stairs just before the housekeeper screamed."

"No, I didn't see a thing," she said, stumbling a bit. "The lights went off, and it was pitch black."

"Did you hear a scream? An argument? Anyone call for help?"

"I heard a lot of screams when everything went dark. But nothing that sounded like someone was in trouble."

"What were you doing up here, Charlotte?"

"Looking for a bathroom," she said, not quite meeting his gaze.

He didn't know what to make of her evasiveness. Charlotte wouldn't hurt anyone. She was a kind, generous person who went out of her way to help people, but there was something she wasn't telling him.

Before he could probe further, he saw the housekeeper hovering in the doorway.

"Mrs. Monroe is still alive?" she asked, taking a few tentative steps into the room. She wore a black dress with dark stockings and flat shoes. Her black hair was streaked with gray and pulled back in a tight bun, no evidence of makeup on her rather plain face.

"Yes," he said. "They're going to take her to the hospital."

"Thank God." She made the sign of the cross on her chest. "I was worried. She was so still. And there was so much blood."

"What's your name?"

"Constance Garcia," she said a bit warily.

"You found her, Constance?" the mayor interrupted, stepping into the bedroom as the paramedics put Theresa on a stretcher.

"Yes," she answered.

"Did you see anyone else near this room?" Joe asked. "In the hallway or on the stairs?"

The maid hesitated for a moment, her gaze darting from him to the mayor and then to Charlotte. She lifted her hand, pointing right at Charlotte. "I saw her."

"Charlotte?" Robert asked in surprise. "What were you doing up here?"

Charlotte stiffened, obviously hearing the accusation in the mayor's voice. "I was looking for a bathroom. I was in the hall when the lights went out. I didn't see Theresa."

"Are you sure? You never liked her," Robert said, suspicion edging his voice.

"That's not true," Charlotte said, paling under his harsh words.

"Theresa didn't want to invite you, but she felt she had to because her grandmother and your mother are friends. She said you'd been horrible to her sister. That you'd always been jealous of them." His voice rose as he took a step forward.

Joe moved quickly between them. "You need to

go to the hospital with your wife. Let us take care of the investigation."

Robert hesitated, then said through tight lips, "You find out who did this, Silveira. I want to know who almost killed Theresa."

"I will."

Charlotte let out a breath as the room cleared. Her eyes were worried. "Joe, you don't think I had anything to do with this, do you? I'm not a thief, and I would never attack someone."

"Is there bad blood between you and Theresa?" he asked curiously. He had never heard of anyone not liking Charlotte.

"Her sister, Pamela, and I didn't get along in high school, but that was a dozen years ago. Theresa and I aren't best friends, but we're civil to each other. She did invite me to the party. I think she wanted to show off her house and her diamonds, but that's just who she is. I doubt half the people here are really her friends."

He knew Theresa well enough to agree with Charlotte's assessment. While he'd managed to maintain a good working relationship with the mayor, he was very aware that while the Monroes thought they ran the place, there were many people who thought they should be run out of town. Unfortunately, the only person in the vicinity of the attack, according to the maid's recollection, was Charlotte.

"Why did you lie about your reason for coming upstairs?" he asked.

She bristled at his words. "I didn't lie."

"You're hiding something. What is it?"

She gave him an irritated look. "Fine. I wanted to leave the house before midnight, but there were too many people between me and the front door when the countdown started. So I came up the stairs, thinking I'd find a bathroom and wait for a few minutes and then go."

"It's a New Year's Eve party. Why would you leave before midnight?"

Her cheeks grew warmer. "I had my reasons."

"I need a better answer."

"That's all I have."

He gave her a long look. "Who were you running away from, Charlotte?"

She stared back at him. "Do you really want to know?"

TWO

Joe's gut clenched. *Did* he want to know? He'd been walking a fine line with her for a long time.

On his way to the party, he'd been thinking about changing that. Soon he would be officially divorced, single for the first time in more than ten years. It was both terrifying and exhilarating to know that he couldn't possibly predict what would happen next.

Charlotte cleared her throat. "Never mind. You wouldn't understand." She glanced around the room. "It looks like someone searched the room. Do you think the thief took more than what Theresa was wearing?"

"Quite possibly," he said shortly. This wasn't the time to think about his personal life. "Why don't we go into the hall?" He led her into the corridor, careful not to touch anything. He needed to preserve the crime scene.

"What happens now?" she asked.

"We'll take names, statements, fingerprints, and

search the guests before they leave. Everyone who was here at the time the lights went off is a suspect."

"Even you?"

"Even me."

"Well, I'm glad to know I'm not alone." An odd look flashed through her eyes. "Someone passed me in the hall after the lights went out. They brushed against my arm."

His pulse quickened. "Man or woman?"

"I'm not sure. The only thought I had at the time was that they seemed to be moving awfully fast in the dark, as if they knew where they were going. I wonder if Theresa saw who hit her."

"That would be helpful. Tell me more about your problems with Theresa."

She sighed. "My grievance was only with her younger sister. And it's ancient history."

"What happened?"

Frowning, she asked, "Do we really have to get into it, Joe?"

"Since the mayor has brought it up, yes. I need to know what he knows."

"Andrew cheated on me with Pamela in our senior year of high school. In return, I called her few names, which she deserved."

"You blamed her, not Andrew?" He never understood why scorned women always seemed to give their boyfriends the benefit of the doubt while laying the blame on the other woman.

A spark of anger lit up Charlotte's eyes. "Of course I blamed Andrew. He betrayed me, broke my trust, and hurt me more than I had thought possible. But Pamela threw their relationship in my face every chance she got. And stealing Andrew wasn't her first offense; she went after a lot of boyfriends. I wasn't the only one who disliked her."

"No, but you were the only one in this hallway tonight."

"But Pamela wasn't attacked. I have no reason to assault Theresa. And where on earth would I even hide a diamond necklace in this dress?"

The form-fitting dress hugged her body like a second skin, which he very much appreciated. Charlotte had full breasts and sweet hips, curves just made for a man's hands.

"Okay, stop undressing me," she ordered, a slight flush reddening her cheeks.

He couldn't help smiling. "You look beautiful tonight, Charlotte."

Her tension eased slightly. "Thank you. So what now?"

"I'll wait here until my officers can seal the room and run forensics."

"The new year isn't off to a very good start, is it?"

"I certainly wasn't anticipating this on my first day back in town."

"How's your father doing?"

"Much better now. I didn't want to leave L.A. until I felt confident he was out of the woods. He still has some rehab ahead of him, but he's a fighter. He won't give up."

"I'm glad. You're close to him, aren't you?"

"We haven't spent much time together in the past few years, but he was a good father to me. Tough, fair, a big believer in doing things the right way. He taught me a lot."

"Now I know who you take after."

He smiled. "I try."

"Did Isabella come back with you?"

"He nodded. "My sister is officially staying at my house, but I doubt I'll see much of her. She and Nick Hartley are spending a lot of time together these days. He came down to L.A. with his daughter over the holidays so he could meet the family."

"Sounds like they're getting serious."

"It looks that way."

He needed to send Charlotte downstairs. He needed to go back into the bedroom and look around. He needed to do a half-dozen other things besides talk to her. None of them involved moving closer to Charlotte—but that's exactly what he did, because it was New Year's Eve and after midnight, and they were alone.

She backed up a step, giving him a wary look. "What are you doing?"

"I came here tonight for one reason." His gaze moved to her soft, pretty pink lips. "A New Year's Eve kiss."

"It's past midnight now."

He looked into her beautiful blue eyes. "Were you running away from me, Charlotte?" He was so close he could see her pulse jump, smell the musky scent of her perfume. So close he could almost taste her.

But almost wasn't good enough. He put his mouth on hers and took what he'd been wanting for so long.

It was even better than he'd imagined. Her lips opened under his, and he explored her warm mouth with rapidly building desire.

When her hands went around his neck, pulling him closer, he pressed against her until there wasn't an inch of space between them. Her breasts met his chest, her hips cradled his pelvis as their legs tangled together. What had started out as a simple New Year's Eve kiss had become a full-out assault on the senses.

But it was the wrong place. The wrong time. He could hear voices growing closer.

"Damn," he muttered, forcing himself to break away.

She looked at him with dazed eyes, as if she couldn't believe what had just happened. He couldn't believe it, either. He'd completely lost his head, and that hadn't happened in a very, very long time.

He stepped back, pushing his hands into his pockets so he wouldn't be tempted to reach for her again. Charlotte pulled down her dress, which had ridden up her gorgeous thighs, and her breasts moved with each quick breath. How he wished he'd had a chance a touch them, to run his thumbs over her nipples, to hear her gasp with pleasure the way she had when he'd slipped his tongue into her mouth.

"Chief," Jason Marlow called out as he turned the corner.

He drew a deep breath and pulled himself together.

Marlow had been promoted to detective just before Christmas, and he was about to get his first big case.

"Colin filled me in," Jason said as he joined them in the corridor. He gave Charlotte a worried look. "Are you all right?" he asked her.

"I'm fine, Jason," she said quickly. "Joe and I were just talking about who could have done this."

"Well, I need you to do me a favor. Your mother is refusing to be searched, fingerprinted, or interviewed. She's starting a mutiny with the other guests. Maybe you could calm her down."

"I rarely have a calming effect on my mother, but I'll give it a shot."

"Don't follow your mother's lead, Charlotte," Joe advised as she moved past him. "Don't look like you have anything to hide."

That brought her head around. "I *don't* have anything to hide. You should know that better than anyone."

He smiled at her pointed words, then quickly neutralized his expression as Jason gave him a speculative glance. Rumors spread fast in Angel's Bay, and the last thing he needed was to put his tenuous relationship with Charlotte under a microscope.

"What was that about?" Jason asked as Charlotte moved toward the stairs.

"Nothing. You'll be in charge of the investigation, since I was on the property when the crime occurred. I'll oversee things from a distance." Although he wasn't sure how much distance he could keep if the heat was turned up on Charlotte. "With the mayor on the warpath, I don't have to tell you how much pressure we're going to be feeling in the next few days. Monroe wants someone to pay for this."

"I hope that won't be Charlotte," Jason replied. "Colin told me she was seen upstairs at the time of the crime."

"According to the housekeeper."

"You can't think she had anything to do with this?"

"No—but we need to find another suspect fast."

Charlotte was not just shaken from the robbery and the sight of Theresa lying in a pool of blood; she was also reeling from Joe's kiss. A lot had happened since she'd impulsively bolted upstairs. What a bad move that had been.

She reached the foyer, where the party atmosphere had turned to fear and worry. Sheila, Joe's assistant and a part-time dispatcher, was patting down female guests, while another officer was taking prints and checking bags on the dining-room table.

Her mother was standing in the living room, speaking quite forcefully with Colin. Kara was also there, a soothing expression on her face, but her mother was clearly not interested in being placated.

Monica Adams was a rail-thin, frosted blonde who had a haughty, unhappy look on her thin face, which was pretty much her usual expression. Her mother had long ago deemed herself the queen of Angel's Bay, or at least of the congregation that Charlotte's father had served as minister. While Monica was magnificently generous in her charity work, she was also a tough, critical taskmaster. She had no patience for fools and refused to put up with anything she deemed to be unjust, which at this moment appeared to be the investigation.

Charlotte wondered where her mother's date was. In the past few weeks, Peter Lawson's presence had made a definite improvement on her mother's mood and lifted the depression she'd been wearing like a heavy cloak since Charlotte's father had passed on.

"Where on earth have you been?" her mother demanded as she joined them.

"I went upstairs to see if I could help Theresa," she said shortly.

"How is she?" Kara asked.

"Unconscious. I don't know the extent of her injuries." She returned her gaze to her mother. "What's the problem?"

"I am not going to allow anyone to search me like a common criminal," her mother said.

"It's not a big deal, Mom. The police are just doing their job."

"It's the principle, Charlotte. I did not do anything wrong, and I will not be treated as if I did. Honestly, this town used to be a quiet place. But lately there's been nothing but trouble."

Charlotte glanced at Colin. Kara's husband was a big, gentle bear of a guy who could be a tough cop when necessary, but he was also polite and understanding when it came to dealing with people like her mother. "Can she go?" she asked.

"Yes," he replied. "I just told your mother that she's free to leave, but her refusal to be searched or fingerprinted will be noted in the report."

"I don't need to be searched or fingerprinted, because I didn't do anything," Monica said. "Now, I want to leave, Charlotte, and I need a ride."

"Where's Mr. Lawson?"

"Peter had to leave just before midnight. His daughter had a problem with her water heater or something. I told him you would take me home."

"All right. But I do want to cooperate with the investigation, so you'll have to give me a few minutes."

Her mother shot her a disgusted look, then took a seat on the sofa, crossing her arms.

"I can't believe what's happened," Kara said, walking with her to the dining room.

"I can't, either."

"Charlotte." Kara put a hand on her arm, stopping her. "Colin said the housekeeper saw you upstairs before the lights went out. I thought you were leaving."

"The front door was blocked, so I ran up the stairs when the countdown started. Then everything went black."

"So you didn't see anything?"

"No. But once again, I was in the wrong place at the wrong time."

"Well, everyone knows you're a good person. You don't have to worry."

"I hope not."

"Andrew was here. He was looking for you, but the police were trying to clear out the party, so he left."

Relief ran through her. With her lips still tingling from Joe's kiss, she wasn't ready to look Andrew in the eye.

"I'd better get my bag so I can take my mother home." Charlotte moved into the next room, gave a brief statement to the officer, as well as her fingerprints, and allowed her bag and her person to be searched. Then she collected her mother and headed out the door.

It was after 1:00 A.M., and they shivered in the cold as the valet ran to retrieve her car.

Her mother complained most of the way home, but Charlotte barely listened, her mind filled with thoughts about Joe.

She could still feel his hands on her body, his solid chest pressing against her breasts. She'd been thinking about kissing him for months, yet the real thing was so much better than she'd imagined. But now what? Was it the start of something more or just a New Year's Eve kiss that would mean nothing the next day?

She didn't even know what she wanted the answer to be. Joe had been forbidden territory since she'd first met him. At the time he'd been an unhappily married man. That wasn't the case anymore. Rachel had moved out months ago, and their divorce would soon be final. Joe was free to be with whomever he wanted to be with, and he clearly wanted her. She wanted him, too. But she had no idea what kind of a relationship he was looking for or what kind of involvement she wanted. A fling with Joe could easily become more than she was ready for. Look what a simple kiss had turned into. He was a risk she wasn't sure she could take.

"Charlotte, you're not listening to me," her mother scolded.

"Sorry. What did you say?"

"I said what a horrible evening this turned out to be. I never should have gone to that party."

"You wanted to see the house," she reminded her.

"True, but it wasn't as impressive on the inside. Theresa needed a better decorator. She didn't do a very good job of mixing the old pieces from the Worthington estate with her own furniture. She came off looking pretentious and silly."

"Seeing as how she's in the hospital fighting for her life, now might not be the best time to criticize her taste."

"Well, of course, I feel bad for her," Monica snapped. "I've already asked Andrew to lead a prayer for her at the New Year's Day service. But I can't help thinking she brought some of this on herself. She's been talking all over town about all the wonderful things they bought from the estate. Obviously, she drew the wrong kind of attention."

"So what happened to Peter again?" Charlotte asked, eager to get her mother onto a new subject.

"His daughter doesn't like us seeing each other."

She shot her mother a quick look. "I thought you were just friends."

"Did I say we were more than that?"

"Well, I can't imagine why his daughter wouldn't want him to be *friends* with you."

"She's jealous. She's divorced and used to someone taking care of her. Now that her husband has left her, she's constantly seeking her father's attention. He goes running every time she sees a spider. It's ridiculous. The woman is in her late thirties."

"You're not used to a man who doesn't put you before all others," she murmured before she could consider the fallout.

"That's not true. Your father put the church before me," her mother replied. "You should know that."

"You were right up there, Mother. Dad did everything you wanted. He might have been the one at the podium, but you called a lot of the shots behind the scenes."

"Your father made his own decisions." Her mother sighed with exasperation. "I don't understand what you're saying, Charlotte. You make it sound like I was some sort of puppet master. That wasn't the case at all."

"You like to control things."

"I like to take care of my family. Everything I ever did was for your father and you kids. My whole life was wrapped up in being a wife and a mother."

Her mother's words were meant to make her feel guilty, and for a second, she wavered. Her mother had done a lot for the family, yet her motivation had always seemed to come from a more selfish place. But maybe she wasn't being fair.

"And you love to control things, too, Charlotte," her mother added. "Isn't that the reason there isn't a man in your life? Because if there was, you'd have to consider someone else's feelings, include someone else in your decisions, and make compromises. When you're alone, you have total control over your life, just the way you like it. But one of these days, you're going to wake up and see just how isolated you are."

"I'm not alone. I live with you and Annie," she defended, although her mother's words hit a little too close to home.

"You should be careful. You'll get so set in your ways no one will have you. Even Andrew is starting to wonder if you'll ever give him another chance."

"I don't want to talk about Andrew with you."

"What a surprise."

"It's late. Why don't we just not speak?" she suggested.

"Fine."

Her mother's angry silence was almost as bad as her sharp tongue. She was a difficult woman to ignore, but Charlotte tried to do just that.

Glancing out the window, she noted that the downtown area was still lively. Music rang out from the local bars, and boats in the harbor were ablaze with lights and full of people. There were couples making out in the shadows of the old buildings and groups of happy, drunken revelers careening through the streets, making their way home.

A reckless yearning filled her heart, and her mother's words echoed through her head. She didn't want to end up alone, but she did have a problem giving up control. Wasn't that the reason she'd dashed up the stairs at the manor? Because she'd been afraid that she wouldn't be able to control the situation?

Andrew and Joe were both attractive, both important to her in different ways, but both came with emotional pitfalls. While she might be impulsive in a lot of areas, when it came to love, she didn't take chances anymore.

It had been far easier to keep love away when she'd been going to medical school, then interning and working seventy hours a week in a residency. Relationships had been short and casual because she was working toward the rest of her life.

Now the rest of her life was here, and she was back in a place filled with family and friends and people she already cared too much about. She should never have stayed this long. Part of her wanted to run right now, to drop her mother off, grab some clothes, and hit the road again. But the other part of her wanted to put down roots, make a home for herself . . . and maybe even let herself fall all the way in love.

Charlotte didn't head for the hills when she returned home. There was no way she could leave her mother or Annie and her baby in the middle of the night. Instead, she spent the night tossing and turning, reliving the good and bad moments of the evening.

In the good category—make that the stupendously wonderful category—was Joe's kiss, the warmth of his arms around her, and the sense of inevitability that had come with their embrace. She'd wanted to kiss him since the day she'd met him, and the real thing had been far better than any daydream.

In the bad—make that horrific—category were the housekeeper's screams, the sight of Theresa lying on the bathroom floor, her blond hair matted with blood, the mayor's panicked fury, and the accusations he'd hurled at her. It was unthinkable that anyone could believe she would hurt Theresa or steal her jewelry, yet she couldn't shake the feeling that there was more bad to come.

She was relieved when daylight came and she could give up on trying to sleep. She took a quick shower, then threw on black pants and a burgundy sweater over a pink camisole. She applied some light makeup to hide the shadows under her eyes and headed downstairs, hoping the new year would get off to a better start.

Annie was seated at the round kitchen table, a stack of pancakes in front of her, her baby boy, Will, asleep in the baby seat next to her. Almost nineteen now, Annie wore her long blond hair in a braid that reached to her waist. Her skin was rosy pink, and her eyes weren't as tired or as haunted as they'd been in recent weeks. Will shared Annie's fair looks, with only a few strands of hair on his otherwise bald head. His eyes, which were sweetly closed at the moment, were a warm gold-flecked brown, the only resemblance he bore to his biological father.

Charlotte had rescued Annie from the streets six months earlier, and a lot had happened since then. Annie had delivered her baby and had had to deal with her own mentally disturbed father and the unsupportive biological father of her baby, Steve Baker. But with Charlotte and Monica's support, Annie had turned the corner. She was coming into her own, not only as an adult woman but also as a mother. Since deciding to keep her baby, she'd embraced her role as chief caregiver, appreciative of Charlotte and Monica's support but determined to do most of the work herself.

Annie was one of the reasons Charlotte hadn't left Angel's Bay. It had been her idea to rescue Annie and offer her mother's house as a refuge, so she hadn't felt she could abandon Annie to her mother. In truth, though, Annie and Monica got along really well, and Monica had made it clear that Annie could stay as long as she wanted.

"Would you like some breakfast?" her mother asked. "I have scrambled eggs, bacon, and pancakes."

Charlotte smiled at the array of delicious, mouthwatering food. Her mother had always been a fantastic cook, and a good, hearty breakfast had been a tradition as long as she could remember. So many things in their lives had changed, but not breakfast, and she was grateful for that.

"I'll have a little of everything," she said as her mother fixed her a plate.

She moved to the table to say good morning to Will. He was just starting to wake up, his eyelids flickering, his little mouth scrunching into a pucker of sweet drooling bubbles. Her heart melted every time she saw him.

For a long time, she'd told herself that having kids wasn't in her future. She'd lost a baby as a teenager, and she'd never really moved past that loss. But little Will was making her want to reconsider that stance. He was such an adorable angel. Who wouldn't want one of these? Then again, if she could love this kid this much and he wasn't even hers, what would it be like to have a baby of her own? She'd spend the rest of her life worried about every breath he took, afraid that something terrible would happen, and she'd never recover.

She knew it was an irrational fear, and it was ironic since her job was bringing babies into the world. But emotionally, she'd always been mixed up on the subject.

Will began to cry. "Looks like he's hungry," Annie said. "I'll get his bottle."

Charlotte unsnapped the safety strap and picked him up. He squirmed and kicked his little legs against her, crying a little. She distracted him by making silly faces, delighted when he reacted with a smile. She rubbed her nose against his as his little hands managed to grab a couple of strands of her hair.

"He loves hair," Annie said, putting the bottle on the table. She reached for Will, gently disentangling his fingers from Charlotte's hair. Then she sat down and cradled Will in her arms, giving him the bottle he eagerly took. Immediately, his little hand reached for Annie's hair, pulling at a few tendrils that had come loose from her braid.

Charlotte watched them for a few moments, noting how confident Annie was now. "He's getting so big."

"They grow fast," Monica agreed, handing Charlotte her plate. "You're not going to wear pants to church, are you?"

"It's cold outside."

"So wear boots. It's not like you don't have good legs," Monica continued. "You get those from me. My mother was all legs, and she wore the highest heels. I remember trying her on stilettos when I was a little girl. I couldn't imagine how she walked in those things."

"I wish I could remember Gran," Charlotte said wistfully. From all the stories she'd heard, her grandmother had been a very interesting woman, not nearly as straitlaced as her mother.

"Do you want coffee?" her mother asked.

"I can get it. Why don't you sit down and eat?"

"I ate hours ago."

She was surprised. "You were up that early? I thought you might sleep in after our late night."

"I didn't get much sleep after all that chaos," her mother said, moving back to the sink to rinse the pans. "It was very disturbing. I hope Theresa recovers."

"So do I. How was your evening, Annie?"

"Not nearly as exciting as yours. Diana and I made popcorn and watched television with her parents. The babies mostly slept."

"It's nice that you and Diana have become friends." Diana was twenty-two years old, living with her parents while her husband was serving in the Navy overseas.

"I'm grateful to Reverend Schilling for introducing us," Annie said. "It's nice to be around another young mother. Oh, and Diana wrote to her husband about Jamie, and guess what—they actually met about a month ago! Some joint-force thing with the Navy and the Marines."

"It is a small world," Charlotte picked up a piece of bacon to munch on. Her younger brother was somewhere in the Middle East, and while he e-mailed as often as he could, he was always vague about where he was and what he was doing.

"I haven't heard from Jamie in a couple of days," her mother interjected, a worried note in her voice. "He's usually so good about keeping in touch."

"He's just busy," Charlotte offered, knowing her mother would worry no matter what.

"I can't imagine how hard it would be to have my child in danger," Annie said. "I've only been a mom for a couple of months, and I don't think I could do it."

"Well, Jamie isn't a child anymore," Monica said, turning to face them. "He's a man now, and he's doing an honorable job. That gets me through."

"He has good friends, too," Annie said. "He's always talking about his lieutenant and his buddies, saying they all watch out for each other. He's not alone."

Monica exchanged a smile with Annie. "No, he's not."

Charlotte took another bite of her pancakes, wondering how Annie was so much better at making her mother feel good than she was.

"Sometimes I wonder what happened to my dad's friends," Annie continued. "Why no one came around to check on him, to help him, after he got injured. Someone had to know he wasn't thinking straight. But as long as I can remember, it was just me and my mom and him. Even before he took us up in the mountains. He was always alone—except in his head. His mind was filled with thoughts of the enemy trying to kill him." She paused. "I would never want that to happen to Jamie."

"Jamie will be fine," Monica said confidently. "His spirit is strong, and if anything were to happen, he would never be alone. I would be there."

Charlotte drew in a quick breath, her mother's words a little painful. At seventeen, she'd needed her mother desperately, and her mother hadn't been there for her. But in her mother's mind, that was different. Jamie's problems would be honorable; hers had only been shameful.

"Diana and I are going to join a group that sends care packages overseas," Annie added. "They need volunteers to keep up their efforts all year long, not just at the holidays."

"That's great," Charlotte said. "I'm glad you're getting more involved in the community."

Annie gave a self-deprecating smile. "That's my New Year's resolution—to stop hiding out."

She nodded in understanding. Annie had branded herself with a scarlet letter, even though most people in Angel's Bay had forgiven her very youthful and naive mistake.

"What's your resolution?" Annie asked curiously.

"Yes, what is your New Year's resolution, Charlotte?" her mother echoed. "Or are you still in the anti-resolution camp? After all, if you don't set goals, then no one is disappointed if you don't meet them. Hasn't that been your philosophy?"

On her mother's sharp tongue, it didn't sound like a good philosophy at all. Fortunately, Charlotte's cell phone began to ring, so she got up to answer it.

Her answering service was on the line. One of

her patients thought she might be going into early labor. After listening to the symptoms, she said, "Tell her to go to the hospital, and I will meet her there." Knowing her patient's penchant for panicking over every little twinge, Charlotte suspected that this was a false alarm, but with the pregnancy at thirty-six weeks, she didn't want to take any chances.

"What about church?" her mother asked when she ended the call.

"If I get done in time, I'll meet you there. Otherwise, I'll see you later tonight. Kara is having a party this afternoon." She picked up her plate and took another bite of pancake as she headed to the sink. "Annie, you're welcome to come to Kara's if you'd like."

"No, thanks. Diana and I are going to take the babies to the park."

"That sounds like fun." She filled a traveling mug with coffee and grabbed her bag off the counter, then headed outside.

She had just stepped onto the porch when Andrew's car pulled up in front of the house. Considering that he was leading a New Year's Day service in less than an hour, she was surprised to see him. He was dressed in black slacks and a black button-down shirt.

"Hey, what are you doing here?" she asked, moving down the steps to meet him on the walk.

"I wanted to talk to you before church, but it looks like you're on your way out."

"I have a patient in possible labor. I'm on my way to the hospital."

"So you won't be at the service?"

"I'll see how it goes. I don't really have time to talk right now."

"I understand. I just wanted to apologize for bailing on you last night. Mrs. Rimmer is having trouble with her teenage son, and she needed my help. He got into a minor car accident last night while he was intoxicated."

"Is he all right?"

"Yes, and I actually think it was a good wake-up call. He's been dealing with a lot of anger issues since his father remarried. He's crying out for attention, and not in a good way."

"I'm glad you were there for him and his mother. Mrs. Rimmer is a sweetheart. She always gives me extra cream cheese when I go into her bagel shop."

"She's a pushover—that's part of the problem. Anyway, I really wanted to spend the evening with you, and I was disappointed." His gaze searched hers. "Were you?"

"Of course." Getting into a deeper answer would take more time than she had, and it wasn't a lie. She liked Andrew. And being attracted to him had never been a problem. But she was conflicted about what kind of relationship she wanted to have with him, partly because of her feelings for Joe.

She opened her car door and put her coffee in the cupholder. "We'll talk when we have more time, but one thing I did want to ask you ... Last night, the mayor seemed to be under the impression that Theresa and I don't like each other, because of what happened with you and Pamela and me."

"That's ridiculous," he said, his eyes widening in surprise. "You don't have a problem with Theresa, do you?"

"No, I don't. I'm not sure where he got that from. Have you kept in touch with Pamela?"

Something flickered in his eyes, and he shifted his feet. Finally, he said, "Not in a long time. Six, seven years, at least."

"So you saw her after her high school, then?"

"We both went to college in L.A."

"And after college?"

"She was around. A bunch of kids from Angel's Bay were down there."

"Right. Do you think Pamela will come back to see Theresa?"

"Possibly." His gaze turned serious. "I know you blame Pamela for our breakup, but I was the one who cheated on you. And as much as I'd like to make her responsible for that, I can't. You say you've moved on, Charlotte, that you don't think about it anymore, but is that true? Because something is holding you back from giving me another chance. And I'd like to know what it is."

"I'm not sure," she said honestly.

"You loved me once. You could love me again," he said persuasively.

She'd been head over heels, crazy, starstruck

in love with him. When he'd loved her back, she'd thought she was the luckiest girl in the world. But that was a long time ago.

"I can't do this now, Andrew. I have to get to the hospital, and you have your service."

"Just promise me one thing," Andrew said.

"What's that?"

He moved closer to her, crowding her between his body and the car. "When you're thinking about us, about whether you want anything to happen again, think about this."

His lips touched hers with compelling, urgent heat, as if he needed her to feel what she'd felt so many years ago. And it didn't take much for the old spark to leap into life. In his arms, she was seventeen again. He was the hottest guy in school, and he wanted her, and that thought was as intoxicating as his kiss.

Andrew broke off the kiss and smiled. "You taste like maple syrup and your mom's pancakes."

"Mom still cooks a big breakfast every day, especially weekends and holidays," she said, reeling a bit. Andrew had been letting her call the shots for the last few months, but apparently, that was over.

"I always loved coming to your house for breakfast."

Another reminder of a simpler time. She slipped into the car. "I'll see you later."

"You will," he promised. "I want you to forgive me, for the way I hurt you before."

She frowned. "Is that what this is about, Andrew? Some sort of absolution for past sins? Because that sounds like your area, not mine."

"This is about letting go of the past so we can have a future together. Just give me a chance. That's all I'm asking."

THREE

Cynthia Lewis and her husband, Johnny, were in their mid-twenties and expecting their first baby. Cynthia had read every book on the subject of childbirth, and Johnny, a musician, had become obsessed with playing classical music to the baby in the womb. Charlotte loved their enthusiasm. She admired their state of readiness. But this was the third trip they'd made to the hospital in the last four weeks, and they still had a ways to go.

"Just Braxton Hicks contractions," she said as she finished her exam.

"I thought they might be," Cynthia agreed. "But Johnny didn't want to take a chance since we're only a few weeks away now." She gave her husband a loving smile that he tenderly returned.

Johnny put his arm around his wife's shoulders. "Cynthia and this baby are the most important people in the world to me. I couldn't stand it if anything happened to them."

"Everything will be fine," she reassured him. Cynthia had had an uneventful pregnancy so far, and there was no reason to suspect that her delivery would go any differently. "A few more weeks, and you'll be welcoming your little boy. Have you picked a name yet?"

Cynthia gave her husband a quick look. "If it was a girl, we were going to name her Charlotte. Since it's a boy—Charles."

She was touched by the gesture. "That's really sweet of you."

"You've been so great," Cynthia said. "My mom died when I was little, and I've had to go through a lot of things without her. But being pregnant with my own child has made me miss her even more. I have so many questions I wish I could ask her. Like how she felt when she was pregnant with me, how her labor was, how she got through it." Cynthia drew in a deep breath. "Your patience with all of my questions made not having her here with me a little easier."

A lump grew in Charlotte's throat as a tear slipped from Cynthia's eyes. "It was my pleasure. Bringing a healthy baby into the world isn't just my job, it's a privilege. I'm honored that I'm going to share such an important moment in your lives." She smiled to lighten the mood. "And I'll make sure I have the good drugs on hand."

Cynthia laughed. "Great. I'm going to try to go as long as I can without anything, but I've never been big on pain."

"We'll make it as easy as we possibly can," Charlotte said. "Now, go home and enjoy your New Year's Day."

After sending Cynthia and Johnny home, Charlotte dropped Cynthia's chart off at the nurses' station, which was still cheerfully decorated with holiday wreaths and garlands. A plate of gingerbread sat on the counter. "Did you make this?" Charlotte asked the nurse.

Peggy Ramsdell, one of their most experienced OB nurses, looked up from her computer. "My mother-in-law did. Try some. It's fabulous." Peggy quickly skimmed through the chart Charlotte had set down. "Another false alarm, I see. Third time this month."

"She's a little anxious."

"I'll say." Peggy filed the chart. "So, you were at the mayor's party last night, right?"

"I was," Charlotte was dismayed at the eager light in Peggy's eyes. Like most of the hospital staff, Peggy liked to gossip. The last thing she wanted to talk about was the night before.

"Is it true that someone stole thousands of dollars' worth of jewelry, including Mrs. Monroe's wedding ring?"

"I don't know the details."

"They've posted a guard outside intensive care," Peggy added.

"I'm sure that's just a precaution." It made her uneasy to think that Theresa might still be in danger. The thief had to be long gone.

"I hope so," Peggy said. "Is there anything else you need?"

"No. Have a good day." Charlotte headed down the hall to the bank of elevators. After a momentary debate, she pushed the up button. She wanted an update on Theresa's condition.

The hospital security guard standing outside the fourth-floor ICU was Bart Hodgkins, an older man whose wife was one of her patients. He gave her a smile and waved her inside.

The unit housed a large nurses' station with a panel of glass that fronted three smaller rooms where patients in acute distress were watched twenty-four hours a day. An elderly man was in one of the rooms. Theresa was in another.

"Hello, Dr. Adams," the nurse on duty said.

"How is Mrs. Monroe?" she asked.

"She hasn't regained consciousness."

"Her husband's not here?"

"The mayor went to get some coffee. He's been by her side all night. The poor man is just distraught."

She was relieved to learn that the mayor was gone for the moment. As the nurse went in to check on the other patient, Charlotte took a quick look at Theresa's chart. The tests showed brain swelling but no bleeds. That was a good sign.

"What are you doing here?" a man asked sharply, his voice cold.

She turned in surprise. The mayor stared back at her with dark, angry eyes. A big man with a square face and a strong jaw, he was a little soft around the middle, and his hairline had receded, but he was still a force to be reckoned with. "I was just checking on your wife."

"I don't want you anywhere near Theresa. That's why there's a guard outside the door. How did you get past him?"

She was taken aback by the intensity of his animosity. She'd thought his reaction the night before had been in the heat of the moment, that he would have calmed down by now.

"I didn't have anything to do with your wife's attack," she said. "I don't have any grudge against Theresa. And my problems with Pamela were a long time ago, when we were kids. I would never try to hurt either one of them."

"Save your explanations for the police. I want you to leave now, and I don't want to see you here again. Is that understood?"

"Yes."

"Good, then get out."

She walked out of the room, mentally kicking herself for coming into the ICU in the first place.

As she reached the end of the hall, the elevator doors opened, and Joe stepped out. He had on gray slacks and a black sweater. His dark eyes and sexy mouth made her heart beat a little faster. Her breath caught as their eyes met. They'd taken a step past friendship last night, but where they were now, she had no real idea. It was impossible to go back, but the way forward was complicated.

"You're working today?" he asked.

"One of my patients had a false alarm."

"Obstetrics isn't on this floor, is it?"

"I wanted to see how Theresa was doing," she admitted.

His jaw tightened. "That wasn't a good idea, Charlotte."

"That's what the mayor just told me."

Joe looked even less happy to hear that. "Want to fill me in on what else he said?"

"Not much. He just wanted me to leave. Do you have any leads?"

"Unfortunately, no."

"Really?" she asked in disappointment. "No fingerprints? No shoe prints in the mud? No tire tracks?"

"You've been watching crime shows, haven't you?"

"I got hooked while I was taking care of Annie's baby a few months ago. There was nothing else on in the middle of the night. You really didn't find any clues? No other eyewitness reports besides the housekeeper?"

"Not yet, but Jason is in the early stages of the investigation."

"Jason is a good officer, but he's a new detective, and you have a lot of more experience. Why aren't you leading the investigation?"

"I was at the party. We'll have a better, cleaner case if I stay out of it. I have complete faith in Jason, but I am watching from a distance."

"I hope you don't watch me get arrested from a distance," she said dryly.

A smile played around his lips. "I wouldn't stand by and let that happen. I'm hoping Theresa will wake up and be able to give us a lead."

"If you're staying out of it, then why are you here?"

"The mayor asked me to give him a personal report."

"I saw the guard. You don't think Theresa is in any danger, do you?"

"I hope not. It's possible that her injury came from a shove and a slip on the marble floor. If that were the scenario, it's unlikely the thief would show up here at the hospital, but then again, it depends on whether she can identify them and how badly they want to cover their tracks." He paused, his expression all business. "Don't go back to the ICU, Charlotte. The fact that you could get past the guard and into Theresa's room will not work in your favor."

"I'm a doctor here. I can go anywhere I want in this hospital."

"Exactly. And that ability will make you more of a suspect if something else happens to Theresa."

"I understand. But I want to help find out who did this to her."

"I appreciate that, but you're going to have to sit this one out."

"I'll try," she said.

"Do better than try," he said forcefully. "You were the only person spotted near the crime scene. You have an alleged grudge against the victim. That gives you motive and opportunity, not a bad start to any case."

A shiver ran down her spine at his very serious words.

He put his hands on her shoulders and gazed into her eyes. "I'll do everything I can to keep you out of the line of fire."

The strength of his touch and his vow reassured her. Joe would protect her. That's the kind of man he was. He stood up for what was right.

"Thank you."

His hands gently kneaded the tight muscles in her shoulders. "I've made you tense."

She was more tense now that he was touching her. She swallowed back a sudden knot in her throat as she remembered the last time they'd been this close, his hands threading through her hair as he angled his head for a deeper kiss.

His massage stopped abruptly, his gaze meeting hers, as if his memories were taking him down the same path. The air between them sizzled with anticipation. They were close but not close enough.

Then the elevator dinged, and they jumped apart.

A woman stepped out, wearing black jeans, spike-heeled boots, and a black leather jacket over a white silk top. Her dark blond hair was long and thick, drifting past her shoulder blades. Her legs were skinny, her bust a triple D.

Charlotte's heart began to pound. She knew that body—that face—those eyes that had once mocked her.

"Oh, my God," the woman drawled, recognition flashing in her eyes. "It's Charlotte Adams, isn't it? Funny that you would be the first person I would see in Angel's Bay. You remember me, don't you?"

How could she have forgotten the girl who had stolen Andrew from her and been picked in their high school yearbook as "Most Likely to Have a Spread in *Playboy*"?

"Pamela."

"That's right. We meet again. You're living here now?"

"Yes," Charlotte said. "I am." She felt awkward and tongue-tied, the way she had when she and Pamela were teenagers. No one had ever gotten under her skin like this girl. With most people, she was outgoing, talkative, and confident, but somehow Pamela always made her feel foolish.

Pamela's attention drifted to Joe. "And you are?" she asked, her predatory gaze making a bold run down Joe's body.

Charlotte frowned, fighting a ridiculous urge to stand in front of Joe and tell Pamela that she couldn't have him.

"I'm Joe Silveira, the chief of police," he said.

"Just the man I wanted to see. I'm Pamela Baines, Theresa Monroe's sister. My brother-in-law didn't tell me much, except that Theresa had been assaulted and her jewelry stolen. What are you planning to do about it?"

"I'd be happy to fill you in on our investigation, perhaps after you've had a chance to see your sister," he suggested. "Her room is just down the hall."

"Thank you." Pamela cast Charlotte a speculative look and then left them alone.

"So that's your old nemesis," Joe said.

"That's her," she said, watching Pamela's sexy swagger. She hadn't changed a bit.

"Are you all right?"

She shook off her feeling of dread. "I'm fine. So what if Pamela is back? She's here to see her sister. It's perfectly natural. Not at all a big deal."

"Are you done?" he asked when she ran out of steam.

"I don't like her. She annoys the hell out of me."

"Really? Because you hide it quite well."

Her mouth curved into a reluctant smile. "Sorry. It's been a dozen years, but she still makes me crazy. And she doesn't appear to have changed at all. She still has that hair, that smirky smile, those skinny legs, and those boobs. God! She flaunted those from the day she got them, and I'm betting they're even bigger now. It's not funny," she added as Joe's grin broadened.

"I've never seen you so worked up."

"You're right. I need to calm down. We're all adults, and I should start acting like one." She pressed the button for the elevator. "But a word of warning: when you talk to Pamela, keep your guard up. Don't trust her. She always had an agenda, and I'm betting that hasn't changed."

*   *   *

Joe thought about Charlotte's warning as he walked down the hall. She normally had good instincts about people, but she might be too caught up in the past to see Pamela clearly now. He wouldn't have that problem.

"Morning, Chief," the guard greeted him.

"Everything been quiet?" he asked.

"Only visitors have been the mayor and the sister. I didn't let the sister in until the mayor gave the okay."

Bart didn't mention that Charlotte had been inside. "I'd also like you to keep track of the hospital personnel going and out of these doors," Joe said.

"Sure, Chief. Dr. Adams was by and Dr. Coulter. A couple of nurses have been in and out. I knew all of 'em by sight. No strangers have gotten past me."

"Thanks." He gave Bart a brief smile and headed into the ICU.

The nurse sent him a quick glance, then returned her attention to her computer.

Pausing in the doorway to Theresa's room, he watched Pamela and Robert conversing in hushed tones. He couldn't hear what they were saying, but their discussion seemed rather heated. He'd need to learn more about Pamela's relationship with both her sister and her brother-in-law.

When Robert saw Joe, he quickly ended his conversation and joined him in the outer room. Pamela remained where she was, but her attention was on them and not her sister, which he found odd.

"What have you learned?" the mayor asked.

"Unfortunately, not much. How is your wife?"

"She's fighting for her life. That's how she is," he said angrily. "I want to know who did this to her."

"So do I. We're going over forensics and witness statements, and we've conducted an extensive search around your property. With the nearby beach and the thick cluster of trees, there's a lot of ground to cover."

"I don't care how difficult it is. I want every officer in the department working on this case. What about Charlotte Adams? Has she been brought in for questioning?"

"She's cooperating fully with the investigation." On a good day, the mayor was impatient, short-tempered, and egotistical, and this was far from his best day. His eyes were bloodshot, and he hadn't slept in twenty-four hours. He wanted someone to blame, and right now the only person in his sights was Charlotte. "When you have a chance, I'd like you to take a look around your house to help us determine if anything else is missing besides the jewelry your wife was wearing."

"I don't know what Theresa had in the way of jewelry. She was always shopping for something." Robert drew in a deep breath as he looked through the glass at his very still and pale wife. "She has to make it through this."

He could hear the fear in the mayor's voice. He'd

never thought of the mayor as a man capable of having deep feelings, but he certainly seemed to be in love with his wife.

"I can't leave here until Theresa wakes up," the mayor added. "Whatever may or may not be missing from the house will have to wait."

"Perhaps your sister-in-law could help with that."

"I doubt that. Just find who did this, Silveira. If you don't, you won't have a job." With that threat, Robert returned to his wife's side.

Pamela moved across the room, pausing in the doorway. "He's worried about Theresa," she said.

"Completely understandable. Are you and your sister close, Ms. Baines?"

"We're sisters," she said with a shrug. "Our blood makes us close."

"When did you last see her?"

"I can't recall. We've both been busy. Robert tells me that Charlotte Adams is a suspect."

It was an adept change in subject. Pamela obviously wasn't going to give him much on her relationship with her sister. "Dr. Adams was one of many people in the house last night," he conceded.

"Charlotte and I have a history. She doesn't like me because I stole her boyfriend."

"And how do you feel about her?"

Pamela shrugged. "I couldn't care less about her. She might have thought we were rivals, but as far as I was concerned, she was no competition whatsoever."

"And your sister's opinion of her?"

"I have no idea. Until I saw Charlotte a few minutes ago, I hadn't thought about her in years. I must admit I'm a little curious about why Theresa invited her to the party, though." She paused, tilting her head thoughtfully. "We should meet later for coffee. You can fill me on the investigation, and maybe I can help you in some way."

It was a good idea. He needed to know the players, and with Theresa unconscious and the mayor stressed out, Pamela was his best bet at getting some insight into the family. "Call the station. They'll get in touch with me."

"I'll see you later, then."

She gave him a flirtatious smile that seemed out of place in this very serious hospital room. Despite the fact that Pamela had rushed to her sister's bedside, she didn't appear to be all that upset about Theresa's condition. Or was her flirting a cover for something else? If she had a hidden agenda, as Charlotte suspected, he intended to find out what it was.

FOUR

After leaving the hospital, Charlotte stopped home to change into jeans and make up a tray of sandwiches to take to the party. Then she headed across town. Kara and Colin lived in a three-bedroom house in a quiet neighborhood filled with young families. The elementary school was only a few blocks away, as was a neighborhood park, and as on most blocks, there was a feeling of community and friendship among the neighbors. It was that feeling of belonging somewhere that she'd missed when she left for college.

But just as she had grown up, so had Angel's Bay. There was a lot more action within the city limits now, more stores and businesses and an influx of people who had come to live here, not just spend their summers near the beach. Yet in spite of the growth, the town still retained its charm. She hoped that would never change.

The street was crowded, so she parked a few

houses away. She had just gotten out of her car when she heard someone call her name. Turning her head, she smiled as Jason Marlow jogged across the street.

Jason, with his light brown hair and brown eyes, had been best friends with Colin and Kara since they'd all met in kindergarten. Charlotte suspected he'd had a big crush on Kara for most of that time, but Kara had only had eyes for her blue-eyed, smiling Irishman.

Fortunately, Jason had found his own love a few months ago when he'd fallen for Brianna Kane. She was a widow and a mother, so Jason was stepping into not just a relationship but a family. He'd never looked happier, and his career was blossoming as well since he'd become a detective.

"I'm glad I caught you before you went inside," Jason said.

"You look like you're in work mode," she commented, his slacks and sports coat a far cry from the usual faded jeans and a T-shirt with a surfboard on it. "Brianna and Lucas aren't coming?"

"No, they're at the Kanes' house. I'm just stopping by for a few minutes. After last night, today is going to be all work."

"I saw Joe at the hospital. He said there hasn't been much progress."

"Unfortunately, no. Which means I'm going to need to interview you again, more formally this time."

"I told you everything I know, Jason. I didn't have anything to do with what happened to Theresa."

"Believe me, Charlotte, you're the last person I want to interrogate, but I have to run this investigation by the book. I hope you can understand that."

She sighed. "We don't have to talk now, do we?"

"Tomorrow will be fine. Can you come in on your lunch break?"

"I suppose so."

"Thanks. Can I carry that inside for you?"

She handed over the heavy tray of sandwiches. "It's the least you can do before you arrest me."

"Well, you wouldn't be a suspect if you hadn't been trying to run away from a kiss."

"Kara has a big mouth," she grumbled. "I can't believe she told you that. You'd better not put it in your report."

He grinned. "It would explain why you went upstairs just before midnight. Who didn't you want to kiss?"

"You're a detective. You figure it out," she said with a smile, then marched up the steps to Kara's house and opened the front door.

Inside, a half-dozen men were gathered around the big-screen television, watching a college bowl game. A few looked up to say hello, then a touchdown drew their attention back to the screen, and a series of high fives broke out.

Charlotte took the sandwich tray from Jason, who'd paused to watch the game. "I'm going to find the women."

In the kitchen, Kara was at the stove, stirring something in a large pot. Her red hair was pulled back in a clip, and she had on a bright red apron over her jeans and T-shirt. Isabella Silveira, Joe's sister, was sitting on a stool by the center island, sipping a glass of wine. She wore jeans and boots with a pink sweater. Her long, curly dark brown hair fell past her shoulders, and her beautiful, unusual blue eyes were bright and happy. She looked like a woman in love, which wasn't surprising, since she'd recently hooked up with local architect Nick Hartley.

Lauren Jamison was another beautiful blue-eyed brunette with the glow of love about her. Lauren was about to be married. She held a box from her bakery and was placing delicious-smelling tarts on a silver tray.

"You're here—finally," Kara said.

"Yeah, finally," Lauren grumbled.

"Am I late?" Charlotte asked in surprise as she set down the sandwiches. "I thought I was early."

"You are, but I'm dying to try on my wedding dress, and I didn't want to do it without you," Lauren answered, her eyes sparkling with excitement. "Isabella brought it here, along with your bridesmaids' dresses."

"I can't wait to see it. I'm betting you outdid yourself, Isabella."

"We'll see," Isabella said. "The only wedding dress I made before this was for an actress in a soap opera, and she wasn't really getting married."

"Did you make these sandwiches?" Kara interrupted with a wary expression as she glanced at the tray on the counter.

"I can make sandwiches," Charlotte retorted. "I tried one, and I'm still alive."

Kara grinned. "Just checking." She unwrapped the tray and tossed the plastic wrap into the garbage. "We have some time before everyone else gets here, so why don't we go upstairs and try on our dresses? Faith is asleep, and the guys won't notice we're gone until halftime or the chips run out."

"Sounds good to me." Charlotte followed the others upstairs to Kara's bedroom, then sat on the bed with Kara while Isabella grabbed a garment bag from the closet.

"I hope it's everything you imagined, Lauren," Isabella said, "but there's still time for changes. I want you to be totally satisfied. Whatever you don't like, I'll fix."

"I'll take it into the bathroom and change there," Lauren said. "That way, you'll get the full effect when I come out."

"I'll help you," Isabella told her. "There are a lot of little buttons."

As the other two left, Charlotte scooted back on the bed, making herself more comfortable. "You talk too much," she told Kara.

Kara raised an eyebrow. "Are you referring to something in particular?"

"You told Jason I ran upstairs last night so I wouldn't have to kiss someone. Now he wants to know who."

"Oh." An apologetic gleam filled her warm brown eyes. "I'm sorry about that. Colin was talking to Jason about why you were up there, and it came out. I didn't think it was a big deal. It was just Jason and Colin."

"They're both cops, and I'm the prime suspect."

"No one would ever believe you're a thief," Kara said with a dismissive wave of her hand. "And you barely wear jewelry. You wouldn't know a real diamond from a piece of glass."

"Yes, but the mayor thinks I hate his wife. Theresa or Pamela must have been talking about me at some point, and I can't figure out why. I haven't had more than a brief conversation with Theresa since I came back to town last year. And before a couple of hours ago, I hadn't talked to Pamela since high school."

Kara raised an eyebrow. "A couple of hours ago?"

"She's back in town. I saw her at the hospital. Robert called her, and she came rushing to Theresa's bedside."

"How did she look? Was she fat?" Kara asked hopefully.

"No, she was the same. Skinny, huge breasts, evil smile . . ." She shook her head, bewildered by her strong reaction. "I don't know why she bothers me so much. It's been more than ten years since I really thought about her at all. But when she stepped off that elevator and looked at me, I felt all my teenage insecurity again."

"Everyone has someone like that in their past."

"Do you?"

"Becky Saunders," Kara said instantly. "She beat

me every damn time, no matter what it was—a math contest, soccer tryouts, cheerleading. And besides that, she had the most gorgeous tan, and all I could do was freckle."

"What happened to Becky?"

"Her family moved away after high school. Her father lost all their money."

"That's sad."

"I know. I tried to feel bad for her."

Charlotte grinned at Kara's unrepentant expression. "Well, at least Becky is out of your life. Pamela is right back in the middle of mine, and now I'm a suspect in her sister's attack. If I was going to give anyone a hefty shove, it would be Pamela."

Kara held up a hand. "Don't say anything more. I don't want to be called to testify."

"This isn't a joke."

"It feels like one. We all know you, Charlotte. We all love you. Jason won't go after you. And Joe has the hots for you, so I don't see him tossing you in jail." She tilted her head. "Speaking of which, who *did* you run away from last night? I thought it was Andrew, but now I'm wondering."

"It was both of them. They arrived within minutes of each other. I couldn't figure out how to handle the stroke of midnight, so I bolted. It seemed like a good idea at the time," she added dryly.

"Really? Because kissing two hot guys doesn't seem so horrible to me."

"They don't like each other, and it's always awkward when the three of us are together." She took a breath. "Frankly, I don't know what I want to do about either one of them. Joe is gorgeous and sexy and a little mysterious, but I'm not sure I want to get involved with someone who's just out of a marriage. He needs a rebound girl, and I'm not cut out for that. Even if I wasn't just a rebound, how do you compete with a first wife?"

Kara's eyes filled with sympathy. "I understand. You don't want to be second. And with Andrew, it's the opposite. He was your first love, but you don't know if you want to go down that road again."

"Exactly."

"They're both good men, and they are both very interested in you. Sounds like you may have a decision to make."

"One of many." Charlotte let out a sigh. "Sometimes I wonder why I'm still in Angel's Bay. I never intended it to be permanent."

"It has to be. I don't want you to leave."

"I can't live with my mother forever."

"So get your own place. You could even get a town house big enough for you, Annie, and the baby if you don't want to leave them with your mother. You have lots of options. I can help you find a place to live. As for the men in your life—just remember you're not getting any younger."

"Now you sound like my mother."

"You don't want to end up alone and single like Mathilda Robertson and her fourteen cats, three birds, and a pond full of fish," Kara said pragmatically. "It's not pretty."

"Would you still visit me if I did?"

"Not a chance. I'm allergic to cats."

Charlotte picked up the pillow and tossed it at Kara's smiling face. "Some friend you are."

Kara caught the pillow and threw it back at her. "Just being honest."

"Are you ready to see the bride?" Isabella interrupted, peeking out the bathroom door. "Here she is!"

Lauren stepped into the room in a swirl of white satin and lace. The neckline was off the shoulder, and the dress tapered in at her waist, then fell in a cascade to the ground. Her dark hair and blue eyes were a perfect foil for the beautiful gown.

"You look amazing," Charlotte said, feeling her heart catch.

She'd met Lauren in kindergarten. They'd spent the first few days walking around the playground holding hands. They'd been best friends until high school, when boys and other things had derailed them for a while. But she'd been there when Lauren had suffered the tragic loss of her sister, Abby, when her family had broken up, and when Lauren's relationship with Shane had ended the first time around. Her friend had been in pieces, her life completely destroyed.

But that was all in the past now. Abby's murderer had finally been caught, Lauren and Shane had reunited and were getting married, and her friendship with Lauren was stronger than ever. They'd all come back to Angel's Bay at exactly the right time.

"I can hardly believe it's me," Lauren whispered, meeting her gaze. "Or that this is really happening."

"It's really happening," Kara cut in. "And you are gorgeous. My big brother's heart is going to stop when he sees you. We might have to revive him."

Lauren tried to laugh, but her eyes blurred with tears.

"Hey, now, no crying," Charlotte said, getting up to put an arm around Lauren's shoulders. "Or we're all going to start, and I am a really ugly crier."

Lauren sniffed back a tear. "I'm just so happy. All those years that Shane and I were apart; I never imagined we'd find our way back to each other."

"You two were meant to be," she said. "A love story for all time."

Lauren smiled. "Thank you, Charlotte."

"You're welcome." Charlotte turned toward Isabella. "You did a fantastic job. It's a beautiful dress."

"Okay, our turn," Kara said. "I want to see the bridesmaids' dresses."

Charlotte was just as curious to see what she would be wearing. Her last three bridesmaids' dresses had been appallingly awful, one a hideous orange that had made her look like a pumpkin, another that was more mother-of-the-bride than bridesmaid, and the third a frilly mess of ribbons and gathered pleating guaranteed to add twenty pounds to even the skinniest bridesmaid.

Isabella opened the second garment bag and pulled out two slinky, strapless, floor-length dresses in a gorgeous dark blue. She held them up with an expectant smile. "Well?"

"Oh, my," Kara breathed, her voice almost reverent. "Really? We get to wear these?"

"I'm stunned," Charlotte said. "You must really love us, Lauren."

Lauren laughed. "Well, I didn't want you to look better than me, but I was afraid you'd both bail if I put you in pink taffeta. Try them on. I want to see how we look together."

They stripped off their clothes and put on their gowns, then the three of them lined up in front of the full-length mirror.

"We look good," Kara said. "One blonde, one brunette, and what group would be complete without a hot redhead?"

"We're grown up," Lauren said, a note of amazement in her voice.

Charlotte smiled, seeing not their adult selves but the little girls they'd once been, playing hide-and-seek in the neighborhood, making up imaginary games in Kara's family tree house, and giggling the night away playing Truth or Dare at a slumber party.

"What do you think, Charlotte?" Kara asked, meeting her gaze in the mirror.

"I'm happy that we all found our way back to Angel's Bay."

Lauren squeezed her hand. "It was the best decision I ever made."

"Well, I was wise enough to not ever leave," Kara

said. "But you two had to see the world first. Thank goodness you finally came to your senses and returned home."

"You all look wonderful," Isabella said. "It's great that you've been friends for so long. I hope you know how lucky you are. I don't have friends who go back twenty years."

"Well, you're one of us now," Charlotte said.

Isabella smiled. "That's generous of you. When I came here a few months ago, I wondered what was so fascinating about this town that my brother couldn't pull himself away. Now I know. It's the community. The people."

"You've fallen under our spell," Kara said with a wise nod.

"Or the spell of one hot guitar-playing architect," Lauren added with a grin. "How are things with you and Nick?"

"Excellent," Isabella said. "I'm going to go back and forth between my projects in L.A. and here until June, and then we'll spend the summer in Los Angeles. Somehow we'll find a way to have the best of both worlds. Of course, Megan is the priority. She has been shuffled around a lot, and Nick and I want to make sure that she's happy with whatever arrangement we come up with."

"Sounds like you're talking long-term," Charlotte said.

Isabella met her gaze. "The first time I saw Nick's face, I knew he was the man I'd been dreaming about."

"Really. It was that clear?" Charlotte asked.

"It was. But then, I'm a little psychic," she said with a grin.

"I knew the first time I saw Colin, too," Kara interjected. "He was eating chocolate pudding in kindergarten, and it was smeared across his face."

"It was first sight for me and Shane, too," Lauren added. "He was racing his motorcycle down the street, and I thought he was the baddest boy in town. I got all hot and bothered but wondered what he'd want with a good girl like me."

"I think we all know what he wanted," Charlotte said with a laugh.

"He was my first," Lauren admitted. "And the best, too. Speaking of first loves, are you and Andrew getting back together?"

"I don't know," Charlotte said.

"Well, it's not always about first love," Kara said. "It wasn't for you, was it, Isabella?"

"No, Nick wasn't the first," she said, her thoughtful gaze coming to rest on Charlotte.

"We should get out of these dresses," Charlotte said quickly, wanting to get everyone off the subject of her love life—especially Joe's sister.

"Before you take yours off, Kara," Isabella said, "I think we need to alter the bust. Can I take a look?"

"Of course. It is a little tight. I love breastfeeding— I actually have a chest! Colin will be so disappointed when these go away," she added with a laugh.

While Isabella worked some pins through Kara's

dress, Charlotte changed into her clothes and then went into the bathroom to help Lauren out of her dress. As she worked her way through the buttons, she said, "How's your father doing? Will he be able to walk you down the aisle?"

"I hope so, but his Alzheimer's has been getting worse. I wish I could have had the wedding earlier, but my mother went on a holiday cruise, and she doesn't get back until this weekend. I want both my parents there, so I'm keeping my fingers crossed that somehow it will all work out. I want to have one day where we'll be a family again."

Charlotte met her yearning gaze in the mirror, knowing how much Lauren needed to have everyone together. While Lauren and her father had been able to work through their differences, her parents were still divorced, and her brother lived on the other side of the country.

"I just wish Abby could be at my wedding," Lauren continued, a sad note in her voice. "She was going to be my maid of honor. When we were kids, we planned out our weddings. She wanted to have hers on a boat. She imagined saying her vows at sunset, surrounded by the sea, a trail of rose petals in the water."

"Sounds pretty. What was your dream?"

"What I'm having," Lauren said with a smile. "At sunset on a bluff, the solid ground beneath my feet, the man I love at my side, and all my friends there to support me. Shane probably would have liked Abby's idea better. He was always more comfortable on the water than on land, but he wants me to be happy. Since this is Angel's Bay, I'm hoping my angel of a sister will be watching from afar. I want it all to be perfect. But whatever happens, I'm marrying Shane."

"And that will make it perfect," Charlotte said quietly.

"Yes, it will," Lauren agreed.

"So did you have your wedding night in mind when you asked Isabella to design a dress with a hundred buttons down the back?" Charlotte teased.

Lauren flung her a mischievous smile. "I'm going to make Shane work for it."

"I hope he doesn't get impatient and rip the dress. Not that that wouldn't be fun."

"Nobody is ripping my dress. I want to keep it in case I have a daughter one day."

Charlotte could picture Lauren with a little girl, same dark hair and blue eyes, and she smiled at the thought of Shane having to deal with another female in his life. He'd always been a moody, reckless loner, except where Lauren was concerned. Then his rough exterior melted to mush. A daughter would probably wrap him around her little finger just as easily.

"I think I've got them all," she said, helping Lauren out of the dress. She took it into the other room while Lauren put on her clothes. Isabella had finished taking measurements and was putting the bridesmaids' dresses away. Charlotte helped Isabella zip up the wedding dress, so that no harm could come to it in the next few days.

When they were all ready, they headed down the

hall. Kara stopped at the first door. "She's awake," she said with delight. "My little princess is up."

Charlotte and Isabella watched from the doorway as Lauren and Kara approached the crib. Kara scooped up the baby and smothered her in kisses before taking her over to the changing table.

"Sweet," Isabella said, exchanging a smile with Charlotte.

"Very," Charlotte agreed. "Shall we keep going?"

"Sure."

As they moved toward the stairs, Charlotte said, "Joe told me that your father is doing better after his stroke."

"He is. Having Joe home really helped his spirits. He could relax, knowing his son was there to watch out for the family. He's very traditional in that regard. My father loves his daughters, but his son has a very special place in his heart. Joe, however, was chomping at the bit once we got past Christmas."

"I'm sure your parents didn't want to see him go."

"No. They were hoping that Joe's return might mean a reconciliation with Rachel."

Charlotte's pulse sped up at the mention of Joe's ex-wife. "Did Joe see her while he was at home?"

Isabella nodded. "Rachel came to visit. She was part of our family for a long time, and she still keeps in touch with my parents. But Joe came back here, and she's still in L.A., so I think it's truly over." Isabella paused, shooting her a quick look. "I got the idea that my brother's desire to get back here by New Year's had a little something to do with you."

"We're just friends," Charlotte said quickly.

"Maybe that will change. Joe is a good guy. I'm biased, but I don't think you could do better."

"I know that. But he has a lot of baggage."

"Don't we all? Some relationships just have their time, and that's it. It took me a while to accept that Joe and Rachel were over. It seemed so sad at first. She was like a sister to me. But I want them both to be happy, and they clearly weren't. You can't hang on to something just because it used to be good."

"I suppose not. But there's something powerful about first love."

"True. But sometimes I wonder if trying to recapture that first love is more about recapturing the person you used to be. And that's what people *really* want to get back." Isabella gave a little laugh. "I'm the last person who should be spouting wisdom on this topic. It took me a long time and a lot of bad boyfriends to find Nick."

Charlotte smiled back at her. "I know just what you mean." But as they made their way into the kitchen, she thought about what Isabella had said. Was it Andrew she wanted back—or herself?

FIVE

Andrew went into the church office and stripped off his minister's collar, which sometimes felt suffocating. He'd been working hard to gain respect from the town he'd grown up in. It had taken time for the congregation, especially the older members, to stop seeing him as the wild teenager who'd never missed an opportunity to party and start seeing him as the conservative spiritual leader of their church.

He'd had some big shoes to step into. Reverend Adams, Charlotte's father, had been a popular and charismatic leader for more than twenty-five years. His death had been a huge loss for the congregation, even worse for Charlotte.

He wondered if one of the reasons she held back from truly allowing him back into her life was that he'd taken over for her father. When she saw him, she saw her dad. When she thought of being with him, she saw her mother in her role as the minister's wife.

But Charlotte needed to realize that they wouldn't be carbon copies of her parents. They would be themselves. They would be who they were always supposed to be.

With a sigh, he rolled his neck around on his shoulders to ease its tightness. It had been a busy weekend, with his normal Sunday sermon yesterday and today's special New Year's Day service. He was a ready for a break.

Hearing the door open behind him, he turned in surprise. He'd thought everyone had gone home.

Surprise turned to shock and wariness as Pamela entered the room.

The last woman he'd ever wanted to see again.

"Hello, Andrew." She gave him a saucy smile as she sauntered toward him. "You don't look happy to see me."

"It's been a long time."

"Seven years."

"Why are you here?"

"My sister was robbed and assaulted last night. Surely you've heard."

"I'm still surprised to see you. When we last spoke, you weren't interested in a relationship with Theresa."

"She's still my sister."

As Pamela came closer, he moved around behind his desk, wanting a buffer zone. Pamela was a born predator. She went after what she wanted with ruthless intensity, willing to do whatever it took to accomplish her goal. Years ago, her goal had been him.

He hadn't put up much of a fight nor had he realized what kind of power she would eventually have over him—how easy it would be to buy into whatever story she was selling. But he knew better now.

She perched on the edge of his desk, the gleam in her eye telling him that she knew she was making him uncomfortable, and she was enjoying it.

"How is Theresa?" he asked.

"She has a severe concussion. They'll know more within the next twenty-four hours. She opened her eyes while I was there, but she seemed very confused and fell back to sleep almost immediately."

"I'm sorry to hear that. Robert must be very concerned."

"He does actually look like he cares," she conceded. "Or maybe he's just worried about losing his trophy wife."

"So cynical."

"Oh, please. Theresa married Robert for his money, and he married her for her looks."

"Maybe they fell in love after they got married."

She shrugged. "Sure, why not?" She stared at him for an uncomfortable length of time. "When you told me you'd found God, I thought it was just the hangover talking. But you actually did what you said you were going to do—you're a minister. Does the church board have any idea of the life you used to lead?"

"How long are you planning to stay in town?" he asked, ignoring her question.

"That depends on how quickly my sister recovers."

"You always hated Angel's Bay. Why would you want to extend your visit? You used to say this town had too many do-gooders in it."

"Yeah, and now you're one of them. Traitor."

"I grew up. What about you? What have you been doing the last seven years?"

"Living it up."

He could see that in the weary lines around her eyes, the limpness of her hair, the paleness of her skin. "You look tired."

For a moment, her hard shell seemed to crack, then she straightened her shoulders and threw up her chin. "I'm great."

"Are you?" She was one of the best liars he'd ever met.

"Why did you come back here, Andrew? You could have gone to any church in the country."

"Angel's Bay has always been home. My family is here."

"Your family? Who cared so little about you when you couldn't play baseball anymore and live out your father's dreams? Where were they then?"

"My father is dead, Pamela."

Surprise flashed through her eyes. "I didn't know that."

"There are a lot of things you don't know."

"And a lot that I do," she countered. "For a while, I was your family."

He shook his head. She was way off the mark.

"Family doesn't describe our relationship. And whatever we were to each other was part of another life." He paused. "I hope Theresa gets better. I'm sure she appreciates your visit, but you and I have nothing left to say to each other."

"You're wrong, Andrew. I have a lot to say. And I have no intention of leaving Angel's Bay until I'm ready. By the way, I saw Charlotte at the hospital."

His heart sank at her sly smile. The last thing he needed was Pamela messing up what little ground he'd made with Charlotte. "You need to leave her alone."

"That may be difficult, considering Robert thinks Charlotte stole Theresa's jewelry and knocked her out."

"That's ridiculous."

"Always to Charlotte's defense. Some things never change. But I know things about you that Charlotte doesn't."

He met her gaze head on. "I know things about you, too. So if that's some kind of threat . . ."

"I was just stating the facts. You're awfully defensive, Andrew."

"Because I know you, Pamela. When you're bored, you like to screw up other people's lives just for fun."

"That's true." She stood up and looked around the office. "What does Charlotte think of you being in her daddy's office, in her daddy's house?"

"Charlotte thinks I'm doing a good job."

"Are you trying to get her back?"

He sighed. "What I'm trying to do right now is

live my life the best way I know how, and I would hope you're doing the same. Can we let the past stay in the past?"

She thought for a moment. "I don't know. I guess we'll see."

And with that, she was gone, leaving him with a very bad feeling in his gut. He'd worked too hard to get his life together. He couldn't let Pamela destroy it.

Joe made it to Kara's house halfway through the fourth quarter. As chief of police, he had to walk a fine line between being friends with his officers and being their boss. In the beginning, he'd kept a distance, but over time, he'd realized that wasn't possible.

His officers and their girlfriends or wives were constantly inviting him over for dinner, a barbecue, someone's birthday party, or another's anniversary. He'd grown tired of saying no, not to mention a little lonely—especially since his marriage had broken up. He had a job in Angel's Bay, but now he needed to make it a life.

When he entered the living room, he saw several of his off-duty officers and their significant others, as well as a half-dozen other people. He exchanged hellos, watched a few minutes of the game, and then decided to find some food.

"Chief, you made it," Kara said, coming through the swinging door of the kitchen with a tray of cookies. "I'm so glad."

"Those look good."

"They're from Lauren's bakery, so they're definitely good. But if you want real food first, there's chili and sandwiches in the kitchen. Charlotte will show you where everything is."

Judging by Kara's smile, she'd either picked up on his interest in Charlotte, or Charlotte had said something. He'd rather not have anyone in his business, but Charlotte had a lot of friends in town. Anyone she dated would come under scrutiny.

Moving through the doorway, he found Charlotte sitting by the island counter next to a baby seat holding Kara's adorable daughter, Faith. Charlotte was spinning a mobile of zoo animals and seemed to be having as much fun as the baby.

"Joe," she said with a smile. "I thought you'd be here earlier."

"I had some things to do."

"Any news on Theresa?"

He shook his head. "Not yet." He glanced around the kitchen, noting the stack of empty plates in the sink. "Is the food gone?"

"Not all. Kara made a killer chili. I'll get you some, but you'll have to take over entertainment duty. Kara told me to keep her daughter happy until she got back."

"I can handle that," he said, sitting on the stool she vacated. He gave the mobile a spin, watching as Faith's eyes lit up, and she kicked out her little legs in pure delight. "Simple pleasures," he murmured.

"Too bad we forget how to enjoy them when we grow up."

"It is too bad," Charlotte agreed as she ladled a generous portion of chili into a bowl. She set it down in front of him and slid a plate of corn bread across the counter. "What else do you need?"

"I'd love a cold beer."

She reached into the refrigerator and pulled out a can. "You're in luck. There's a few left."

"This is good," he said, digging into the chili. "Much better than the one you and I made for the chili cookoff."

"I never said I could cook. I thought you could."

"I have a mother and a lot of sisters. They tend to dominate the kitchen on family occasions."

"And what do the men do?"

"Watch sports, play pool in the basement, drink beers out on the patio."

"Being a man is a pretty sweet deal in your family."

He grinned. "I can't lie. It's not bad. Why don't you cook, Charlotte? Your mother is the epitome of the perfect homemaker. I can't imagine she didn't teach you."

Charlotte rested her forearms on the counter. "She tried to teach me, but I was all thumbs when it came to cooking and crafts. I'm better at stitching up people than at altering hemlines."

He grimaced. "I can't imagine doing that."

"I wouldn't take you for the queasy sort," she said with a grin.

"I'm not a big fan of blood, although I've seen quite a bit of it."

"I bet you have," she said more seriously. "Have you ever shot someone?"

He wasn't sure he wanted to answer, but there was something about Charlotte that always made him want to spill his guts. "A couple of times," he admitted.

Her gaze softened. "Was it hard to pull the trigger?"

"No. It was instinct, training, self-defense." Did that sound cold to her? "There's no place for emotion when someone's life is on the line. You know that as well as I do."

She nodded with understanding. "Yes, I do. But sometimes later . . ."

"Yeah, that's when it can get hard." He paused. "Even the worst criminals have families—mothers who cry over their death, fathers who wish they'd done something differently, sisters, brothers, friends, who wonder how they could have stopped the worst from happening."

"But the other side is that you were protecting someone else, or at the very least yourself."

He took a sip of his beer. "Let's talk about something else. How was your Christmas? You went to San Francisco, didn't you?"

She straightened. "Yes, we all went—my mother, Annie, and little Will. We visited my sister Doreen and her husband and kids. We rode the cable cars, went to Alcatraz, shopped in Union Square, did all the touristy things. And the rest of the time, we just talked. It was great to see my sister—we reminisced a lot. Annie was very curious about how we'd grown up, so we told her every family story we could remember." She gave a self-deprecating smile. "I didn't come off too well in most of them. Doreen and my mother seem to remember every stupid mistake I made in my life. And the stories just get wilder year after year."

"Family lore can never be believed."

"Exactly." Her expression turned wistful. "I do miss the past, though. Everything is different now. My dad is gone, and Jamie is in the Middle East somewhere. Holidays aren't what they used to be."

"I'm sorry your brother couldn't get home for Christmas."

"My mother was very upset about it. She adores Jamie. He's still her baby boy, and she misses him so much. Sometimes when we video chat with him, I barely recognize him. He's grown up so much, seen things I'm sure no one should ever see. But he loves the military. It was all he ever wanted to do. We were tripping over toy soldiers from the time he was in kindergarten." She drew in a big breath, as if talking about Jamie was too stressful. "Can I get you some more chili?"

"No, thanks. I'm moving on to these chocolate things," he said, reaching across the table for the dessert plate.

"Good choice."

"Why are you hanging out in the kitchen? Not a football fan?"

"I was keeping Kara company, but she seems to have deserted me and her baby."

Joe glanced over at Faith, who was fast asleep. "She doesn't seem to be upset about it."

Charlotte smiled. "She's a sweet thing."

"They always look like angels when they're asleep."

"True. I learned that when Annie was missing and Will screamed for hours on end, making me want to tear out my hair. But asleep, he was an angel." Charlotte paused, a question in her eyes. "It's not my business, Joe, but—"

"You're going to ask anyway," he finished, thinking he knew where she was about to go.

"Why didn't you and Rachel have any kids?"

"A lot of reasons."

"Any that you want to share?"

He hesitated. He wasn't used to sharing details about his marriage. But his marriage was over; there was nothing left to protect. "We never wanted to have a baby at the same time. In the beginning, we waited because we didn't have any money, but after a few years, I convinced Rachel that we should start trying. Unfortunately, nothing happened. Then she got busy with her career, and I wasn't handling my own stress too well. Throwing a baby into the mix didn't seem like the best idea.

"At some point, she went back on birth control, and I stopped asking. Maybe we somehow sensed that we weren't going to stay together. I'm glad now that it didn't happen, because I wouldn't have wanted to put my kid through a divorce." Some days, though, he wondered if he'd missed his chance to be a father.

"Has it been difficult for you—the divorce?"

He nodded. "I don't like to fail, and divorce is the ultimate failure."

"But staying together—"

"Wouldn't make the marriage any less of a failure," he said. "That's true, but it doesn't feel that way."

"Are you sure it's really over?" she asked tentatively.

"Yes," he said, holding her gaze. He didn't want there to be any misunderstanding between them. "It's over. Rachel knows that, and so do I. We got married too young. We grew up and apart. I wish her the best; I hope she can find someone to make her happy."

"You're hard on yourself," Charlotte observed.

"So are you," he pointed out. "Something we have in common."

She nodded. "You're right. I don't like to fail, either."

He got up and took his dishes to the sink, then moved next to her.

She tensed, her lips parting as their eyes met. "Stop looking at me like that."

"Like what?" he challenged, crowding her against the island counter.

"Like you want to go somewhere and get naked."

He grinned as her cheeks pinked. He'd like to see

that rosy flush all over her body. "Sounds like a good idea to me."

"It's a bad idea. A very bad idea."

"Are you trying to convince me or yourself?"

Before she could answer, the kitchen door swung open. Charlotte jerked away from him, busying herself with cleanup, while Kara and Colin and a crowd of people descended on them.

"We're going to the park to play some football," Colin told Joe. "Want to come?"

"I'm not dressed for it."

"Go home and change. We're meeting at Maplewood Park in twenty minutes. That goes for you, too, Charlie."

Joe turned to see Charlotte's reaction. She was frowning and shaking her head.

"I don't think so," she replied. "The last time I played football with you, Colin, you said I threw like a girl."

He grinned. "You do throw like a girl, but we need you to even out the teams. Lauren is in, Isabella, Tracy, Joanne . . . we need one more."

"My sister is going to play?" Joe asked in surprise.

"Yeah, Isabella and Nick," Colin answered. "Come on, Charlotte, we need you."

"What about Kara?"

"I have to babysit," Kara said. "You should play, Charlotte. You're a fast runner."

"Yeah, it's the catching and the throwing I don't care for."

"What about you, Chief?" Colin asked. "Can we count on you?"

"If Charlotte's in, I'm in."

She made a face at him. "Don't put it on me."

"If you're getting out of it, so am I."

"Neither one of you is out of it," Colin said firmly. "Go home, get changed, and we'll meet at the park. It will be fun."

"Charlotte, you can borrow some clothes and tennis shoes from me," Kara interjected.

"I'll meet you at the park," Joe told her. He just hoped they were on opposite teams. If he was going to cover someone, he wanted it to be her.

Andrew dug his hands into his pockets as he stood next to Kara, watching the game. He'd arrived at the party just as everyone was heading out to play football. Since the teams were even, he'd been sidelined with Kara. She was one of his favorite people, but he didn't like being out of the action while Joe was in the game. He couldn't help but notice how often Joe and Charlotte seemed to be chasing after each other.

"What's bugging you?" Kara asked. "You've sighed like three times in the last two minutes. Or should I guess?"

"You're not encouraging that, are you?" he asked.

"You mean Charlotte and Joe? I'm not encouraging it. I'm not discouraging it, either. I'm neutral. I'm Switzerland."

He frowned as he looked at her. "The chief is married, Kara."

"Almost officially divorced," she pointed out.

"*Almost* isn't officially anything," he grumbled. "What I don't understand is why Charlotte would want to be someone's second choice?"

Kara's brows knit together. "I don't think she's looking at it that way, Andrew. Or any way, for that matter. Joe has been gone for almost a month. He just got back yesterday."

"He's been hanging around her for months. He used Annie's disappearance as a way to get closer to her. Now he's probably going to use this burglary at the mayor's house to do the same thing."

"Joe isn't the problem, Andrew," Kara said abruptly.

"What do you mean?" he asked, surprised at her tone.

"You're the problem."

"Me? What have I done?"

"It's not what you've done; it's who you are. You're the guy who hurt her. You're the bad boyfriend from the past. I know it was a long time ago, and everyone's changed, and you're a wonderful, respectable man now. But Charlotte may not see the guy you are now. She still sees the boy who broke her heart."

"I couldn't have broken her heart if she hadn't loved me. And if she loved me once, she can love me again. I would think you, of all people, would understand, Kara. You married your high school sweetheart. I'm sure your relationship wasn't perfect all the time. Colin must have made at least one or two dumb-ass moves in the past."

"More than one or two," she said with a soft smile. "I do get it, Andrew. But Charlotte is very guarded when it comes to love, and if you want her back, you're going to have to work for it."

"Then that's what I'll do." He glanced back at the action in the park. "You need to get me into this game, Kara. I can't fight for Charlotte if I'm on the sidelines."

"What do you want me to do?"

"I don't know. Tell Colin he has a phone call or something. Then I'll take his place."

"You want me to lie to my husband?" she asked in mock astonishment. "What would the church elders think?"

"You're not going to help me?"

"I'm thinking about it. First, tell me about Pamela."

"Pamela?" he echoed, stalling for time.

"Charlotte said she's back in town to see her sister. Do you think you'll see her again?"

"I already have. She came by the church earlier."

Kara raised an eyebrow. "That was quick."

"There's nothing between us, Kara."

"What's Pamela's story? Is she married? Does she have a job? Where does she live?"

"We didn't discuss her personal life. We just talked about Theresa. It was a short conversation." He shifted his weight, watching the game for another minute. "I feel like an idiot standing here. I should just go."

"I thought you were going to fight."

"How can I do that while she's rolling around in the grass with him? Did anyone tell the chief this wasn't tackle football?"

"Colin!" Kara shouted as the group headed into the next huddle. "Can you come here for a second?"

"Babe, we're in the middle of a game!" Colin yelled back.

"Andrew can play for you."

Colin looked as if he wanted to say no, but he'd made a habit of giving Kara whatever she wanted.

"Thank you," Andrew said.

"Don't hurt Charlotte. Or you'll have me to contend with."

Colin came over and tossed Andrew the ball. "You're in. Don't lose my lead."

Six

The game got more intense with Andrew replacing Colin, Charlotte thought. Each play seemed to become more competitive. Andrew had been a star baseball player when he was young, and he was good at football, too. He threw the ball far better than Colin did, and their team quickly racked up more points. Joe was no slouch, either. He was agile and fast and played with the same drive he brought to everything else.

Charlotte was trying to stay out of the action as much as possible, always relieved when the ball went somewhere else. Finally, someone called a halt as the sun sank lower in the sky, and they all headed toward the sidelines.

"I wish I'd gotten here earlier," Andrew said, falling into step next to her. "I was just getting into it. I can't remember the last time I threw a football around—probably high school."

"Well, it came right back to you. I'm not surprised. You were a good athlete."

"At one time, baseball was what I lived for. I never imagined there would be a day when I couldn't do it anymore. When my dream would die a brutal death."

She stopped abruptly, surprised by his words. "What are you talking about?"

"I tore up my knee in junior year of college," he explained. "I had to have surgery. I was out that year and wasn't in good enough shape the next year to play. I thought you knew that."

"No one ever mentioned that you got hurt. I thought you just quit after you finished school."

"No. I wanted to go pro, and I had some interest. A few weeks before I got hurt, a couple of scouts talked to me. I was going to be drafted, but that was put on hold with the injury. Then it became an impossibility."

The pain in his voice matched the shadows in his eyes. Andrew had always been the golden boy, the one for whom things came easily and quickly. He'd never seemed to struggle for anything; he was just naturally good. But to have his dreams ripped away from him—that must have been tough.

"I'm sorry," she said. "I had no idea. Your father must have been disappointed, too. He spent so much time with you at the batting cage."

"My father was furious."

"Why? It wasn't your fault you got hurt."

"He thought it was a result of poor conditioning. I was partying too hard, not paying enough attention to my training. He didn't speak to me for almost three years."

"I can't believe that," she said in amazement.

"You weren't the only one who had a parent with high expectations. He wasn't completely wrong, either. I *was* partying a lot. Eventually, we made peace with it. Actually, we just didn't talk about it anymore. And then he died, so that was that."

She slid her arm around his waist. "Well, you may have lost one dream, but you found another. You're a good minister, Andrew."

"That's nice to hear from you."

"I'm sure you hear it from a lot of people."

"But you're different, because you know me better than most."

Did she? She hadn't known about his injury, which shocked her a little; it made her realize that maybe the years in between mattered more than she'd thought.

"Charlotte, I want to tell you something before you hear it from someone else," Andrew said.

"What's that?" she asked warily.

"Pamela came by the church a few hours ago. We had a short discussion about Theresa. It wasn't important, but I'm telling you because I wouldn't want you to think I was keeping it from you."

"I saw her earlier, too, at the hospital."

"She told me. I meant what I said earlier today,

Charlotte. I want to go forward, not backward. Don't let Pamela's presence drag us into the past, into problems we've rehashed a dozen times."

"Hey, you two, are you coming back to the house?" Kara interrupted, coming over to join them.

Charlotte started, realizing that most of the crowd had dispersed. Colin was pushing the baby stroller back and forth on the sidewalk while talking to Joe. "Sure, I'll come back for a little while."

"What about you, Andrew?"

He glanced down at his watch. "I wish I could, but I have some business to take care of. I'll talk to you later, Charlotte." He kissed her on the cheek, then walked across the grass, saying good-bye to the others before heading to his car.

"You and Andrew were chatting it up. Did you have fun today?" Kara asked, a mischievous gleam in her eyes.

"What's making you so happy?" Charlotte asked suspiciously as they walked across the grass.

"Watching you dodge two men."

"I was playing football. I had to dodge a lot of men."

"That's not what I'm talking about, and you know it. Andrew practically bribed me to get into the game."

"Is that why you made Colin come out?"

"Are you going to thank me?"

"It was your choice," Charlotte said. "Nothing to do with me."

Kara made a face at her. "It had everything to do

with you. So what's the deal? Are you into Andrew? Or is Joe the one giving you goose bumps?"

"Shh," she said warningly. "He'll hear you."

"That's not an answer."

"I like them both."

"Well, there's nothing wrong with that. Andrew is a blond god, and Joe is a sexy hunk of a man. Dating them both could be a lot of fun. Maybe I *did* get married too young," Kara said with a wistful sigh. "I missed all this excitement."

"It's not always exciting," Charlotte said dryly. "If you'd seen some of the losers I've dated, you wouldn't be admiring my single status. I've made a lot of mistakes when it comes to men."

"It's not the mistakes that matter; it's how you recover from them. But neither Andrew nor Joe is a loser. It looks like a win-win situation to me."

"Stop trying to marry me off. I have a lot of other things in my life to figure out. In fact, I think I'll take you up on that offer to show me some real estate."

"Anytime."

As they joined the men, Joe's cell phone rang.

After listening for a moment, he said, "I'll be there in fifteen minutes." He gave them a look of apology. "I have to take off. Thanks for the invite."

"I'll catch up to you, Kara," Charlotte said, wanting a moment to speak to Joe.

"Was that call about Theresa?" she asked as the others moved down the sidewalk. "Has something new developed?"

"That was Pamela. I'm going to meet with her to learn more about her sister."

"Why not ask the mayor? He's married to Theresa."

"The mayor has tunnel vision. I need another perspective."

"And you think Pamela will give it to you?"

"It's just routine, Charlotte."

"Then why isn't Jason handling it?"

"Because I am. It's not personal. Nor is it anything for you to be concerned about. It's just a simple conversation."

"Nothing is simple where Pamela is concerned. She doesn't like me, and she would probably love to see me go down for attacking her sister, even though it's not true. She's going to try to railroad me."

"Do you think I'd let that happen?"

"Men lose their minds when they're near Pamela's triple Ds."

A smile played around his lips as his gaze met hers. "You're jealous."

"I'm pissed. There's a difference," she said, crossing her arms in front of her chest.

"You're pissed because you're jealous."

She wanted to smack the knowing smile off his face, but there was too much truth to his statement. "Just remember that whenever Pamela is around, there's trouble."

"I hate to break it to you, Charlotte, but you seem to be a magnet for trouble yourself." He leaned in close. "But I've always liked trouble, especially when it comes in such a pretty package." He gave her a tender kiss, then stepped back. "Don't worry about Pamela. She's not going to put anything over on me, and the last thing I would ever let her do is hurt you."

Joe entered the Java Hut fifteen minutes later. Pamela was seated at a corner table, sipping coffee as she perused the local paper. A young man on his computer was the only other patron in the café. Joe sat down across from Pamela.

She gave him a smile. "Can I buy you a coffee, Chief?"

"I'm good. Thanks."

"Did I pull you away from something?" Her gaze ran down his body. "You don't look like you're on duty."

"I'm not. I just finished up a football game. How's your sister doing?"

"Confused and in pain. The doctor says that's normal. They're keeping her heavily sedated to give her brain a chance to rest. They're not sure she'll remember the attack. I'm very concerned that we're not going to find out who did this to her."

"We're in the early stages of the investigation. It's too soon to be discouraged."

"Aren't the early stages the most critical? Doesn't the trail grow colder with each passing minute?"

"My officers are working very hard on this case, Ms. Baines."

"It's Miss," she said with a flirtatious smile. "What about you, Chief? Are you a single man? Or a married man who doesn't wear a ring?"

He'd worn a ring until a few months ago, but it was amazing how quickly he'd stopped feeling its absence. "I'm divorced," he said shortly.

"Someone let you go? That's surprising."

He didn't like the gleam in her eyes. "Let's talk about you, Miss Baines. What kind of relationship do you have with your sister?"

"The usual kind," she said with an offhand wave.

"Yet you can't recall the last time you saw her?"

"A few months ago. I thought I was going to be the one asking the questions."

He ignored that. "Whoever attacked your sister knew how to get in and out of that house very quickly. We got a list of friends and workers who were involved in the renovation from the mayor, but sometimes sisters know more than husbands."

"I doubt my sister's list of friends is all that long. She loves to brag about her jewelry, her house, her money, and her clothes. And since she moved into that mansion, her head has gotten even bigger."

"It doesn't sound like you're a big fan of Theresa's."

"I know her better than anyone. I think she shot off her mouth a little too much, opened up her house to a lot of people she doesn't even like just so she could impress them, and she didn't hire any security. I'm sorry she got hurt, that she lost her wedding ring, which I know is the most important piece of jewelry she owns. But I can't help thinking that someone wanted to get back at her for something." She paused. "Maybe Charlotte."

"Why would Charlotte want to hurt your sister?"

"To get back at me for stealing Andrew."

"That's a stretch. As far as I can tell, Charlotte had no problem with Theresa."

"Well, the fact that Charlotte was discovered upstairs just after Theresa was attacked speaks for itself. I hope you won't let your friendship get in the way of your job, Chief. Or is there more between you and Charlotte than friendship?"

"I don't let anything get in the way of my job. Where do you live now?"

She stiffened. "I have a place in Los Angeles."

"How long are you planning to stay in Angel's Bay?"

"As long as my sister needs me."

"Were you invited to the New Year's Eve party?"

Her gaze turned cool. "No, I wasn't. But that's not surprising; I don't live here."

"So geography was the only reason you didn't get an invitation?" he queried.

"You'll have to ask Theresa or Robert."

"I will."

"Fine. Now let's talk about you," she said with an interested smile. "When did you leave your wife?"

"Do you flirt with every man you meet?"

"Only the ones I might want."

"You should stick with Andrew."

"Well, I've never done it with a minister. Not

that it's easy to think of Andrew in those terms. When I knew him, he was about as far from a saint as you could get."

"Care to elaborate?"

"I could be persuaded. How badly do you want the information?"

Not badly enough to take her up on the invitation in her eyes. He got to his feet. "Thanks for the chat."

"You don't know what you're missing, Chief."

"I have a pretty good idea," he said dryly.

Pamela might have played the boys in high school, but he wasn't seventeen, and more important, he wasn't a fool.

After leaving Kara's, Charlotte drove past Joe's house, debating whether she should stop. It was past seven, so it would be smarter to go home, touch base with her mother and Annie, and get ready for work tomorrow, but she was dying to know how Joe's conversation with Pamela had gone. She didn't want him to think she was stalking him, but in the end, her curiosity won out. She parked in front of his house and hurried up to the front door.

Rufus started barking, and she could hear voices inside. Was Pamela there? Her stomach turned over at that thought. She was just about to bail when the door opened. As Isabella and a barking Rufus greeted her, she smiled with relief.

"Charlotte. You're just in time."

"For what?" she asked as Rufus jumped up to smother her in wet kisses.

"Rufus, down," Joe said firmly, grabbing hold of the dog's collar and pulling him away from her. "Sorry about that."

"It's fine."

Joe had changed into worn jeans, his green T-shirt clung to his broad shoulders, and his dark hair was damp as if he'd just gotten out of the shower.

"Come on in," Isabella said. "We're just about to start the movies."

Charlotte stepped inside and nodded to Nick Hartley, who was walking down the hallway with a bowl of popcorn. "I don't want to interrupt," she said.

"You're not interrupting at all. Is she, Joe?" Isabella gave her brother a pointed look.

Joe didn't look quite as excited about her staying as his sister did. "Did you need to talk to me?"

"I did," she began, but Isabella cut her off.

"You two can talk later. Nick and I only have a short time before we have to pick up Megan." She grabbed Charlotte's hand and pulled her into the living room. "You're going to love this. I brought back home movies from L.A. to show Nick."

No wonder Joe looked so uncomfortable. "Really?" she said, shooting him an amused look. "Any naked baby pictures of you in the mix?"

"God, I hope not," he muttered.

They settled in the living room. Nick sat in the big armchair, Charlotte took a seat on the couch, and Joe sat next to her, Rufus at his feet. Isabella perched on the chair nearest the television, a box of DVDs on the table next to her.

"My sister Valerie had our old movies transferred to DVD, and she made copies for all of us," she explained.

"That's great," Charlotte said. "I need to do that with my mom's old films."

"You should. You'll want to show your childhood to your kids one day. Let's see—where should we start?"

"Let's hit the high points," Nick interjected. "We can watch the rest later."

"When you have insomnia," Joe said cynically. "It will put you right to sleep. Nick, I can't believe you're encouraging this."

Nick grinned. "I know what's good for me, and that's keeping your sister happy."

"Smart man," Isabella said, exchanging a warm smile with Nick.

"You don't have to stay for this, Charlotte," Joe said. "We can go in the other room and talk."

"Are you kidding?" I would love to see the younger you."

"Great." He sighed as Isabella turned on the first DVD.

"This is the summer we moved into the new house," she said, her hand on the remote control. "We had the best backyard, tons of grass and trees. So much better than the other place."

"I can't believe you remember the other place,"

Joe commented. "I think you were about five when we moved."

"I remember there were a lot of cars on the street, and Mama never let me play out front."

"That was a tough neighborhood," Joe said. "It wasn't safe for anyone to be out front."

"Look, the Slip 'n Slide!" Isabella pointed to the screen, where a dozen bathing-suit-clad kids of varying ages were taking turns running and sliding down a wet piece of red plastic. "And there's me."

"Love the polka-dot bikini and the heels," Charlotte said with a smile.

"I liked to make a statement even back then." Isabella fast-forwarded for a few moments, pausing at a hill and some skateboarders. "And here's Joe on the street behind our house, giving our mother a heart attack."

Charlotte watched as a dark-haired, dark-eyed, teenage Joe flew down the hill on a skateboard, jumping over the curb, onto a bench, and then down a flight of stairs. "Wow, that was crazy!"

"Young and stupid," Joe agreed. "By some miracle, I survived."

"And here he is on his bike, no hands, cocky as hell," Isabella said.

"Hey, I thought we were looking at *your* movies, Izzy," Joe complained.

"We're getting there; relax." Isabella hit fast-forward again, and for the next few minutes, they watched the seasons pass: the Halloween parade, Thanksgiving dinner, decorating the tree at Christmas. Isabella pointed out parents, grandparents, sisters, and cousins. Charlotte couldn't keep track of the names, but one thing was clear. "Every occasion in your family was big," she said.

"My parents loved a crowd," Isabella agreed. She fast-forwarded again, slowing down to show a teenage Joe and his father standing in front of an old Mustang. "The hot rod," she said, shooting Joe a smile. "How many hours did you and Dad work on that car?"

"Too many to count," he muttered. "Keep going."

Isabella hit play again, narrating more Silveira events. Then she said, "Look, Joe, your high school graduation. There's you and Rachel in your caps and gowns."

Joe stiffened as Rachel's face came on the screen. Charlotte cast him a quick look, then focused her attention on the video. Rachel and Joe looked happy, optimistic, ready to take on the world, exactly what graduation was all about. But their future hadn't turned out the way either of them had anticipated.

"I'm going to get something to drink," Joe said abruptly.

Isabella paused the tape, shooting a guilty look at Nick and Charlotte. "He's pissed."

"I don't think he's enjoying the trip down memory lane as much as you are," Nick said. "Why don't we do this later?" he added, getting to his feet. "In fact, let's take the DVDs to my house, and we'll show them to Megan."

"All right." Isabella ejected the DVD and put it in the box. "Sorry, Charlotte."

"No need to apologize. I enjoyed seeing you both as kids, especially Joe. He's so private; he's a little hard to get to know."

Isabella smiled. "He doesn't let a lot of people in, but those he does he treats really well. Tell him we're gone, will you?"

After Nick and Isabella left, Charlotte went into the kitchen.

Joe was drinking a glass of orange juice and kicking a ragged tennis ball to Rufus.

"You don't have to hide out anymore," Charlotte said. "Isabella and Nick left, and they took the DVDs with them."

"Good. Do you want something to drink?"

"No, thanks." She tilted her head, considering his restless mood. "I had no idea you were such a daredevil. I suppose it makes sense, though. You can't be a coward and be a cop."

"I was stupid back then. I thought I was invincible."

"Most kids do. You were pretty hot, though. I bet a lot of girls had crushes on you." She gave him a teasing smile to coax him out of his bad mood.

"I did all right." And I'm still hot," he teased back.

She smiled. "And cocky, too."

He grinned. "Part of my charm."

He was right about that. "So you and your dad worked on cars together, huh?"

"Yeah, every weekend for years. It was our thing. The garage was where we got away from the women. Where we talked about engines and horsepower and speed."

"Man stuff," she said with a grin.

"Oh, yeah. I loved speed. Whether it was a skateboard or a bike or a car, I liked to modify things so they went faster. That Mustang was the first car I ever drove. At sixteen, I was very cool—the envy of all my friends."

"What happened to it?"

A shadow crossed his eyes. "I had to sell it."

"Why?"

"For cash, why else?"

She didn't like the way he avoided her gaze. "I don't think that's the whole story."

He hesitated, then said, "I sold the Mustang to buy Rachel a bigger wedding ring on our fifth anniversary. The diamond was so small on the first one I gave her, you could barely see it. She wanted something more impressive, and I wanted to give it to her. She didn't force me to sell the car. It was my choice."

"Why are you so defensive about it?"

His lips drew in a tight line. "My friends thought I was a fool to sell that car. And my father didn't speak to me for weeks. He was hurt. The car was something we'd built together. But you have to make choices sometimes. It wasn't that big a deal. And who knows, maybe someday I'll buy another old wreck and try to restore it." He drew in a breath.

"But we've gotten way off the subject—why you came over here tonight."

"Oh, right. Pamela. I'm dying to know what you talked about."

"Not much. She was cagey, far more interested in flirting with me than providing information."

She stiffened. "She was flirting with you?"

He quirked an eyebrow. "You just said I was hot. Now you're surprised someone hit on me?"

"I'm surprised Pamela hit on you. You're investigating an attempted murder on her sister. I'd think she'd be more interested in how that was going."

"Yeah, me, too." He paused, a speculative gleam in his eyes. "Why do you let her get under your skin? You're a successful doctor, Charlotte—smart, beautiful, with a ton of friends. Why do you care at all about her?"

"She reminds me of a time in my life I'd rather forget."

"I'm all for you forgetting Andrew, but it's not just his cheating you're talking about, is it?" His gaze softened. "It's the baby you lost."

His words sent the old pain through her heart. "I don't want to talk about that. She had nothing to do with that."

"Didn't you tell me that you slept with someone else after Andrew cheated on you, because you wanted to prove it didn't matter? And that it could have been his baby as much as it could have been Andrew's? You never said who he was, by the way."

"And I'm never going to. None of that matters

anymore, Joe. I don't know why we're even talking about it." She ran a hand through her hair, desperately needing to change the subject. "I just don't
want Pamela to mess up my life now."

"I suspect Pamela gets a kick out of stirring up
trouble. And I don't think you're the only one she's
interested in messing with. She hinted that Andrew
isn't nearly the saint this town believes him to be."

"Andrew has never professed to be a saint."

"Are you sure? I've been to a few of his sermons."

"His job is to inspire faith and to encourage people to behave well. Not to pretend he's never done
anything wrong. He may be better equipped to help
people avoid temptation because he *wasn't* always
perfect."

"You're quite his defender."

"Because you're usually accusing him of something," she said bluntly.

He gave her a half smile. "Point taken. Cynicism
tends to go with my job."

She held his gaze. "Your dislike of Andrew has
nothing to do with your job."

"No, it has to do with you," he admitted. "If
you're considering getting back together with him,
shouldn't you know who he really is?"

"If you think I have Andrew up on some pedestal,
you're mistaken. I don't have any illusions about him."

"His collar doesn't change the way you look at
him?"

She hesitated. "Maybe a little, because I can see
that he's grown into a better man than the teenager

he used to be. But that's probably true of all of us. And I never said I was getting back together with him."

"He wants you. But so do I." Joe closed the distance between them and cupped her face with his hands. "What do *you* want, Charlotte?" he asked in a deep, husky voice that sent a thrill of desire down her spine. His thumb traced her lips, making her tingle all over.

"I don't know," she murmured, her heart pounding hard in her chest.

"Yes, you do. You just don't want to say it."

"Now you're reading my mind?"

"That would be impossible. You're such a contradiction. Strong but soft, fierce but vulnerable, impulsive but a little cautious. You're generous with your life, opening your house to strangers, but you're selfish when it comes to love. You guard your heart like it's Fort Knox."

How did he know her so well? "It makes life easier."

"Easier, maybe. Better? I don't think so." His gaze clung to hers. "I want you to let me in."

"I don't know if I can," she said honestly.

His gaze darkened. "Why not?"

"I don't do serious, Joe. And you're a serious kind of guy."

"I can be fun, too. You saw the home movies."

"That was before you grew up. Now you like to be in control, and so do I."

"We can duke it out."

The sparkle in his eyes made it hard to to keep saying no. "Mostly, it's just too soon. You're just getting out of a marriage."

"I've been telling myself that for months, but it doesn't feel soon. It feels like it's taken forever for us to get here, to this moment."

He lowered his head and gave her an enticing kiss that made it really hard to remember why this was a bad idea.

She drew on every last ounce of strength she had in order to break away from him. "I have to go."

He stared back at her, his eyes challenging. "Do you?"

Desire warred with reason, but in the end, caution won out. "Yes, I really do," she said, then left before she could change her mind.

SEVEN

Joe drove across town Tuesday morning, relieved to be back at work. He knew how to be a cop, and he was good at it. His personal life was another story. He shouldn't have pushed Charlotte, but damn, every time he was with her, he wanted her more. The fire between them had been simmering for months, but since he'd come back from L.A. after Christmas, he couldn't stop thinking about her. He couldn't stop wanting her. And she wanted him—she was just scared. In truth, so was he.

His thoughts were interrupted by a call from dispatch. There had been another break-in at Sandstone Manor.

Making an abrupt U-turn, he headed quickly down the highway. It took him ten minutes to reach the turnoff. The narrow road twisted through a thick patch of trees to the edge of the bluff, where the manor rose up in elegance against a light blue morning sky. It would have been a peaceful scene if there hadn't been a squad car in front of the house.

He got out of his truck and strode forward, noting the shattered glass on the pavement and the smashed panel next to the front door. "What happened?" he asked Jason.

"Mrs. Garcia said when she came out to get the newspaper, the front door was open, and the glass was broken. She called nine-one-one and came outside to wait. I checked the house and then sent her back in to see if anything is missing."

"Where's the mayor?"

"At the hospital. I told him we were checking things out and will get back to him. He wasn't happy."

"I'll bet. What else?"

"Mrs. Garcia didn't hear anything, but her room is on the other side of the house. I haven't been able to locate a rock, a brick, or any sort of weapon that was used to break the glass. I've got a call in to Davidson for more forensics, but considering we came up empty the last time, I'm guessing that's going to be the case here as well." His expression was grim. "What do you make of this, Chief?"

Joe stared at the pattern of glass pieces sprayed across the steps. "Looks like the window was broken with some force. Is there anyone else in the house besides the housekeeper?"

"The gardener has a room over the garage. The rest of the help comes in during the day only. Mrs.

Garcia said the mayor came back to change his clothes last night, but she hasn't seen him since."

"What about Theresa's sister?"

"If she was here, no one saw her," Jason replied.

Joe put his hands on his hips as he studied the situation. One of his favorite parts of police work was putting together the pieces of a crime. "This doesn't fit," he said thoughtfully. "It's too clumsy, unsophisticated, loud."

Jason nodded in agreement. "Could be a sign of desperation. First plan didn't yield the results the thief was looking for, so he came back. Or we have two different crimes to deal with."

"Or someone wants to throw us off the track," Joe added. "Give us something else to investigate, as a distraction. What do you know about this place?"

Jason shrugged. "What everyone knows. It was owned by various generations of the Worthington family. The last owner, Edward Worthington, was a recluse. He lived here for thirty-plus years, but no one saw much of him."

"What about the housekeeper? Did she come with the Monroes, or did she work for Worthington?"

"She worked for Mr. Worthington for twenty-five years. Mrs. Monroe asked her to stay on when the house was sold. The gardener has been here about eight years, and he seems to speak less English than Mrs. Garcia. The day help is mostly new since the Monroes moved in."

"Well, someone knew this house well enough to shut down the lights and get in and out of the house quickly. We need to take a close look at anyone who fits that description."

"The employees have access to the house. They wouldn't need to break this window."

"True. Could be two separate events or the same person with a different motive. What else could a thief want, besides the jewelry they already took?"

An odd look passed through Jason's eyes. "This is going to sound ridiculous, but there are rumors that the Worthingtons stashed some of the gold from the shipwreck in the house. But the house has passed through several generations, so I can't put much credence in that story."

"Are there any Worthingtons still alive?"

"I don't believe so. That's why the house went up for sale. But I'll double-check." Jason paused. "I've asked Charlotte to come in on her lunch break today to give a more detailed statement. The mayor wants her interrogated, and I can't put him off again. Not that I anticipate getting any useful information; she's completely innocent."

Joe's gut clenched at the thought of anyone grilling Charlotte, but he knew Jason would make it as painless as possible.

"Do what you have to do. I'm heading to the station now. I'll talk to you later."

As he drove down the road and back onto the main highway, Joe saw a familiar figure a half mile down the road. Charlotte was jogging in the bike lane. She had on black leggings and a bright blue T-shirt, and her blond hair was pulled back in a ponytail. He remembered the silky feel of her hair in his hands, the softness of her skin, the sweet taste of her mouth. God, one look, and he was right back where he'd been the night before.

He needed to get a grip and focus. While he loved the way her hips swayed with each running step, he didn't love the fact that she was so close to the Sandstone property. Why would she come out here when she lived on the other side of town?

He drove past her and pulled off to the side, getting out of his car as she ran toward him.

Her smile was surprised as she slowed her steps. "Joe, what are you doing out here?"

"I was going to ask you the same question. You don't usually come this way, do you?"

"I felt like a longer run. I did a lot of eating yesterday."

"And you thought the best place to run would be right past Sandstone Manor?" he asked sharply, because snapping at her made it easier to keep his hands off her.

Her gaze narrowed as she planted her hands on her hips. "What kind of question is that?"

"You're a suspect in a burglary that took place a half mile from here."

"So?"

"So someone threw a brick through the glass panel next to the front door of the Monroes' house earlier this morning."

Her jaw dropped in astonishment. "Seriously?"

"Do I look like I'm kidding?"

"I didn't jog on their property. I stayed on the road."

"Can you prove that?"

She threw her shoulders back, anger tightening her lips. "Obviously, I can't."

"Any cars pass you on this road?"

"A couple."

"Anyone you know?" he pressed, not sure whether he wanted witnesses. But he'd learned a long time ago that asking detailed questions saved him trouble in the long run.

Charlotte thought, then nodded. "Mr. Owens waved to me. And Jane Bentley was driving her kid to school."

"Once again, you've ended up at the wrong place at the wrong time, and we have witnesses."

"I didn't do anything!"

"You shouldn't have come up here, Charlotte. Why would you? It's not anywhere close to your house."

"I've made this run lots of times. And how would I know someone was going to break into the house again?"

"You need to stay away from the house, from the hospital, from the Monroes, and from anyone or any place with a link to what happened."

"I can't stay away from the hospital; I work there. And I shouldn't have to hide out. I'm not guilty of anything. You know that."

"Knowing it and being able to prove it are two different things."

She stared at him for a long moment. "What did they take this time?"

"I don't know yet. Jason was starting to investigate when I left." As a car passed by them, a woman giving them a curious look, he realized that *he* was making the mistake this time. He shouldn't have had this conversation on the side of the road, creating even more speculation. "I'll drive you into town."

"I'd rather run. I need the exercise."

"You need to be farther away from here," he said bluntly, moving around the vehicle to open the door for her.

After a momentary hesitation, she got in. "Fine. You can drive me to Elm Street, then I'll run the rest of the way in."

He slid into the driver's seat, started the engine, and pulled onto the highway. Charlotte folded her arms in front of her chest, staring straight ahead for a few long minutes. He didn't like the tension between them, but he didn't know how to diffuse it. Every subject he thought to bring up seemed fraught with potential problems. So he stayed silent.

"You can let me off here," Charlotte said.

He pulled over to the side of the road. "Are you sure you won't let me drop you off at home?"

"This is fine." She put her hand on the door, then paused. "How much trouble am I in?"

He glanced at her, seeing the worry in her eyes. "I'm sure you weren't the only runner on that road this morning, and it's unlikely that someone would break in without some means of transportation to make a quick getaway. But I want you to be more aware of your surroundings, Charlotte. This second break-in could be a distraction or another attempt to get something that was missed. Whatever the reason, it means this isn't over yet."

"I understand." She drew in a breath and let it out, her gaze still clinging to his. "Should we talk about last night?"

He hesitated, not sure he wanted to have that conversation now. "I need to get to work, and so do you."

She nodded. "Okay. Then I'll see you later—not in a police lineup, I hope."

He tried to smile at her attempt at a joke. Despite Charlotte's innocence, circumstantial evidence was piling up against her. They needed to come up with another suspect and another theory that would get her off the hot seat.

Police lineup . . . What a stupid joke, Charlotte thought as she ran home. Joe hadn't laughed, either. He'd had his serious chief-of-police face on all morning. In fact, he'd been harsher and colder than she'd ever seen him. Did his bad mood have something to do with her abrupt departure last night? She couldn't blame him for being pissed at her; she'd been sending him mixed signals. Things were happening too fast, so she'd slowed them down.

Sighing, she sprinted the last block and jogged up the steps to her house. She stretched on the porch for a few minutes, then went inside to take a shower. She was looking forward to going into the office and losing herself in work. Being a doctor was one thing she did really well.

After getting dressed, she stopped into the kitchen to fill her travel mug with coffee. Her mother was at the breakfast table, reviewing her daily planner. Despite the early hour, her mother was stylishly dressed and perfectly made-up. Involved in numerous charities at the church and within the community, she always seemed to have a busy schedule.

"Pretty flowers," Charlotte commented as she paused to inhale the sweet scent of pink roses in a vase on the counter. "Did Mr. Lawson give you these?"

"Those aren't mine," Monica replied, pushing her reading glasses to the top of her head as she lifted her gaze. "They're for you, from Andrew. He stopped by a half hour ago."

"Oh, that was sweet of him." Roses before breakfast? Andrew had certainly learned how to romance a woman in the decade since she'd first gone out with him. She felt a little guilty, though. She hadn't been thinking about Andrew at all when she'd been kissing Joe yesterday.

"Andrew is worried about you," her mother added. "And now so am I. Why didn't you tell me you were upstairs at the time of the robbery? I didn't realize you were on the second floor when the lights went out."

Her heart sank. She'd hoped to keep her mother out of it as long as possible. "It wasn't a big deal, and I didn't want to upset you."

"Not a big deal? Detective Marlow called a few minutes ago and asked me to confirm that you'd be going to the station on your lunch break."

"Boy, people get up early around here," she muttered.

Her mother's mouth drew into its familiar disapproving line. "What on earth is going on?"

"Nothing. I went upstairs to find the bathroom, and the lights went out. I had nothing to do with Theresa's assault."

"You should have told me. I don't like to be caught off guard by rumors around town involving my children."

"I'm not a child anymore. I'll handle this."

"Does it ever cross your mind that I might be able to help you?" her mother asked in exasperation.

There was a tremendous amount of irony in that question. Her mother hadn't helped her when she was a teenager, when she had confessed the biggest secret of her life, that she was pregnant. No, she'd been criticized and condemned and made to keep the secret until her mother could figure out what to do. The miscarriage had solved her mother's problems but not hers. And their relationship had never recovered.

In the past few months, she'd been trying to get

past the old hurts, to see her mother as she was now and not as she was then. To forgive and forget. She'd thought her mother was trying to do the same thing, but it was difficult for them to step out of the roles they'd always played with each other.

"Charlotte," her mother prodded. "Are you even listening to me?"

"Yes, I'm listening. Jason's interview is just a formality," she said. "It's nothing to be concerned about."

"I'll go with you."

"I can go on my own. You'll make it a bigger deal than it is."

"Charlotte—"

"No. Look, you refused to be searched or finger-printed the night of the assault. I don't need the police to think you're covering for me."

Her mother's widened eyes reflected her shock. "They couldn't think that. I had no idea at the time that you were in any way involved."

"Of course. But what if I had stolen the jewelry and handed it off to you?"

"That's ridiculous."

"Nothing we can prove beyond a shadow of doubt. If you go with me, there's a good chance someone will ask you questions. I'd prefer to do this on my own."

"You prefer to do everything on your own, which is usually the problem. Your father would turn over in his grave if you were charged with burglary or assault." She shuddered at the thought. "One of the last things he asked me to do was look out for you. As if you'd let me."

She stared at her mother in amazement. "You never told me that. In fact, when I asked if Dad had had any last words before he died, you said no."

"Well, they weren't his last words. They were just part of one of the many conversations we had after he got sick."

"I didn't know I was on his mind," she said, grappling with that fact. She'd often felt invisible where her father was concerned. She couldn't remember having any deep, personal conversations with him growing up. She'd always felt on the outside of the circle. It was partly why she hadn't rushed back when he was sick; she'd been unsure of what to say to him or if he even really wanted her there.

"Of course you were on his mind. This family was everything to him."

It certainly hadn't felt that way. But sharing that thought with her mother wasn't a good idea, so she grabbed an apple out of the fruit basket and turned toward the door. "I'll see you tonight."

"Don't forget the fund-raising meeting at the church—seven o'clock."

She paused at the door. "I'll be there if I don't have to work late."

Her mother frowned. "This is important, Charlotte. We're discussing plans for the new children's classroom. It was an important project for your father, and Andrew has decided to continue efforts in that direction."

"I said I'd be there."

"I just want you to know that I'm carrying out your father's wishes."

There was something odd about her mother's words. "Why would I think anything else?"

A frown crossed Monica's lips. "Because of Peter."

"Mr. Lawson?" she echoed in surprise.

"You don't like that I'm seeing him."

"That's not exactly true," she said slowly. "I'll admit it's a little strange to see you with another man. But I'm not against it."

"You're not?" her mother asked, a hopeful look in her eyes, as if her answer was important.

That thought threw Charlotte. Her mother didn't ask for her opinion ever. "If you like him and he treats you well, then I have nothing to say."

"He does treat me well, with the exception of deserting me at the party. Other than that, he's been very attentive." She sighed. "It's just that our friendship feels a little . . . wrong."

The uncertainty in her mother's eyes also surprised Charlotte. Monica Adams was the epitome of confidence. She was always sure of what was right and what was wrong. Now she was looking to Charlotte for some sort of confirmation.

She chose her words carefully. "Dad's main goal in life was to make you happy. That was the most important thing to him. I'm certain he'd want you to be happy now."

"With another man?" her mother asked doubtfully.

"The wedding vows are only till death."

"But I never imagined a time when your father and I wouldn't be together." Her mother blinked quickly, as if fighting tears. "He died too young. He had so much more to offer—not just me but everyone. The world was a better place with your father in it."

"He was a good man," she agreed.

"He's missing so much," Monica said, her voice thick with emotion. "So many important moments in our family."

Charlotte swallowed hard, wishing her mother wasn't going down this road. She'd had her own sad thoughts on the subject, and she tried not to think about it.

"He's not going to see our grandchildren grow up or celebrate another birthday, another holiday," her mother said. "He's not going to walk you down the aisle, see you get married or have a baby of your own.'"

Charlotte sucked in a painful breath, her mother's words conjuring up a dream that she wasn't sure would ever happen.

Monica gave a helpless shake of her head. "I know death is final, but feeling it, living with loss every day, is so different. I wake up and think he's in the next room. Sometimes I hear his footsteps in the hall. They're so familiar. I look up and expect to see him in the doorway."

"I know, Mom," she got out, tears blurring her vision. Not having had the chance to say good-bye to her father had left her with a hole in her heart that might never be repaired. Because he wasn't coming back. She would never be able to talk to him again.

Her mother met her gaze. "I want you to have the kind of love I had, Charlotte. A man in your life who will stand by you, love you, and take care of you. A career won't keep you warm at night, won't comfort you through hard times, won't be enough to fill your heart. You think I don't know you, but I know you want more than you have."

"Maybe I don't know how to get more."

"Maybe you don't try."

Her mother had a point; she'd never made getting a man a priority. Love was always put off for another day, down the road, far into the future.

"Start by opening your mind to the possibilities," her mother continued. "Like Andrew."

She sighed. "I'll think about my future, but how did we get onto me? We were talking about you and your relationship. Is it serious with Peter?"

"I don't know," her mother said with a vague gesture. "He's not your father."

"No one could be. You can't replace Dad."

"No, I can't."

"But you like Peter."

"He's intelligent, interesting, and well read."

"And he's not bad to look at it," Charlotte interjected with a mischievous smile.

"That's beside the point," her mother said sharply.

"Actually, it's a big part of the point. If Mr. Lawson makes you happy, then you should feel free to do whatever you like."

"I'm not sure some ladies of the congregation would agree with you."

"Well, who cares what they think?"

"I do."

"But it's *your* life, Mom. You need to live it."

Her mother stared at her for a moment, weighing her words. "Thank you."

"You're welcome."

Her mother adjusted her glasses and returned her attention to her paperwork.

Sharing time was over. Their relationship would always be on her mother's terms. But at least she was starting to feel as if they *had* a relationship. That was something.

EIGHT

One thing Joe didn't like about his job was the amount of paperwork and administrative duties. Sometimes he felt more like an office manager than a cop. On the other hand, he enjoyed the power to get things done. No more bucking against the top brass, because that was him now. He did have a city manager and a mayor to answer to, both of whom were breathing down his neck at the moment. But he could take the heat. His focus wasn't on pleasing them but on getting to the truth and arresting the right person. That wasn't going to be Charlotte.

He got up as a knock came at his door. Fiona Murray had asked to see him, and he was curious. In her mid-eighties, with a sharp tongue and an even sharper mind, Fiona was the matriarch of Angel's Bay. She was descended from one of the shipwreck survivors and ran the Angel's Heart Quilt Shop, along with just about everything else in town. She didn't mince words, worry about feelings, or apologize for her beliefs, however crazy they might be. He liked that about her.

"Thank you for agreeing to see me, Chief," Fiona said as she entered.

"No problem."

Fiona had a strong grip for an elderly woman, and her eyes were bright, her hair a fiery shade of red that reminded him of her granddaughter, Kara. But Kara was a lot softer and warmer than her grandmother. With Fiona, he needed to stay on his toes.

"Can I get you some coffee or something else to drink?" he offered.

"No. I won't take up much of your time. I'm concerned about the robbery at Sandstone Manor."

"What concerns you, exactly?" he said as they both sat down.

"That the thief was after more than jewelry."

"Like what?"

"Gold." She clasped her hands together as she sat up straight. "Ingots, gold bars from the San Francisco gold rush, worth millions in today's market."

"Go on," he said with interest.

"When the *Gabriella* went down in the 1850s, it was laden with gold. Most people believe that gold is lying on the bottom of the ocean in a wreck that no diver has been able to find. However, others think that some of the gold was brought ashore by George Worthington. He built half the town, and rumor has it that he had a stash of gold hidden away somewhere." She took a breath, then continued her story.

"George and his teenage son, Grant, survived

the shipwreck while his wife and daughter perished. It was supposed to be women and children first, yet somehow George and his son managed to survive while the females in the family did not. Some think he sacrificed them to get the gold."

"Sounds like a hell of a guy."

"To pay penance, he built the church, which was one of the first buildings in town. He also built a number of other structures over the years, including Sandstone Manor. He remarried about six years after the wreck, but he still couldn't find happiness, and ten years to the day after the wreck, he killed himself. He left a note for his son, apologizing for not saving his mother and sister and for letting his greed destroy their family. He said he was sorry for leaving Grant behind but that he hadn't left him without anything—there was more gold than anyone had imagined."

"There's an actual suicide letter?" Joe asked in surprise.

"It was written about in one my ancestor's journals."

"Did the letter say where this gold was?"

"Unfortunately, no."

"That would have been too easy."

"Life was never easy for the Worthingtons. Grant fell off a horse and died before he was forty. His son came down with pneumonia and died just after his marriage in his twenties. The males in the family seemed to be cursed, including Edward Worthington, the most recent owner of the manor."

"He lived to be an old man, from what I understand."

"Yes, but he lost his wife and child in a car accident. He became a hermit after that."

"Let's go back to the gold. Why wouldn't the Worthingtons have put it in a bank?"

"Because the ingots were stolen."

"And these bars were valuable?"

"Yes. During the gold rush, the miners would take their gold to the assayer's office, and it would be melted into a bar, stamped with the date and the assay office, and then it could be used as money. A few years ago, such a bar was discovered in a shipwreck off the coast of Mexico, and it was valued at eight million dollars."

She'd finally said something that he could wrap his mind around. A rare gold bar worth millions of dollars would be quite a prize. "What I don't understand," Joe said, "is why anyone would believe the gold bars still exist and weren't sold off decades ago and why they would still be the house. Surely the last Worthington would have made certain that the gold was willed to someone in the family. Are there any other Worthingtons?"

"No. Edward was the last, which is why the house was put up for sale by his attorneys. Very few people were allowed into the manor for the last thirty years. It's interesting that once the house changed hands and was opened up for a big party, there was suddenly a robbery. And the fact that the necklace Theresa was wearing was from the

Worthington estate . . . well, there seems to be a connection."

"While you present a good motivation for robbery, it's difficult to believe there would still be gold hidden somewhere in the house or on the property. The mayor and Theresa did some renovation work; wouldn't they have looked for the gold?"

"Maybe they already found it," Fiona said with a sharp smile.

"If they did, they haven't mentioned it to me."

"I'm sure they searched. Theresa was always looking for some connection between her family and the shipwreck. She couldn't find one, so she bought one. That's why she purchased a lot of the furnishings and pieces of jewelry from the estate. Here in Angel's Bay, people who are related to descendants of the wreck are part of a special group."

"A group Theresa wanted to get into."

"Yes. I know it's not important to you that your blood goes back to the shipwreck survivors, but others value the connection to the past. And there's enough truth in our town legends to take them seriously. Think about it."

"I will. And as long as all of the angel and shipwreck stories don't get in the way of good police work, I'm fine with them," he said with a smile.

She got to her feet. "You're a very polite young man. I appreciate that. One of these days, you're going to understand what it means to have faith in things you can't see or touch."

"You don't think I have faith?" he asked curiously.

She gave him a long look. "Isn't that why you came here—to get your faith back? Many people come here because they've lost their way, and this town heals them. There's magic here. Maybe it's goodness, faith, hope . . . or the angels. But whatever it is, it works."

He drew in a deep breath. She knew nothing about his past, yet there was a lot of truth in what she'd said.

"Thanks for your time, Chief."

"You're welcome." He walked her to the door, and as she made her way through the squad room, he went over to Jason's desk.

"What was that all about?" Jason asked curiously.

"Hidden gold in Sandstone Manor."

Jason raised an eyebrow. "Did Fiona bring a map with her?"

"Unfortunately, just a lot of rumor and speculation. Tell me you've discovered something more concrete than an old legend and a bunch of cursed Worthington men?"

"I've been reviewing the guest list. Approximately ten people left the party before we started taking names. One of those individuals was Peter Lawson, Mrs. Adams's date to the party. Colin noticed an agitated discussion between Mr. Lawson and Mrs. Adams a little before midnight. Then Mr. Lawson left. Since Mrs. Adams refused to give a statement or be searched and Charlotte was near the scene of the crime, Mr. Lawson's absence could be construed as being interesting."

Joe frowned, hating that the facts were leading them back to Charlotte and her family. "Have you spoken to him?"

"I've left several messages. No return call yet. I'm going to ask Charlotte about him when she comes in this afternoon."

"We need a different angle. One that doesn't involve Charlotte or anyone connected to her."

"Got any ideas?"

"Theresa. The theft was personal. Someone literally ripped the necklace off her neck and the ring off her finger. Talk to her friends. See if she had any enemies."

"I've already spoken to a few people. She's not well loved, but no one can imagine anyone wanting to hurt her."

"Keep digging. What do you know about Pamela Baines?"

"Super-slutty in high school. Just arrived back in town."

"Someone must have more recent information on her. Start with Reverend Schilling. They have a past, from what I understand."

"I'll get on it. Anything in particular you're looking for?"

"We'll know it when we find it."

Problems were just challenges, Andrew told himself as his car refused to start. Unfortunately, today had been filled with a few too many challenges, and

it was only noon. His determinedly optimistic out-
look was taking a beating. First, Jason had called to
quiz him about Pamela. Then the mayor had asked
him to visit Theresa in the hospital. And now his car
wouldn't start.

While he was used to making hospital visits for
those in the congregation, he wasn't sure why the
mayor had called. Robert and Theresa weren't par-
ticularly religious and usually showed up only at
Christmas and Easter. He couldn't help wondering
if Pamela was behind the request, finding another
way to get to him. She'd probably love to watch him
in action, her mocking eyes making him feel like a
phony.

But he wasn't a fraud. This was his life now—a
life that he enjoyed, that made him feel proud, that
made him happy.

A car pulled into the lot next to his, and Tory
Hartley Baker stepped out. A slender, petite woman,
Tory wore a dark red sweater dress with a floral scarf
and a pair of boots. Her short light brown hair was
straight and angled around her face, the front longer than the back, and her bright green eyes sparkled
with friendly curiosity.

"Problems?" she asked as he got out to speak to her.

"Car won't start."

"Maybe it's the battery. Does it just click when
you turn the key?"

"Yes. You know about cars?"

"A little. I can give you a jump. I have cables in
my car."

"Really? I'm impressed," he said. "What are you doing here?"

"Bringing flyers for the winter theater classes. Marjorie said I could put a few up on the community bulletin board."

"Of course, no problem," he said, walking with her to the back of her car. She had bags of clothes in the trunk. "What's all this?"

"Donations. I did some spring cleaning."

"A little early. It's only January," he said, his smile dimming when he realized that one of the bags was filled with men's clothes. After discovering that her husband, Steve Baker, had fathered Annie's baby and lied about it for months, Tory had thrown him out and filed for divorce. A few months ago, she'd been happy, in love, and hoping to adopt a baby. Then she'd had the rug pulled out from under her. He was impressed that she was holding it together so well.

"It's a new year, so out with the old," she said. Following his gaze, she added, "I gave Steve every opportunity to take what he wanted with him. Our marriage is over, and I don't need to be storing his clothes."

"There's no chance for reconciliation?" he asked tentatively.

"Not one little bit."

He could hear the pain in her voice. Divorce was never easy, but Tory's was especially difficult. Her infertility and inability to have a child had been tough to handle, but her husband having a baby with a teenager and then trying to pretend to adopt it had hurt even more. Tory had had to choose between keeping the marriage going so she could be a step-mother to Annie's baby, which might be her only chance to be a mother, or letting Steve go. It had probably been the hardest decision of her life.

"I'm sorry things ended so badly for you and Steve," Andrew said. He'd gotten to know them during the adoption process and had never imagined that their marriage was anything but rock solid. "If I can do anything to help during this transition . . ."

"Thank you, but I'm all right. I'm done crying, and now I'm cleaning," she said with a forced smile. "The cables are in here somewhere," she added, digging through the bags. "I had to give my grandfather's car a jump a couple of weeks ago."

"If the theater gig doesn't work out, you can get a part-time job with Ernie's Auto Body," he teased.

She smiled. "I'd probably make better money." She held up the cables.

"Will I complete destroy my reputation if I tell you I don't really know what to do with them?" he asked.

She laughed. "I'll keep your secret. I'm surprised your father didn't teach you."

"He was too busy instructing me on the finer points of hitting a baseball."

"Ah—about as practical as my mother teaching me one of Hamlet's soliloquies."

Within minutes, Tory had the hoods up on both their cars and was attaching the cable. She told him to start the car, and his engine kicked into life.

He left it running as he got out of the car to thank her. "You're a lifesaver."

She shrugged. "At least you won't have to wait for a tow truck."

"Who taught you how to jump-start a car?" he asked, suddenly curious about her life. Tory was a few years younger than him, and he really didn't know much about her.

"Nick. My brother and I learned early on that being self-sufficient was the key to surviving in a family of actors and dreamers. They're not big on practical matters." She removed the cable and tossed it into the back of her car. "I'd let it run for a few minutes before you go. Then maybe stop by Ernie's to see if you need a new battery."

"I'll do that right after I go to the hospital."

Her eyes filled with concern. "Is someone ill?"

"The mayor asked me to come down and give his wife a blessing."

"That's nice," she said with a nod. "I hope Theresa recovers. It's terrible, what happened to her."

"Were you at the party? I got there late, so I'm not clear on who was there."

"No, I celebrated New Year's Eve in my jammies with a half gallon of praline pecan ice cream. I'm sure your evening was much better."

"Not really. Certainly not what I expected it to be."

She grabbed the flyers off the front seat of her car. "I'll see you tonight. I'm coming for the meeting."

"Good. Thanks again," he said, watching her walk away. She really was an attractive woman. Some man would be lucky to have her. Realizing that he was staring a little too long, he got into his car and headed to the hospital.

Fifteen minutes later, he was getting off the elevator at the fourth floor. Hospital visits were his least favorite part of his job. It was in a hospital room after knee surgery that he'd realized that his dreams of a baseball career were over.

It wasn't just his personal experience that made him uncomfortable, though. He felt awkward trying to soothe not only people who were dying but also their families, who were looking for answers he couldn't give them. Faith didn't come with guarantees, and in the end, that's what people were looking for: a promise he couldn't make. Not everyone got well. Sometimes the worst happened.

But this visit wasn't going to be that dire. Theresa was recovering. He gave his name to the guard, who checked it off on a list and opened the door for him.

He slipped quietly into the outer room. The nurse was speaking in quiet tones on the phone and gave him a quick glance, then waved him on.

As he moved toward the center room, he could see Theresa asleep in the bed. Pamela and Robert were by the window, their backs to him. Pamela had her arm around the mayor's shoulder as if she were comforting him. But there was something about the way they were standing that was far too personal for a brother-in-law/sister-in-law relationship. Had there been something more between them? And if so, what did that mean?

His stomach began to churn, the way it always did when Pamela was about to turn his life upside down. He shouldn't have come here, but it was too late now.

Pamela looked over her shoulder and quickly stepped away from Robert. She didn't look guilty exactly, but there was something awkward in the way she cleared her throat and shifted her feet. The mayor, too, appeared unsettled.

"If this is a bad time . . ." he began.

"No, it's fine," Robert said, straightening his shoulders. "I'm glad you're here, Reverend." He cast a look at his wife. "Theresa is sleeping again. We can't seem to keep her awake for very long."

He nodded. "What can I do for you?"

"We haven't been very good about going to church, but would you mind saying a prayer for her? Pamela thought it might help, and I don't know what else to do."

The mayor looked exhausted and a little deflated. He was a big personality around town. When he was in the room, everyone knew it. But today the life was gone, as well as the overconfidence.

"I'd be happy to say a prayer. Would you like to join me?"

"Okay," Robert said somewhat gruffly as they all moved closer to the bed.

Andrew turned his attention to Theresa, noting

the bandage around her head, the paleness of her skin, the fragility of her limbs. The slight woman also had a big personality, one that didn't always win her a lot of fans, but her injury had made her very human.

"When she goes to sleep, I'm always afraid she won't wake up again," Robert said, fear in his eyes.

Andrew gave a smile of reassurance, then put his hand on Theresa's cool arm and led them in several minutes of quiet prayer. When he finished, Robert and Pamela echoed, "Amen."

"Thank you for coming," the mayor said. "I won't forget this. If the church needs something, you let me know."

"I appreciate the support, but I came for your wife, no other reason. I hope she recovers quickly."

"I'll walk you out," Pamela told him.

He breathed a little easier once they were back in the hall and heading toward the elevators.

"You were very impressive in there," Pamela told him as he pushed the button for the elevator. "Why don't we get a drink or coffee or something? It's hard for me to sit in that room hour after hour."

"I can't."

"You can't or you won't?"

"Why don't you go back to the house? Or are you staying in a hotel?"

"Robert suggested I stay at the Seagull Inn since the house is considered a crime scene," she said, an edge to her voice. "But that's not the real reason. He doesn't want me in his home."

"Why not?" He paused, giving her a hard look. "What did you do? Did you and Robert hook up?"

"It was a long time ago," she admitted. "Theresa doesn't know."

He should have been shocked, but he wasn't. "Are you sure about that?"

"It was before they got married, after the rehearsal dinner. We were both drunk. But we swore never to say anything, and we didn't."

"Then why did you tell me now?" He didn't want to be the keeper of any more of her secrets.

"Because I want you to trust me again," she said, a plea in her eyes.

He shook his head. "That's not going to happen."

"I'm not that bad a person. You know I'm not. A lot of it is just an act."

"Then why don't you stop acting?"

She sighed. "I don't know how. Maybe you can help me."

"I'm not the man for that job. Did you put the mayor up to calling me?"

"I suggested it. I didn't think you'd come unless you had a reason."

"You should go back to L.A. You've made your sisterly appearance, done your duty. Why hang around? Or is there something you're not telling me?"

She frowned, glanced around the hall, and then said, "Things aren't so good for me back in L.A. Mitch got out of prison a couple of months ago."

His stomach turned over. Mitch Harding was a local kid who'd gone off track after leaving Angel's Bay. "I thought Mitch had another couple of years."

"Apparently, he got off on good behavior, if you can believe that. I don't want to get involved with him again, but he's been coming around, pressuring me. When Robert called, I figured it was a good time to leave L.A."

Andrew could understand that; he just wished she hadn't come to Angel's Bay. The last thing he needed was for their former friend to make an appearance, too. "Does Mitch know where you are?"

"Who knows? He's always been good at finding me."

He pushed the elevator button again, impatient to get out of the hospital, away from Pamela, and far from the past that was threatening to catch up to him.

"I could use a friend, Andrew," Pamela wheedled. "Is that really so much to ask? We used to mean a lot to each other."

"We never meant anything to each other," he said harshly, because subtlety was lost on Pamela. "We just used each other to escape from our lives. We were toxic, and you know that as well as I do. I've made a new life for myself, and you should do the same."

"It's not as easy for me, Andrew. I don't have God in my corner. He's never answered my prayers. Not once."

The minister he'd become wanted to help her take a better path. But the man in him was afraid that he wouldn't pull her up, that she'd pull him back down to a place he never wanted to go to again. "I'll give you the name of someone you can talk to in L.A."

Hurt filled her eyes, along with anger. "You think you can get rid of me just like that, Andrew? Because you can't. And if you don't want to help me, I'll help myself."

He had a feeling he'd just made things worse.

NINE

"It's not that bad, is it?" Charlotte asked Jason. She'd spent the past fifteen minutes in the interrogation room at the police station, and while he was her friend, she still felt very uncomfortable. Despite her innocence, having to repeat her simple story over and over again was almost making her doubt herself.

"I'll be honest, Charlotte, it's not great." He looked past her toward the mirror, and she followed his gaze.

"Is someone watching us?" Was it Joe or one of the other officers? "It's not the mayor, is it?" Dismay filled her.

"It's no one. Relax."

"Relax? I feel like you're about to throw cuffs on me."

"You're safe for the moment. Now, let's go over your story one more time."

"Jason, I've told you everything," she said in frustration.

"You didn't tell me when you saw Mrs. Garcia."

"The housekeeper?" she asked, a little confused. "I didn't see her. She saw me. The only person I saw was a younger woman coming down the stairs when I first went up. Did you question her?"

"We're not sure yet who that was. None of the servers or help that night admitted to going upstairs."

She frowned. "Well, someone is lying."

"Yeah," he said heavily. "That's what we have to figure out."

"I also felt someone brush by me in the dark," she said. "But I have no idea who that was."

Jason nodded. "Maybe some clue will come to you—a scent, a flash of something."

"I hope so. I do want to help. I just don't know anything."

He nodded. "Now, what can you tell me about Peter Lawson?"

She was surprised by the abrupt change of topic. "My mother's friend? What do you want to know?"

"Did you talk to him at the party?"

"Briefly. He left early. His daughter had some sort of emergency."

"Do you know where he is now?"

"I have no idea. Why are you asking me about him?"

"Just covering all the bases. Do you know what he does for a living?"

"He's semiretired. He does some sort of consulting work. That's all I know. If you want more information, you'll have to talk to him or to my mother."

"I'd rather face a wild bear than question your mother," he said dryly. "Then I might have a fighting chance."

"Well, along those lines, I wouldn't go accusing her boyfriend of anything unless you have some evidence."

"Boyfriend, huh?"

"She might not call him that, but they spend a lot of time together."

"I wish your mother had allowed herself to be searched the night of the party, Charlotte. It's a little suspicious that she didn't."

"My mother had nothing to do with the robbery. And I doubt Peter Lawson did, either. Has Theresa said anything?"

"She has no memory of what happened."

"Well, at least she didn't say I robbed her."

"Not yet, anyway."

She sighed. "I've gotta say, Jason, that since you've become a detective, you're a little on the gloomy side."

"I'm worried," he admitted. "We don't have much to go on, and what we do have keeps leading back to you. The chief is under a lot of pressure to solve this case. His job could be on the line." Jason paused, looking into her eyes. "And he likes you."

She wasn't quite sure how to take the concern in his eyes. "Is that a problem?"

"It might be if he tries to protect you."

"Joe is incredibly honest and ethical. You don't have to worry about that." The doubtful expression on Jason's face disturbed her. "What aren't you saying?"

"You were jogging by Sandstone Manor this morning. I canvassed the neighborhood to see if anyone was in the area. A local gardner told me he saw a blond jogger talking to the chief of police."

"Joe stopped me and asked me where I'd been."

"Which was where?"

"On the road, Jason. I didn't go on the mayor's property."

"Why did you run in that direction?"

"It's one of my routes when I want to work the hills. I've run it many, many times before. I told Joe that. I don't see the problem."

"The chief didn't tell me he saw you, and he should have."

She was surprised that Joe would have kept their meeting to himself. "I'm sure he just hasn't had a chance."

"He's had a chance, Charlotte."

"Joe knows I'm innocent, Jason. I thought you knew that, too."

"I want to be able to prove it. And right now, I can't."

"It's supposed to be innocent until proven guilty, not the other way around."

"Yeah, it's supposed to be. But if you're smart, Charlotte, you'll stay the hell away from anything or anyone connected to the Monroes or that house until we solve this case."

"I will. I promise."

Charlotte's promise didn't last more than a few hours. But it wasn't her fault, she told herself as she watched Pamela walk into the church auditorium and take a seat. How was she to know that Pamela would show up at a church meeting? She'd never set foot inside the church as a teenager. She certainly hadn't been in any of the youth groups. And in her short, clingy blue dress and spike-heeled boots, she looked even more out of place. Not that she seemed to care. As their gazes met, Pamela gave her a sly smile.

Charlotte focused her attention on the front of the room. Andrew sat next to a podium where her mother was leading the meeting. He gave her a subtle shrug, as if to say he had nothing to do with Pamela's arrival. Unfortunately, that didn't make Pamela's presence any easier to take. She fidgeted in her seat, trying to listen to her mother, but all she could think about was why Pamela had come. What was she up to now? She should be at the hospital with her sister, and if her sister didn't need her, then she should be heading back to wherever she came from.

"Don't let her get to you," Kara whispered.

It was good advice, and she tried to take it, but

two minutes later, her nerves were drawn so tight she thought she was going to snap. "I have to get out of here."

"That's what Pamela wants."

"I don't care. I need fresh air." She paused. "But I also need a distraction. Stand up and ask my mother a question."

"No way. Your mother doesn't like to be interrupted. And where are you going to go, anyway? We're breaking up into small groups at the end of this, and you're one of the leaders."

"I'll be back. Please, Kara."

"Fine, but next time I need a babysitter, you're it."

"No problem."

Kara waited for a pause and then stood up, blocking Charlotte from her mother's view. As Kara asked some vague question about logistics, Charlotte slipped down the aisle and through the side door. She moved quickly down the hall, taking a grateful breath of air when she hit the church steps.

More relaxed now, she walked through the church grounds, enjoying the quiet, cold night. When she'd been growing up in the house next door, the church grounds had always been an extension of her backyard, with trees to climb, gardens to explore, and a bell tower perfect for dreaming.

Turning abruptly, she ducked under some low-hanging tree branches and moved quickly toward the side of the church. The heavy door swung open with a groan, and she made her way up the narrow, winding spiral staircase to the tower. The bell was long gone, but the wide, open windows offered dazzling views from every angle.

There wasn't much to see in the dark. The ocean was just beyond the rim of trees, and she could hear the sound of waves breaking on the rocks. While the surrounding grounds were in shadows, the night sky was clear and sparkling with stars. She took a long, deep breath and told herself that everything would work out—the same speech she'd given herself here numerous times before.

This bell tower, this night sky, had seen her through some hard times—childhood conflicts, then more serious issues: Andrew's cheating, her own sexual misadventures, pregnancy, and her miscarriage. In this quiet oasis, she had cried buckets of tears and let out emotions that no one else would ever see. During most of those times of crisis, she'd reassured herself that life would get better when she left Angel's Bay. And in some ways, it had. College, medical school, and residency had driven Angel's Bay from her mind. She'd been too busy to think about her hometown, too driven to succeed and make something of herself, to consider that the community she'd taken for granted wouldn't stay exactly the same.

But it had changed, just as she had. Her father was dead. Her family home was gone. Her brother was overseas. Her sister was hours away. Even her mother was moving on, dating another man. And she was in limbo. Caught between two lives, afraid to choose the next path to take.

Resting her arms on the window opening with a sigh, she tried to quiet her mind, to stay in the moment, let the past rest and the future be determined. A flash of wispy white caught her eye. There was someone moving in the dark shadows, slipping in and out of the trees. A woman, maybe a girl, her hair a white blond. It flowed out behind her as she ran, and her billowy dress scraped the ground in a swirl of fabric.

A distant memory plucked at her brain. She'd followed that girl once before, when she'd been eleven or twelve years old. They'd climbed onto the rough branches of an old tree that looked down over the church garden where a wedding reception was being held.

"What are you doing?" she asked as the girl scrambled higher.

"Looking for the bride. I love weddings. Everyone is in love. I wish I could get married."

"You're too young to get married."

"And I'll never get old. I had a boyfriend. His name was Christopher. He gave me my first kiss, right before we sailed away."

"Why are you wearing that old dress?" Charlotte asked with a frown, distracted from the girl's story by her odd clothing.

"It's all I have." The girl smiled at her. *"I know who you are. You're Charlie. The one who always gets into trouble."*

She frowned. "Not always."

"You're in trouble now. You're supposed to be serving punch."

That was true. But she'd gotten bored and had snuck away when her mother wasn't looking. "How do you know my name?"

"I know everyone's name."

"What's yours?"

"Mary Katherine. I used to get in trouble, too. My father would get so angry with me. He didn't like me spying on him. He was afraid I'd get him in trouble. But instead, he got himself in trouble." The girl stopped abruptly. "You should go back. Someone is coming. Don't tell anyone you saw me; they'll never believe you. You'll just get into more trouble for making up stories."

"How do you know I get into trouble for telling stories?"

"I heard you in the garden. You were talking to the flowers."

"You were there?" she asked in astonishment.

"I'm everywhere, but not everyone can see me. They have to believe."

Charlotte wanted to talk to her some more, but her sister Doreen was calling her name. "Coming!" she yelled.

When she glanced back at Mary Katherine to say good-bye, the girl was gone.

Charlotte shivered as she stared out into the darkness, wondering where that old memory had come from. Mary Katherine was an imaginary friend she'd made up to escape the boring hours she had to spend at the church. She wasn't real. Although they had had some interesting conversations—

Another flash of blond hair in the moonlight made her heart race. She could almost see a face in the shadows with a laughing yet sad smile, almost hear the words whispering on the wind, *"It's me, Charlie. I missed you. I didn't think you'd ever come back."*

Charlotte shook her head. There was no one out there, just shadows from the trees and old memories. The stress of the last few days was getting to her, that's all.

A sudden clattering of footsteps made her jump. Then a man came up the stairs.

"Joe," she said with relief, putting a hand to her pounding heart. "You scared me."

"Sorry," he said with an apologetic smile.

He was still wearing his dark gray suit, but his tie hung loosely about his neck as if he'd been tugging at it most of the day.

"What are you doing up here?" she asked, her heart beating faster for another reason. Joe had a way of getting her pulse pounding without even trying.

"Looking for you. I stopped in at the auditorium. The meeting was still going on, but Kara said you'd taken a walk to clear your head. I remembered you telling me this was one of your favorite places when you brought me up here a few months ago, and I thought I'd check it out."

"Has something else happened? I've been right

here, trying to stay out of trouble and away from Pamela, as instructed."

"Nothing has happened. And I appreciate your efforts regarding Pamela," he said with a dry smile. "I saw her in the church. That was a surprise."

"I'll say. She was never religious when I knew her. She had to have another reason for coming."

"Andrew?"

She shrugged. "I don't know. So why did you come looking for me?"

"I wanted to see you. I didn't like the way we left things this morning—or last night, for that matter," he added.

"You said earlier today that you didn't want to talk about last night," she reminded him.

"Maybe I changed my mind."

His hesitant tone did not match his words. "We should leave it alone, Joe."

"Leaving you alone doesn't seem to work for me."

She caught her breath at the intense look in his eyes. It would be so easy to kiss him, to throw herself into his arms and escape her life for a little while. But she didn't want to use him for an escape. And she didn't want to begin something she wasn't sure she could finish.

"There's too much going on in my life right now," she said. "I feel like I'm on a runaway train and have no idea how to get off."

"You're not on it alone. I'm here for you."

"How can you be? You're the chief of police, and I'm a suspect. That puts us on opposite sides."

His jaw tightened. "Not for long. We'll break this case. We just need a little time."

"I hope you're right, but until then, we should keep our distance."

"That's not a good idea."

"Isn't it?" she challenged. "Jason told me that we were seen talking by the highway this morning. You didn't tell him that I was there, and he was concerned about that."

Joe's lips drew into a frown. "He shouldn't be giving you that kind of information."

"We're friends. And while you're Jason's boss, he's your friend, too. He's worried about both of us."

"He has a job to do. That's all he should be thinking about."

"It's not that simple. And I don't want either of you to end up in this mess along with me."

"That won't happen."

"I'd like to believe that, but every time I turn around, another shoe drops. Now you're looking into Peter Lawson, my mother's boyfriend? Is my mother going to be next in line to be questioned?"

"God, I hope not!" His emphatic words broke the tension between them. "The last person I want to bring down to the station is your mother."

"Wise man."

He gave her a small smile. "Let's table this for the moment."

"And do what?"

"Take a breath. Isn't that why you came up here to your hideaway in the sky?"

"Yes."

He moved closer, his hands sliding around her waist. "Lean on me, Charlotte. Let the stress go."

His tempting words were impossible to resist. She wrapped her arms around him and rested her cheek against his broad chest. Her head came to just under his chin, and as he tightened his embrace, she felt safe and secure for the first time in a long while.

She'd been standing on her own for so many years, she couldn't remember the last time she'd leaned on someone. Closing her eyes, she did exactly as he'd suggested and let herself just breathe. The quiet night surrounded them like a warm blanket, and in Joe's arms, there was no uncertainty, no worry that she'd lose her balance or her way. Because she wasn't trying to get somewhere—she was exactly where she wanted to be.

If only she could capture this moment and keep it forever . . . but nothing lasted forever. And in her experience, when something was too good, bad usually followed.

"You're tensing," he murmured.

"No, I'm better, thanks," she said, forcing herself to pull away from him.

A chill ran through her as their bodies separated, but she was grateful for the cold. It woke her up to reality. She couldn't afford to lose herself in another fantasy. Being with Joe was fraught with too many complications, no matter how good he looked and smelled and tasted.

Clearing her throat, she turned her attention to the view.

He leaned against the wall next to her. "How long are you planning to hide out up here?" he asked.

"Until the meeting is over."

"It didn't look like that would be anytime soon." He folded his arms. "What do you think about when you come up here?"

She shrugged. "Whatever is on my mind. When I was younger, I spent a lot of time plotting my escape from Angel's Bay."

"You never brought any friends up here with you?"

"Oh, no. This was my place, and mine alone."

He nodded. "Because this is where you hide from everyone else but not from yourself."

His words touched her to the core. "That's very perceptive."

"Are you surprised?"

"Not really. You're good at reading between the lines. But it's a little disconcerting. Most men I've dated have been pretty clueless about what I was thinking or feeling."

"They believed whatever you told them."

"Because I told them what they wanted to hear," she agreed.

"Not big on conflict, are you?"

"Conflict means someone wins and someone loses. No conflict, and everyone is even."

"See, this is where you confuse me," he said.

"Why?" she asked, surprised.

"Because you're always in the middle of some conflict. You jump into trouble to help people. You risk your life to make good things happen. You're not a coward."

"When it comes to relationships, I am."

"Because of Andrew? Or was there someone else who broke your heart?"

He was veering into dangerous territory, and she changed the subject. "Did you have a place you used to go to as a hideaway?"

He sighed. "Nice deflection."

"Did you?"

"No. Our house was crowded, and there was no privacy. We lived in the city, so there was no open land to wander. My escape was on my skateboard or my bike and later in the Mustang. That's where I found freedom—where I could fly out of my life and into the world of the impossible. There's nothing like a steep hill, the wind at your back, and a lot of speed."

"You were never afraid?"

"When you're young, you don't think anything bad can happen to you. I'm sure you did some crazy things, too."

"Not really. I was a science geek."

He laughed. "I can't imagine you as a geek of any sort."

"Oh, I was. In eighth-grade biology, I was the first in line to dissect the frog. It was my first surgery," she said with a smile. "But the frog was dead.

When I got to medical school, I couldn't wait to work on a real person."

"Operating on someone is a lot of pressure."

"So is being a police officer, running into a dangerous situation when everyone else is running out. I can't imagine that."

"But Charlotte, that's exactly what you do."

Her eyes widened in surprise. "I don't."

"Remember Annie's father? You jumped out of the car when he turned a gun on me."

"That was just instinct."

"Exactly. Your instinct is to help, no matter what it costs you. I get paid for doing what I do. You're much more altruistic."

"And you're giving me way too much credit for not thinking before I act."

He smiled and moved closer. "I like it when you don't think."

"You're the only one."

"Good. I want to be the only one. What are your instincts telling you to do now, Charlotte?"

"I have some very risky ideas going through my head right now."

"Are you going to act on them?"

Her senses tingled as his warm breath touched her cheek. "Yes," she said, putting a hand behind his head and pulling him down for a kiss. His mouth was warm, inviting, intoxicating.

He took the kiss deeper, sliding his tongue into her mouth.

Burning need ran through her soul. Why was

she fighting him? This was wonderful, incredible. As their hot breaths mixed in the chill air, a cloud of desire surrounded them. Then it wasn't nearly enough just to have his mouth. She wanted the rest of him, too.

She pulled on his loosened tie and yanked it over his head. He shrugged out of his coat as she pulled his dress shirt out of his slacks, then ran her hands over his hard abs. He was all man. And she'd never felt more like a woman in her life.

His fingers worked the buttons of her top until it fell open, and then he flipped open the clasp of her bra, and his hot hands palmed her breasts as his mouth slid down her neck. He backed her up against the wall, and the cold roughness of the cement barely registered.

"We can't do this here," he said hoarsely, yanking his head away. His eyes glittered as he stared down at her. "Can we?"

"Maybe. I want you, Joe."

"I want you, too." His head swooped down for another heated kiss, and she reached for his belt buckle, wanting no more barriers between them.

Then her mother's voice hit her like a cold shower.

"Charlotte?" her mother called. "Charlotte, where are you?"

"Oh, my God," she said, pulling Joe down to the tower floor. "That's my mother."

"Just stay down. Maybe she won't know we're up here."

She grabbed the edges of her bra and clasped it, buttoning up her blouse as quickly as possible. "It's like she has some sixth sense for when I'm doing something wrong."

"I thought it felt exactly right."

"Button your shirt," she hissed, wondering why he wasn't getting dressed.

"She might leave," he said hopefully.

"Or she might come up here and find us half-naked."

"Andrew, have you seen Charlotte?" her mother demanded. "I swear that girl is always disappearing."

Great, now Andrew was there, too. She looked over at Joe, who appeared amused. "This isn't funny."

"I'm tempted to blow your cover. I'd like to see Andrew's face, and I'd love to hear your explanation."

"Shh," she said, putting her hand over his mouth. "They're right below us."

"I don't know what's gotten into Charlotte lately," her mother complained. "She keeps disappearing on me, and now she's caught up in that terrible mess at the mayor's house."

"I'm sure that will all get straightened out," Andrew said. "Maybe Charlotte got called to the hospital."

"Her car is in the parking lot. She's out here somewhere—she always loved wandering these grounds. She used to come over here and make up games with some imaginary friend."

Charlotte frowned. She didn't remember telling her mother about Mary Katherine.

"Imaginary friend?" Joe whispered.

"Shh," she said again.

"It's cold out here," Andrew said. "Let's go back into the auditorium. If Charlotte doesn't show up, I'll give you a ride home."

"You're so thoughtful, Andrew. And much wiser than you used to be. Charlotte needs someone like you to keep her grounded and on track. I know she's a smart girl, but she doesn't always use her head when it comes to anything besides medicine. She's a brilliant doctor, but her personal life is a mess. I didn't always like you. You and Charlotte got way ahead of yourselves in high school. But I respect the way you've turned your life around."

"I appreciate that."

"I hope Charlotte doesn't let her resentment of me, or the way she grew up as the daughter of a minister, get in the way of a potential relationship with you."

"I share that hope," Andrew said. "Let's go back inside."

Charlotte let out a breath of relief as they walked away.

"So your mother wants Andrew for a son-in-law," Joe mused.

"Of course she does. If I marry him, I'll be living her life, which she always wanted for me."

"You need to tell Andrew you're done with him," Joe said as he grabbed his tie and stood up.

She didn't like his commanding tone. "It's none of your business. Just because you and I made out a little—"

"A little? We would have had sex if your mother hadn't come looking for you."

"Well, we didn't," she said, not wanting to think about how far they would have gone.

Joe put on his coat and stuffed his tie into the pocket as she stood up and rearranged her clothes. The silence between them grew tense.

"Why don't you go down first, and I'll follow in a bit?" Charlotte suggested.

"I'm not leaving you up here alone."

"I've been alone up here many, many times."

"Well, it's not happening tonight," he snapped.

"Joe, I realize that you're used to ordering people around, but that doesn't work for me," she said, frustrated with far more than just his tone. Her body was still tingling with the heat of his kiss, she was irritated with her mother for talking to Andrew about her, and now Joe was getting into her business.

"You don't want him anymore," Joe said decisively.

"How could you possibly know that, when I don't even know that?"

"You do know—but for some reason, you don't want to let him go."

"Even if I do, it doesn't mean you and I will end up together."

"You should go find your mother," he said coolly. "I'll wait here and make sure no one sees us together. Does that work?"

"Fine. Have it your way."

He caught her by the arm. "My way would be the two of us in bed together. No interruptions, no excuses, and no pretending that what's happening between us isn't happening. And that *will* happen, Charlotte. You can count on it."

TEN

Charlotte hit the gym early Wednesday morning. She had a lot of frustration and energy to burn off, and she didn't want to run into another crime scene inadvertently. The two-story health club was a fairly recent addition to Angel's Bay and offered a vast array of exercise equipment, as well as classes in yoga, Pilates, kick-boxing, and spinning.

After working up a sweat on the elliptical, she toweled off, grabbed some water, and walked down the hallway to make an appointment with one of the personal trainers. She wanted to work with some weights and needed to have someone set up a program for her. The door to the office was closed. She lifted her hand to knock, pausing when she heard a man and a woman having a heated argument.

"Do you think I'm stupid? I know what's going on, Larry. You were doing a lot more than training her."

"You're paranoid."

"No, I'm not. She had a thing for you."

"So what? Most of my clients do."

"Most of your clients don't have a lot of money."

"Baby, relax. She's not going to be needing my services anytime soon. She's in the hospital."

"Well, when she does, you'd better say no, or I'm going to have a little chat with her husband."

"Don't threaten me."

"That's not a threat. It's a fact."

The door flew open, and Charlotte jumped back as an angry brunette flew out of the office.

She stopped when she saw Charlotte. Then she glanced back at the head trainer. "What is it with you and blondes?" Without waiting for an answer, she stormed down the hall.

"Sorry about that," Larry said, clearing his throat. "Were you looking for me?"

Larry was a tall, tanned, muscled man with very short blond hair and several tattoos across his shoulders and down his arms. He had offered to set up a program for her when she'd joined.

"I wanted to schedule my fitness-program evaluation," she said.

His gaze drifted down the hall, and she saw worry in his eyes.

"Do you need to go after her?" she asked.

"I think I do. My girlfriend gets a little jealous. Why don't you wait in my office? I'll be right back."

"Sure, no problem."

She walked into the office, wondering if she wanted to work with a trainer who had a very jealous girlfriend. She didn't need to get in the middle of yet another volatile situation. Maybe she should ask for Anna, the female trainer.

Wandering over to the bulletin board, she perused a series of articles on nutrition and fitness. Then her gaze moved to the glass case of photographs taken around the club, and caught on one in particular. It looked as if it had been taken at a club Christmas party. The main focus was the manager dressed up as Santa, but in the background was Larry whispering into the ear of a skinny blonde—Theresa Monroe.

Her pulse leaped as her mind flashed back to Larry telling his girlfriend that the woman he'd been training was in the hospital. Was Theresa Monroe the blonde his girlfriend had referred to? Her gaze lingered on the photo, on Larry's hand resting on Theresa's hip. She was on to something; she could feel it.

"Sorry about that," Larry said, startling her again. "You were looking for an appointment?"

"Yes, in the evening, preferably."

He moved around the desk to look at his planner. "We're pretty booked this week. Since it's the first of January, everyone is working on their New Year's resolutions."

"Next week is fine." She paused. "Do you ever train off the premises? I was thinking about having someone come to my house."

"That could be arranged, but it will cost more."

"And who is available to come?"

"I am," he said with a smile. "Anna only trains here at the club."

"Would that upset your girlfriend?"

His smile dimmed. "You overheard?"

"She was yelling pretty loudly."

"She's possessive. I found it attractive at first; now it's getting to be a little much. But she's not a problem. If you want a personal session, we can do it. How's a week from Wednesday night?"

"That sounds good," she said. "Let's do the first session here and then see how it goes."

"All right. Seven o'clock work for you?"

"Yes. I'm Charlotte Adams," she said.

He jotted down her name. "You're all set. I'll see you then, if not before."

"Thanks."

After leaving the office, she headed straight to the locker room. She showered and dressed quickly, then drove across town to the police station.

Charlotte intended to speak to Jason but he wasn't in yet. She only had about ten minutes, before she had to be at the office, so she asked if Joe was available. She would have liked a little breathing room before seeing him again, but this was too important to wait.

A few minutes later, she entered his office. As he stood up, her body reacted with a fluttering stomach and a racing heartbeat.

Joe gave her a wary look. "I thought after last night, you'd be avoiding me for a while."

Clearing her throat, she said, "That was the plan, but something has come up. At the gym this morning, I overheard an argument between the trainer, Larry, and his girlfriend. She accused him of cheating on her with one of his clients. I saw a photo of him with Theresa, and I think there's a possibility she was having an affair with him."

She was so excited about her theory that it took a moment for it to register that Joe looked less than enthused. "This could be important," she said. "Why aren't you excited?"

"First of all, you're supposed to stay out of this case."

"I can't help what I overhear. And you're missing the point."

"I'm not missing anything. You heard an argument. Was Theresa's name mentioned?"

"No, but the girlfriend called the client a skinny blond bitch, and that fits."

"That's all you've got?"

"Larry mentioned that his client was in the hospital. And there was a photo of him with his hand on Theresa's hip. You said that the crime was personal. Maybe Larry went after Theresa. Or maybe his girlfriend did," she said, the idea gathering steam. "It was obvious that she hated her. Maybe the girlfriend went to the party to confront her. They fought, and she ripped off Theresa's jewelry."

"It's a theory," Joe conceded.

"It's a good theory," she said with a proud smile.

He reluctantly smiled back. "I'll have Jason look

into it. But Charlotte, I have to warn you again: this isn't one of those mystery party games. Someone almost killed Theresa. Leave the investigation to us."

"I came straight to you, even though I was planning on avoiding you for a few days. So that should tell you how important I thought my information was." She got to her feet. "I'm off to work."

He stood up and walked around the desk. "You have to promise me something." Her heart beat a little faster as he drew closer. "Stay away from Larry until we can clear him."

"I already made an appointment with him for a training session."

"Cancel it."

"You really need to work on this autocratic thing you have going on."

"I'm sorry. Would you please cancel your appointment until we know if Larry was involved in Mrs. Monroe's assault?"

"That's better."

"Is that a yes?"

"Yes. I'd rather train with Anna, anyway. At the gym, Larry seems to spend as much time looking at himself in the mirror as he does watching what his client is doing." She drew in a breath. Joe was so close to her; it would be so easy to jump back into his arms. "I'd better go back to avoiding you now."

He leaned forward and kissed her mouth. "Don't stay away too long. I'll miss you."

She'd barely left his office when she started missing him. She really did need to keep her distance.

Halfway to her car, her phone started to ring. She had the crazy thought that it might be Joe, but Andrew's name flashed across the screen.

She let it go to voice-mail. The men in her life were on hold—at least until the end of the day.

Andrew frowned as Charlotte's voice-mail picked up. He could never get hold of her. He'd thought he'd have a chance to talk to her last night, but Pamela's appearance at the meeting had sent her into hiding. And when she'd returned from her walk, she'd grabbed her mother and headed home with barely a glance at him. He was getting a little pissed off. He was willing to give her time, but he didn't want to be stupid. Maybe he needed to stop letting her call all the shots. He'd certainly never let her do it the first time around.

When they were teenagers, she'd adored him. She'd drop everything to hop into his car and go for a ride at a moment's notice. He remembered long phone calls after midnight, when he'd talked about his dreams and she'd always listened. But she hadn't done much talking, he realized. It had always been about him, back then.

Now it was all about her, what she wanted, what she needed. Only he didn't know what that was, and she *still* wasn't talking. He had to find a way to get her to open up, to tell him what she was really afraid of. Then he could reassure her that the future would be a lot different from the past.

A knock at his door interrupted his thoughts. He set down his phone. "Come in."

"Andrew, are you busy?" Tory asked as she stepped into his office.

"Not too busy to see the woman who saved me a trip to the auto shop. How are you?"

"I'm good, but I'm looking for a little advice. I'm hoping you might be the man to give it."

"Of course." He got up from his desk and waved her toward the more comfortable couch along the wall. "Do you want some coffee? A soda?"

"I'm fine, thanks. Last night's meeting went well, I thought."

"We made some progress. Mrs. Adams has a strong will."

"That's what it takes to get things done. Believe me, I know. I've spent most of my life bringing in funding for our family theater."

"Which makes your willingness to help out here at the church even more impressive."

"I'm just trying to fill up my days."

"What's on your mind?"

She gave him a worried look. "You're going to think I'm crazy."

"I doubt that."

Clasping her hands together, she breathed deep. "I'm thinking about having a baby on my own."

"Okay," he said slowly. "That's a big decision."

"I'm sure everyone will think it's too soon, since I'm just in the process of divorcing Steve, but wanting a baby isn't new. I've been thinking about it for years, and I don't want to wait anymore. The thought of having to meet someone and fall in love and then plan a wedding and figure out when to have children is overwhelming. Who knows how long it will take even to meet the right person? I don't have years."

"Or it could be weeks," he suggested. "You don't know what's around the corner."

"But I *do* know that I want to be a mother."

"Raising a baby alone is a huge responsibility."

"Don't you think I'm up to it?"

"I didn't say that. I just want you to think about it. It also may not be as easy to adopt, as a single woman."

"I know. I've thought about that. I could try to adopt a child from another country, which would probably be more expensive." She drew in a big breath. "Or I could maybe ask someone to give me their sperm and try to carry the baby myself."

He swallowed hard, suddenly feeling completely out of his depth. They'd never covered the topic of sperm in seminary.

"Andrew?" she prodded. "You still with me? You look a little pale."

He cleared his throat. "You surprised me."

"I just want a baby. I don't need a husband or someone to give me financial support. I have enough money to raise a child on my own. And I have my parents, my grandparents, and Nick to share with a baby, so there will be a family."

"Just not a father," he said.

"No, not a father." She met his gaze. "Am I being selfish?"

"Ideally, every child deserves two parents."

"What about if one parent loves them beyond belief?"

He leaned forward, resting his elbows on his knees. "Tory, you'd make a wonderful mother. There's no doubt in my mind about that. But wouldn't you feel that your child was missing something by not having a father? You just mentioned your own parents. Can you imagine not having one of them?"

"Actually, my parents weren't around all that much growing up, but I hear what you're saying. Maybe I wouldn't be single forever, though. There could be a man who would want me and my child, and we'd make a family then. I just don't want to wait anymore—and at some point, it'll be too late."

"You and Steve had problems conceiving, didn't you?"

"Yes, and I've had several miscarriages. So there's a possibility I couldn't carry a child to term." She got to her feet, pacing in front of the couch. "I want to take action, Andrew. To go for it. I don't want to spend the rest of my life wondering, what if I'd had the courage to make a family of my own? Steve thought I was obsessed with having a baby, and he was partly right. Maybe I did drive him into Annie's arms. Who's to say I wouldn't do that to the next guy? So it makes sense to do this on my own and then maybe find a man who wants to be a part of something real—not something we hope might happen one day, a day that might never come."

Her passion for motherhood was unmistakable, and her decision to regain control over her life after her husband's infidelity was understandable, but he didn't know how to advise her. He could see a mountain of obstacles in her path and possibly a lot more pain.

"Did you ever want something so much you'd do anything to get it?" Tory asked.

His mind flashed back to the past. "I had a big dream, and I took for granted that I would get it. But when things got hard, I didn't try harder—I gave up. I succumbed to self-pity."

"That doesn't sound like you."

"You don't know the man I used to be."

She sat back down on the couch. "Do you look back and say *what if?*"

"More times than I can count."

"Is it too late for your dream?"

"Far too late, but I've made my peace with it. And I believe what I'm doing now is better. Sometimes God's plan is different from your own."

"I can't imagine that God planned for me to marry a cheater," she said harshly.

He didn't try to talk her out of her anger. She would have to find her own way to come to terms with what had happened in her marriage.

"What do you think I should do?" she asked.

"I can't tell you what to do, but I'd be happy to help you research your options. Then you can make an informed decision."

She gave him a warm smile. "Thanks for listening. Just saying it all out loud helps. I didn't want to talk to my parents or Nick until I heard myself say it to you. I thought you'd probably be less judgmental or less inclined to dramatize with some scene from some play you'd been in. My parents love to go into character when there is some family problem. I guess that's their way of escaping reality and pretending the problem will end after a good last scene."

"Your parents sound wild and crazy."

"They're all that. But I love 'em."

"I'm happy you felt you could come to me, Tory."

"Really? Because when I mentioned needing some sperm, I was afraid you might pass out," she said lightly.

He grinned. "They didn't teach us how to talk about sperm donation in the seminary."

"How would you feel if a woman asked you to do that for her? Would you? And I'm not asking," she added quickly. "It's just hypothetical."

Shaking his head, he said, "I couldn't be a father and not know my kid. That wouldn't work for me."

She sighed. "I have a feeling most good guys would feel like you. So adoption seems like the best option, especially since my ability to carry a child is also in question."

"I have connections with some agencies. Let me

make some calls and see what I can find out about single mothers and adoption prospects."

"I really appreciate that." Getting to her feet, she said. "So, are you excited about officiating at Lauren and Shane's wedding?"

"Yes. I've done a few weddings, but none where I knew the two people when they first met."

"Are you going to be sitting with Charlotte at the reception?" she asked curiously.

"She's in the wedding, so I think she has a lot of responsibilities."

"But you two are getting together, right?"

"I don't know. I let her go once. I'm not sure I'll get her back."

"Well, if you want her back, you'd better fight for her. Otherwise, you'll have something else to think *what if* about."

"I don't know how hard to push Charlotte. She's opened the door about this big," he said, demonstrating a narrow space with his hands. "And if I mess up, that door is slamming shut."

"You need to stick your foot in the door, so she can't close it. Tell you what—you help me research adoption, and I'll help you get Charlotte back."

"How would you do that?" he asked curiously.

"By dating you. Women always like guys who are with other women."

He was a little unsettled by the idea but also intrigued. "Charlotte wouldn't just say, 'Great, he's found someone else'?"

"Since when you do have so little confidence? You've got dozens of women dancing around you after every Sunday service."

"Charlotte knew me when," he said simply.

"That can work both for and against you. What do you say?"

He thought about the many messages he'd left for Charlotte to return. "Why don't we go to dinner and discuss it?"

She gave him a big smile. "Excellent plan."

"You're a very generous and giving person, Tory. Any child would be lucky to have you as a mother."

Her mouth trembled, and her eyes teared up. "Thank you."

"I mean it. Don't give up, no matter what anyone says."

"I won't."

"Good. I'll pick you up at six-thirty."

"Perfect, I have to be at the quilt shop by eight to help finish Lauren's quilt tonight. Charlotte will be there; maybe you can drop me off." She smiled mischievously.

"I shouldn't be playing games," he said hesitantly. But he was feeling a little desperate.

"We'll only take it as far as you want to go. We'll just give Charlotte something else to think about."

ELEVEN

Joe couldn't keep his mind on work, so he decided to have lunch at Dina's Café. The hotbed of town gossip, Dina's Café also offered up good food and a warm, comfortable place to sit for a while. It was after the lunch rush, and he was happy to see that his usual booth in the back corner was open.

Dina, the gregarious middle-aged woman who ran the café, appeared with a coffeepot and a warm smile. "You're in luck, Chief. Today's special is chicken enchiladas with rice and beans."

"Ah, a taste of home. I'm in."

She poured him a cup of coffee. "How's it going today?"

"I'm keeping busy."

"I wish I was. The holiday tourists have gone home, and everyone here is on a diet," she grumbled.

"Give 'em two weeks, and they'll all be back."

She grinned. "That they will. Nobody gives up my pie forever." She glanced over her shoulder and told the other waitress to bring him the special, then sat down in the booth across from him. "I'm glad you came in. Any luck finding whoever knocked out the mayor's wife?"

"We're still investigating."

"Well, it sounds to me like you're investigating the wrong person. Charlotte Adams certainly didn't do it. She doesn't have it in her." Dina gave a quick glance around the room. "If you ask me, Theresa's sister is the one you should be looking into."

"Pamela?"

"Yes, that girl was trouble from the day she was born. She used to come here in high school and run out on her check—dine and ditch, they used to call it. By then, her parents had passed on, and she and Theresa were living with their grandmother, who didn't know where they were half the time. Those girls just ran wild. They were always fighting with each other, too; they had a lot of screaming matches in here. One time, I thought Pamela was going to rip out her sister's hair. She had a violent streak in her."

"Pamela did rush back here after Theresa's attack, so there must be some family loyalty."

"Did she come back? Or was she already here?" Dina said with a quirk of her eyebrow.

"What do you mean?" He'd had a few thoughts about Pamela's arrival himself, but he was curious about what Dina had to say.

"I think Pamela was jealous of Theresa. Let's face it, her sister is a rich woman. She married a success-ful man, and she now owns one of the biggest houses in town, along with some fabulous jewelry. That couldn't have made Pamela happy. Maybe they had a fight, and Pamela stole her sister's jewelry."

He'd considered a similar scenario but, like Dina, had no facts to back it up. As far as he knew, the mayor's phone call was what had brought Pamela to town, and it seemed a little unlikely that she'd stick around if she'd committed the crime. Unless she was staying to find out what her sister remembered, which at the moment seemed to be next to nothing.

"Something to ponder," Dina said as she slid out of the booth. A minute later, she returned with his lunch. "Enjoy."

"Thanks." The cheesy chicken enchiladas reminded him of home, of his father's spicy tamales and his grandmother's salsa. They also reminded him that he was due to call home. He'd been checking on his father's progress regularly, but it had been a few days. He was just taking his last bite when his cell phone vibrated. The number gave him immediate indigestion. It was Rachel.

He debated answering for as long as it took the phone to stop vibrating. A moment later, his voice-mail gave a little *ding*. Did he want to know why she'd called? If it was something to do with his father, one of his sisters would have been on the phone. So her call had to be about the divorce or something along those lines, lines he didn't care to travel. She'd been the one to file, but he was the one now who wanted everything finalized.

He drank his coffee, stared at his phone again,

and finally punched the button to retrieve her voice-mail.

Rachel's voice brought with it a mix of emotions.

"Hi, Joe. I know it's almost officially over between us, and you probably don't have any second thoughts, but if you do, call me. I can't stop wondering if we moved too fast, if we should have tried harder, if things would have been different if you'd been willing to move back home. Your answer is probably no, but I had to ask one more time. Because we meant a lot to each other once. Anyway, that's it. 'Bye."

"Joe?"

He blinked in surprise as Isabella slid onto the bench across from him. His sister's eyes grew worried as she stared back at him.

"What's wrong?" she asked. "I saw you on the phone. Nothing's happened to Dad, has it?"

"No. Rachel left me a message."

"Oh, she called you, too."

"You spoke to her?" he asked.

"She wanted me to persuade you to talk to her."

"We're done, Izzy. I don't know how I can say it any more clearly. And I find it ridiculous that she's now acting like she never wanted a divorce. She's the one who followed Mark Devlin back to Hollywood after his accident here. I saw her the night he got hurt. She was destroyed. She wouldn't leave his bedside. That's why she filed for the divorce. She was in love with him."

"I don't think things worked out for them."

"That's not my problem."

"She's used to you forgiving her," Isabella said quietly.

He thought about that for a moment. "I'm not angry with her," he said, knowing it was true. "To be completely honest, I'm relieved it's over. I was fighting to hang on to something that wasn't there anymore, that hadn't been there for a long time. It was exhausting. Now I've let go, and I feel good." He picked up his phone and deleted the voice-mail.

Isabella smiled. "I'm glad. I loved Rachel like a sister, but I wasn't oblivious to how needy she could be or how unhappy the two of you were the last few years. Now I'm going to grab my salad and go."

"Where are you off to?"

"The theater. Tory's mother asked me to help them go through the costumes for their spring production."

"You're getting as sucked into this town as I am."

She smiled. "I didn't just fall in love with the town, I fell in love with Nick."

"It doesn't bother you that he was married before?" he asked curiously.

"No. It was a long time ago."

"That would make a difference," he mused. "He's had plenty of time to get his head straight."

She gave him a thoughtful look. "Are we talking about Nick or about you?"

He tipped his head. "I was wondering how long it would take someone to feel like they weren't the rebound person."

"I don't think it's about time," she said, her expression turning more serious. "It's about the quality of the new relationship, the depth of the feelings, the trust, the honesty. Sometimes that happens fast. Sometimes it takes a while. I knew Nick was the man for me from the first minute I met him. But he fought it a little longer."

"Are you going to marry Nick?"

"Well, he hasn't asked, but if he did . . . maybe."

"Taking on a teenage stepchild wouldn't be easy."

"Megan looks like a rebel on the outside, but on the inside, she's a marshmallow. Just a little girl wanting to be loved, and I've got plenty of that to give."

"You deserve to be happy, Isabella. I'm glad you found Nick and Megan."

"Me, too. And you deserve to be happy as well." She slid out of the booth just as Jason approached. "Hi, Jason. You can have my seat."

"Are you sure? I don't want to interrupt," Jason said.

"I was on my way out. See you both later."

"What's up?" Joe asked Jason as he sat down.

Jason didn't answer right away, as Dina came by to pour coffee.

"I have your favorite peach pie," she told him.

He groaned. "You're killing me, Dina. Fine, bring me a slice."

"Warmed up with ice cream on the top?"

"Do you have to ask?"

She laughed. "What about you, Chief?"

"No, thanks. I'm stuffed."

She cleared his empty plate. "I knew you'd like that. I'll be back in a minute with that pie."

After Dina left, Jason said, "I spoke to the fitness trainer, Larry Craig. He got very nervous when I asked him about his training sessions with Theresa and admitted that he'd been seeing her two days a week for the past couple of months, but he assured me his relationship with her was completely professional."

"What about Larry's girlfriend?"

"Still trying to get in contact with her. She wasn't home and called in sick to work." He paused as Dina set down his pie. "Thanks, this looks good."

"Enjoy," Dina said, and left.

Joe didn't like the fact that the trainer's girlfriend seemed to be unreachable. People in Angel's Bay weren't usually that difficult to locate. "Make it a priority to locate the girlfriend before the end of the day."

"Will do," Jason replied.

"Anything else?"

Jason shook his head as he dug into his pie. "Nothing," he said between bites. "On a lighter note, you're coming to Shane's bachelor party on Saturday night, right? We've got the back room at Murray's reserved for a little pool, a lot of beer, maybe even a stripper," he added with a grin.

"A stripper here in Angel's Bay?" Joe asked in amazement.

"I know a couple of girls who are willing to travel for the right amount of cash."

He raised an eyebrow. "Does Kara know that you and Colin are bringing in strippers?"

Jason shrugged. "It's a bachelor party. What happens in the back room of Murray's stays in the back room."

Joe smiled to himself. Somehow he didn't think that would be the case.

Charlotte could see the roof of the police station from her office window. If she were a floor up, she could probably see into Joe's office. She could imagine him there now, working at his desk that always seemed to be stacked high with files, a cup of coffee by his elbow, the computer next to him, his brow furrowing with concentration or irritation because they weren't finding the answers they needed. He cared a lot about his job and about the people in the community. He also cared about her.

Her heart leaped at the memory of last night, stripping his clothes off his body with a reckless impatience that went way beyond her usual romantic or sexual encounters. She would have made love to him in the bell tower if her mother hadn't come looking for her. Another few minutes, she probably wouldn't have cared *who* was nearby, because when she was with Joe, she was with him all the way. His kiss drove all rational thinking out of her head. But Joe could hurt her badly, because the feelings swirling inside her felt dangerously like love.

Her office intercom buzzed, reminding her that

she had another patient to see. Staring out the window at the roof of a man's office building was not an efficient use of her time. Smiling at her foolishness, she turned away from the window and got back to work.

After spending the next ten minutes on a routine physical, she left her patient to get dressed and headed to the front desk to fill out a prescription slip and check the rest of her schedule. While she was doing so, her gaze caught on a patient being led down the hall into an examining room.

It was Constance Garcia, the housekeeper of Sandstone Manor.

Charlotte's pulse began to race. Constance wasn't her patient, but what a golden opportunity to get some information. She headed down the hall, knocked briefly on the exam-room door, and turned the knob as Mrs. Garcia said, "Come in."

The woman was dressed in black pants, a white blouse, and a heavy gray sweater, her black hair pulled back in a severe knot. She was sitting in a chair by the exam table, reading a magazine. When she saw Charlotte, her eyes widened with surprise and what appeared to be a little fear.

"Hello, Mrs. Garcia. I'm Dr. Adams," she said with a cheerful smile. She wasn't guilty, and she wasn't going to act guilty. "We met the other night at Mrs. Monroe's house."

"I know who you are. And you're not my doctor."

"Dr. Shaw is finishing up a surgery. She'll be a little late. I wanted to let you know."

"The nurse already told me," she said warily.

"Good. I was hoping you and I could have a little chat about what happened the night Mrs. Monroe was assaulted."

The woman immediately shook her head and put a nervous hand to the cross that hung around her neck. "I don't have anything else to say. I told the police what I knew."

"I'm sure you did. I'm just curious about where you were when you saw me. Were you on the stairs? Or in the hallway?"

The woman hesitated. "I'm sorry you're in trouble. I just told them what I saw."

"As you should. But I wasn't near Mrs. Monroe's room. I was at the other end of the corridor, and I don't remember seeing you at all. I passed another woman when I came up the stairs. A young woman wearing a black dress, with dark hair. Do you know who I mean?"

Constance licked her lips. "I—I don't know. I'm not sure." She jerked to her feet, the magazine falling to the floor. She grabbed her big purse and held it in front of her like a shield. "I'll come back when Dr. Shaw is here."

"I'm sorry. Please don't be upset," Charlotte said quickly, holding up her hands in apology. "I'm just trying to figure out who could have hurt Mrs. Monroe, because it wasn't me, which means it was someone else."

The woman stared back at her for a long moment. "You seem nice. I'm sorry. I can't talk to you. They told me not to."

"Who?" she asked. "The police?"

Mrs. Garcia started shaking her head again, visibly more upset. Then she darted past Charlotte and practically ran down the hall, almost knocking over Charlotte's nurse, Leslie, in the process.

"What happened?" Leslie asked.

"She didn't want to wait," Charlotte said shortly.

"I guess not," Leslie said, giving her an odd look. "Are you all right? I just put Mrs. Rogers in room three."

"I'll be there in a minute." Charlotte hurried into her office, closed the door, and breathed in and out, unsettled by the housekeeper's words. *They told me not to talk to you.*

Who were *they?* Somehow she didn't think Constance was referring to the cops. There had been fear in her eyes. And her cryptic apology made Charlotte wonder if the housekeeper had seen her in the hallway at all.

Who was the woman she'd passed on the stairs? There must be a list of all the employees who had been at the party that night. She needed to get it, go through it, identify the woman she'd seen. Put some pressure on someone else for a change.

Her mind whirled in a dozen different directions. She glanced at the phone, wondering if she should call Joe or Jason. Neither one wanted her involved, and she doubted they'd appreciate her talking to Constance. But something was off about the housekeeper's behavior. She just had to figure out what it was.

Andrew jogged down the stairs of his house as his doorbell rang, three impatient times in a row. He finished buttoning up his shirt and ran his fingers through his damp hair as he headed toward the front door. He was just about to leave to pick up Tory for dinner.

On his porch was Pamela, wearing a dark red minidress under a black leather jacket with black tights and high heels. She brushed past him, taking off her coat and tossing it onto the couch before he could tell her she wasn't welcome. Her dress was cut low, her generous cleavage front and center. She'd always been bold and uninhibited, but he didn't intend to let her provocative clothes or her sexy smile get to him. He'd been to Pamela's version of fantasy land, and he had no intention of going back.

"What do you want?" he asked.

"To finish our conversation from the other day. Did I get you out of the shower?" she asked, her gaze trailing down his body. "Too bad I didn't get here a few minutes earlier. We were always good in the shower."

He cleared his throat. "I'm on my way out, and we have nothing to say to each other."

"Why don't you offer me a drink?"

"All I have is soda and orange juice. Hardly your style."

"Or yours. Fine, I'm not thirsty, anyway." She glanced around the living room, giving a disbelieving shake of her head. "It's weird that you're living here in Charlotte's house. Do you lie in bed at night and think about her? Do you go into the room she used to sleep in and imagine her dreaming about you?"

He knew better than to answer either of those questions. "I'm not discussing Charlotte with you."

"Is she the one you put on cologne for?" She gave him a speculative look as she sat down on the couch. When she crossed her legs, her dress slid higher up her thigh, which was probably not an accident.

"I'm going to ask one more time. What do you want?"

"Sit down, Andrew."

Her determined tone told him she wasn't leaving until she'd had her say. Taking a seat in the chair across from her, he said, "Talk."

"Charlotte's not for you. You never saw her for who she was, and she never knew the real you. You were like the couple on top of the wedding cake, all dressed up and completely fake."

He shook his head. "This is what you want to talk about?"

"I'm trying to stop you from making a mistake, going back to someone you didn't love enough to stay with in the first place. I've always had your back, Andrew. I'm the best thing that ever happened to you."

He looked at her in amazement. "How can you say that?"

"When you were with me, you were yourself, your real self. With Charlotte, it was all a big act. I bet she doesn't even know you now."

"You're the one who doesn't know me now. We've been apart for seven years. I've turned my life around."

"Was your career choice some sort of penance?"

"It was my calling."

"It didn't seem like it was calling you when we were roaming the streets of Hollywood at three o'clock in the morning, going from club to club, drinking ourselves into oblivion, waking up with people we didn't remember meeting."

He swallowed hard. He'd never gone as far off the deep end as Pamela or some of his other friends, but he'd come close. And he thanked God every day that he'd found a way out of that life.

"I regret the choices I made back then, which is why I want to help people avoid the mistakes I made. I intend to have a life I can be proud of."

"And you need Charlotte to complete your transformation," she said with a bitter twist of her lips. "When she forgives you, then you can forgive yourself, right?"

"She's already forgiven me. And my relationship with Charlotte is none of your business." He didn't want to admit that she was right, but she'd come damn close.

"I could wreck it again," she said in a matter-of-fact voice.

His stomach rolled. "Why would you want to do that?"

"You left me behind, Andrew. You went off and saved yourself, and you didn't give one thought to me."

"I told you I was leaving."

"But you didn't offer to take me with you."

"You wouldn't have gone. You were sleeping with Mitch. How long did you stay together?"

"Until he went to prison, but I only stayed with him because you left. You were the one I loved, Andrew. Even Mitch knew that."

"You need to leave Angel's Bay," he said abruptly.

"Why should I? You might have everything to lose, but I have nothing."

"Are you sure about that? Because I've been thinking about the robbery at your sister's house."

She gazed back at him, giving nothing away. "So?"

"You always liked to borrow your sister's jewelry. And then there was that girl in college, who lived in Beverly Hills. We partied at her house one night, and you somehow ended up with a pair of diamond earrings."

"You think I did it?" Her eyes widened with surprise that could have been feigned or real. Pamela was a very good actress.

"I think you had a fight. Maybe you shoved Theresa. Maybe she just slipped and fell. And there was that big fat ring on her finger and that beautiful necklace, and you wanted them."

"Nice story. Are you planning on telling it to the cops?"

"I might."

"That sounds a little like blackmail, Reverend Schilling. It's nice to know you haven't lost all of your edge," she said sarcastically.

"Most of it is gone." He took a moment, wanting to find the right words to make her understand, to make her leave. "My life is completely different now, Pamela. I'm not the guy you ran around with in Hollywood. I give sermons, run youth groups, counsel people on their marriages, and visit the sick. I host bingo night and work with the ladies' auxiliary to organize fund-raisers and plant gardens. I rarely drink, and I don't touch anything stronger than aspirin. Would you really want to be a part of this life?"

"It does sound boring, I admit. But maybe I'm looking to change, too."

"Then change—but don't do it here," he said as he rose. "You never liked Angel's Bay, and the town is just as dull as you thought it was when you were seventeen."

"I liked the excitement we made together." She stood up and walked over to him. She put out a hand, but he backed away. "Are you afraid you'll want me again if I touch you?"

"Would that make you feel better?" he asked gently.

Her lips turned into a pout. "Now you *do* sound like a counselor. I hate people who humor me."

"Then maybe you should go." He walked to the front door and held it open for her.

After a moment's hesitation, she followed. "Do you really think I stole my sister's jewelry? That I would leave her bleeding on the floor?"

He hated to think Pamela was that cold, but he couldn't dismiss the idea. "Maybe you felt guilty, so you ran to the hospital, or maybe you just went to find out what Theresa remembered. Since she remembers nothing, you're off the hook."

"And you think I cut the lights at the party, too?"

That part didn't sound like Pamela. "You could have had help. You said Mitch is out of jail now."

Her gaze was steady and ice-cold. "You really believe that?"

"The only thing I know for sure is that you're the best liar I've ever met."

"There was a time when you were pretty good yourself. Perhaps this is one of those times. Your minister gig could just be one big act. And the perfect way to seal that deal is to marry the former minister's daughter. Excellent plan, Andrew."

"It's not a plan. I love Charlotte." He said the words as forcefully as he could, not just for her sake but for his own.

Pamela shook her head, giving him a pitying look. "You want to love her, but you don't. I'm not sure you ever did. And that's not a lie, Andrew, that's the truth. I'd be doing you a favor if I broke you up. I'd be preventing you from ending up with the wrong person."

"Just like I'd be doing you a favor by turning you in to the cops," he returned. "Stopping you from going any further down the wrong path."

She gave him a mocking smile. "Looks like we have a stalemate. I guess the question is, how far are you willing to go to protect your past?"

"And how far are you willing to go before you stop trying to destroy your own life? All you've ever done is sabotage yourself, Pamela. You don't think you're worth anything, so you make sure that everyone else thinks the same thing. But you can change. It doesn't have to be like this."

Her smile faded, her lips tightening. "You think you can save me?"

"No, I think you can save yourself."

Pamela gave him one last look and then stormed out of the house, slamming the door behind her.

Andrew drew in a deep breath, his heart beating fast. He needed to do something about Pamela before she ruined his life again. This time, he had a lot more to lose than just Charlotte.

TWELVE

Charlotte stopped in at Lauren's bakery on her way to the quilt shop Wednesday evening. She'd been so caught up in the Monroe case and her own problems that she'd been a little remiss in her bridesmaid duties. She not only wanted to check in on Lauren, but she also had a very special piece of jewelry that she wanted to drop off before the wedding.

The Sugar and Spice Bakery, which Lauren had opened a few months earlier, was officially closed, but the lights were still on, and Charlotte could see Lauren through the windows. She was talking on the phone, her body language tense and her expression frustrated. The door was unlocked, so Charlotte stepped inside.

Lauren gave her a distracted wave, her attention clearly on the phone call.

Charlotte wandered over to the counter and took a piece of banana walnut bread from the sampler tray, trying not to eavesdrop, but it was clear that

Lauren was talking about her father and that the news wasn't good.

Ned Peterson had been suffering from early-onset Alzheimer's for the past year, and his battles with the disease were beginning to take their toll—not just on him but also on the people around him. Lauren had originally come back to Angel's Bay thinking that she might move her father to San Francisco, where she was then living, but it had soon become clear that he had no intention of leaving the town he called home. Fortunately, Lauren found love and a new career, so everyone ended up happy.

"Thanks, I'll be by in about an hour," Lauren said, then tossed her cell phone onto the counter in frustration.

"That doesn't look like good news," Charlotte commented.

Lauren pulled the band out of her hair and shook it out. "My dad had a bad day. He got very agitated, and they had to sedate him. He kept yelling that someone was trying to hurt his daughter. Even in his dementia, he thinks about Abby. He still wants to find some way to turn back the clock and bring her back to life. It's hard to watch, because I wish I could do the same thing. Anyway, I need to go over there."

"Do you want company?"

"Don't you have some super-secret thing to do at the quilt shop?"

"I could probably get out of it."

"Don't bother. It's better if I go on my own. More people will only confuse him." She gave a sad smile. "So why are you here? Sweet craving? Or did you just come by to see me?"

"I wanted to bring you something." She handed over a small jewelry box.

"You bought me jewelry?" Lauren asked in surprise.

"I wouldn't say that, exactly. Open it."

Lauren flipped open the lid. "Oh, my God, the daisy chain," she said, pulling the beaded bracelet out. "We made these in eighth grade." She gave Charlotte a nostalgic smile. "We used to go to that garden you found by the beach and pick the daisies."

"And play the game, 'He loves me, he loves me not,'" Charlotte finished with a grin.

"I remember. Yours always ended up on 'he loves me' and mine on 'he loves me not.'"

Charlotte laughed. "Well, you beat me to the altar, so there you go. Anyway, I wasn't sure if you still had yours, but I wanted you to have something from me for the wedding—something old and borrowed. You don't have to wear it, though. It might ruin the look of your dress."

"Are you kidding? I'm definitely wearing this." Lauren put it on her arm, letting the white beaded daisies dangle from her wrist. "This means a lot to me, Charlotte. Our friendship was really special, and I'm glad we have it back."

"Me, too. The best part about coming home was getting to be friends with you again—you and Kara and all the others." Unexpected moisture filled her eyes. She was getting far too emotional these days.

Lauren tilted her head, giving her the same misty-eyed look. "Don't you start crying, or I will."

"I'm not crying," she said with a sniff. "It's silly. I had other friends in medical school. But for some reason, none of those friendships ever went as deep as ours."

"Because we knew each other when we were kids, when we were growing up into our lives. That's why I wanted you and Kara to be in the wedding. It feels right to have you two standing by my side. We've known each other the longest."

Charlotte nodded. "And you know how honored we are—and even happier now that we've seen our bridesmaids' dresses."

"They are spectacular." Lauren touched the daisy bracelet. "I haven't been out to the garden since I came back to town. Is it still there?"

"I haven't been out there, either. I've thought about going a few times, but part of me is afraid it won't be there anymore."

"Well, there was never any reason for it to be there. It was magical."

Charlotte smiled. "I wouldn't go that far. Anyway, I'll let you go see your dad."

Lauren walked with her to the door. "By the way, Charlotte, Shane has a couple of single good-looking friends coming to the wedding. Just in case you need some more men to complicate your life."

She laughed. "That's the *last* thing I need."

"I'm still working on the seating chart. Anyone in particular you want me to put next to you?"

"How about you?"

"You can't go home with me. I'm already taken," she teased.

"I'm not going home with anyone."

"You never know. Weddings can be very romantic. Now, get out of here, and go work on my super-secret wedding quilt." Her eyes sparkled. "Is it pretty?"

"It's amazing. You're going to love it."

"I know I will." Lauren's eyes blurred with tears. "There I go again."

"It comes with being a bride."

"I just feel so happy I'm afraid something will go wrong. It's like it's too good to be true."

"Nothing will go wrong," Charlotte assured her. "You've had all the bad luck you're going to have. And I can't wait to see you and Shane finally tie the knot."

"Me, either." Lauren paused. "Can I ask about you and Andrew?"

Charlotte sighed. "You can ask, but I don't have an answer."

"That might be your answer."

"Maybe I should ask the daisies," she said lightly.

Lauren smiled. "I don't think the question is whether he loves you—but whether you love him."

Charlotte was still thinking about Lauren's comment when she walked around the corner to the Angel's Heart Quilt Shop. Housed in a converted barn, the two-story shop was the heart of the community. Quilting had been a tradition in the town for more than a hundred and fifty years. One of those traditions involved making a wedding quilt for every new bride, and that's what tonight's meeting was all about.

As Charlotte approached the shop, she was surprised by a couple coming from the opposite direction. Tory and Andrew were sipping coffees from the Java Hut, and Andrew had his arm around Tory's shoulder while she laughed at something he'd said. Charlotte hadn't seen Tory look that animated in months. And Andrew looked happy, too. Funny, she hadn't thought of them as being friends.

When he saw her, Andrew quickly dropped his arm from around Tory's shoulders. "Charlotte, hello. Are you doing the quilting thing, too?"

"Yes, of course. I'm one of the bridesmaids."

"Right. Sure."

She wondered about his sudden awkwardness. "I'm sorry I didn't get a chance to call you back."

"No problem. I figured you were busy."

"It was a long, hectic day. Everyone who put off their appointments before Christmas suddenly wanted to come in."

Tory interrupted. "I'm going inside. I'll see you upstairs, Charlotte. Thanks for dinner, Andrew. Next time, it's my treat."

"You're on," Andrew said.

Charlotte was surprised at the way Andrew watched Tory walk to the door. She'd seen him surrounded by women on many occasions, but it was usually their gazes following him, rather than the other way around.

"So, why did you call?" she asked, drawing his attention back to her.

"I was hoping you might have time for dinner, but when you didn't call me back, I figured that was a no go."

"So you found a substitute?"

"Tory's great, isn't she? I admire the way she's handled all the tough things she's had to go through the last couple of months."

"Are you counseling her about the divorce?" she asked, still trying to find a reason for why they were together.

"Not really. She knows what she wants and what she needs to do to get it."

"I'm glad. She deserves to be happy." Charlotte genuinely liked Tory, but for some reason, seeing them together bothered her a little. She almost felt jealous—which was ridiculous, since Andrew had made it clear that she could have him back if she wanted him.

"What's going on with you, Charlotte?" Andrew asked. "I heard you were questioned yesterday at the police station. Is everything all right?"

"It's fine. They're just running things by the book. Have you spoken to Pamela again?"

His jaw tightened as he gave a brief nod. "She came by the house earlier. Be careful around her, Charlotte. She has it in for you."

That surprised her. "Why?"

"It bothered her that I never felt for her what I felt for you."

"I can see why that might have upset her a long time ago, but now? I'm sure she's been involved with dozens of other men since then."

"Probably. But now that we're all here again, she's reminded of the past—just as we are."

"Does she want you back?" Charlotte asked bluntly.

He gave a shrug. "If she thought it would bother you, I'm sure she would."

"I doubt that would be her only reason. She obviously had a thing for you that lasted beyond high school."

"Well, I have no interest in restarting anything with Pamela, only with you. We need to find some time to get together, Charlotte."

"Maybe tomorrow night," she suggested.

He hesitated. "I'm sorry, I can't. Bible group. What about Friday?"

"Uh, maybe. I'm not sure if the bachelorette party is going to be Friday or Saturday. Why don't you call me, and we'll figure something out for this weekend?"

"Are you going to call me back?" he asked somewhat cynically.

She *had* been putting him off, wanting to deal with her feelings for Joe before she dealt with him. "I will call you back," she promised.

"Okay, then." His smile was warmer now. "I'll see you soon."

The second floor of the quilt shop was crowded when Charlotte arrived upstairs. Most of the women were chatting and enjoying refreshments, while a few worked on the beautiful silver, white, and gold-trimmed quilt that would be officially presented to Lauren at her bridal shower.

Charlotte joined a table with Kara and Kara's youngest sister, Dee, a petite, tomboyish blonde. Isabella and Tory were at the table, too.

"Looks like you're taking care of the drinking portion of the evening," she commented, picking up the empty wine bottle with a raised eyebrow.

Kara giggled, a sure sign that she'd had more than one glass of wine. "You're late, Charlotte."

"What have I missed?"

"A lot of drinking," Dee commented. "And my sister here getting tipsy."

"I'm fine," Kara declared.

Charlotte smiled. "You'd better pace yourself, Kara. We still have Lauren's bachelorette party to get through this weekend."

"Speaking of which," Kara said, "Lauren wants to do dinner at the Bella Vista and then crash the guys' party at Murray's."

"Does she think Shane will be happy to see her at his bachelor party?" Charlotte queried.

Kara shrugged. "She doesn't much care. She wants to keep an eye on her man. So I said okay."

"Because you want to keep an eye on *your* man," Charlotte said, seeing right through her.

"Hey, I'm just going along with the bride," Kara protested. "But there have been some sneaky conversations between Jason and Colin. They're up to something, and I want to see what it is. So we'll meet at the Bella Vista at nine and see what we want to do from there."

Their conversation was interrupted by the arrival of Kara's grandmother, Fiona, who fixed them with a stern eye. "I need the bridesmaids. We're down to the last few threads, and Kara and Charlotte should do the honors."

"I've had a little wine, Grandma," Kara confessed.

"You'll manage. Charlotte will help you."

"I don't want to ruin the quilt," Charlotte protested. Quilting had never been her thing.

"You won't do that. Just imagine you're sewing up someone's insides, minus the blood, and you'll be fine. Now, come with me."

They followed her to the quilting table. As Charlotte glanced down at the beautiful quilt, a lump came into her throat. The dreamy, romantic pattern incorporated parts of Shane and Lauren's love story in the detailed quilting: the outline of a sailboat, a tree house, a pair of white doves. Everything was subtle, sophisticated, and stitched to perfection. "It's fantastic," she said.

A tear fell from the corner of Kara's eye. "Isn't it? Lauren will love this."

"What's left?" Charlotte asked, taking a seat.

Kara sat next to her. "Just this little bit of stitching here. Grandma didn't leave us much to do."

"Thank goodness."

"I wonder if Lauren and Shane will have a baby right away," Kara said as she threaded a needle.

"Hey, let them have a honeymoon first, would you?"

"I'd love for Faith to have a cousin close to her age. My brother Patrick's kids are older, and they live far away. It would be perfect if Shane and Lauren had a girl, too."

"Well, put in your order. I have to say, I never imagined your moody bad-boy brother as a father."

"Love changes people. You should try it sometime."

"Let's not talk about me," Charlotte said quickly.

Kara's eyes narrowed. "Why? Has something happened?"

"How do you want me to stitch this?" she asked as Kara handed her the needle and thread.

"You know how. Answer the question," Kara commanded.

Charlotte slipped the needle through the material, stalling, but Kara's silence was just as compelling as her voice. "Joe and I made out last night in the bell tower," she said finally, shooting Kara a quick look.

"Wow! While I was sitting through your mother's

incredibly long meeting, you were getting it on? Your life is much more exciting than mine. How was it?"

"Very, very good," she admitted. "Head-spinning, toes-curling, heart-melting good."

"Wow again," Kara said, clearly impressed. "What happened? Did you go all the way?"

"No, but only because my mother came looking for me."

"Did she see you?"

Charlotte shook her head. "Fortunately, she didn't look up."

"So things are moving along with you and Joe."

"Too fast," she said. "I've decided to slow it down."

"Why? A kiss that good doesn't come along every day."

"It's too soon. Joe is not even officially divorced."

"He is except for the paperwork. You're just using the technicality as an excuse to push him away."

"And there's Andrew."

"*Is* there Andrew?" Kara asked pointedly. "Because I'm beginning to think the guy doesn't have a chance."

"He kissed me, too—the morning before your party."

"Whoa," Kara said in surprise. "You've been holding out on me. This is good. You can compare, see who you like better." She gave Charlotte a thoughtful look. "Although you didn't give me any description of Andrew's kiss, so I'm guessing it didn't shake you up quite as much."

"Andrew and I have chemistry; we always did. And there's an emotional connection that goes way back. With Joe, it's new, different."

"Exciting," Kara finished.

"Unpredictable," she added. "Joe is dark and mysterious, and I don't really know who he is all the way through, you know? With Andrew, I've seen the worst of him and the best. There aren't so many un-answered questions. But it's still good."

"Joe is a bigger risk," Kara conceded.

"Yes, he is."

"He might be worth it."

She met Kara's wise eyes. "How will I know?"

"Sometimes you just have to trust your instincts."

"My instincts aren't always right." She looked up as Fiona joined them to evaluate their work.

"Not bad," Fiona said. "Although you two have been doing more chatting than sewing."

"Just like you and your friends, Grandma," Kara said with a smile. "When I got here tonight, you were all gossiping about the Worthingtons and hid-den gold at Sandstone Manor."

Fiona's eyes sparkled. "Well, with the second break-in, one has to wonder what else the thief was looking for. It only makes sense that it's the missing gold from the shipwreck. Those gold bars would be worth a huge fortune today."

"But there couldn't still be gold in the house after all this time," Charlotte interjected.

"You never know," Fiona returned. "I told the chief about the Worthingtons and their history with the shipwreck. He was his usual cynical self, but he did listen."

"What did you tell him, exactly?" Charlotte asked curiously.

"I told him that I thought George Worthington brought more gold to the shore than anyone realized, and he might have sacrificed his wife and daughter to do it. To atone for his sins, he built the church and the manor house and some of the other buildings in town, but despite his good works, his family seemed to be cursed for the rest of time."

An uneasy feeling ran down Charlotte's spine as Fiona's words tugged at some distant memory. She'd heard this story before. The voice in her head was that of a little girl, an imaginary friend telling her about her father and her brother. Swallowing hard, she said, "What was her name—the girl who died?"

"Mary Katherine," Fiona said.

Her heart skipped a beat. That was the name of her imaginary friend. "How old was the girl?"

"Twelve," Fiona said, giving her a sharp look. "Kara, would you get me some coffee?"

"Sure, Grandma." Kara got to her feet.

Fiona slid into the empty chair. "What do you know about Mary Katherine, Charlotte?"

"Nothing."

"I don't believe you. Talk," Fiona ordered.

"Well . . . I used to have an imaginary friend when I was growing up. A girl I'd see running through the church grounds or playing on the beach near the garden." She shook her head. "I sound like a crazy person."

"And her name was Mary Katherine?"

"That's what I remember," she admitted.

"When did you last see her?"

"Years ago." Or had she caught a glimpse of her the night before? But that had just been the clouds, the fog, the shadow of the trees—hadn't it?

"Grant used to tell everyone that he saw his sister all over town."

"I'm sure he wanted to. This is just a story I made up in my head. She wasn't real. She wasn't an angel."

Fiona gave her a speculative look. "Why are you so afraid to believe, Charlotte?"

"I'm not afraid. I just don't believe."

"I have something you might be interested in. We'll meet tomorrow, and I'll give it to you."

"What is it?"

"You'll see."

Before Charlotte could ask another question, Kara returned with the coffee.

Fiona rose and took the cup from her granddaughter's hands. "Thank you, dear. You girls enjoy yourselves, now. I'll see you later."

"Okay, why did Grandma want to talk to you alone?" Kara asked immediately.

Charlotte sighed. "She wants me to find the missing gold."

Kara raised an eyebrow. "How are you going to do that?"

"I have no idea."

Thursday morning, Charlotte got up at 6:30, threw on her running clothes, grabbed a bottle of water from the fridge, and headed out the door. The morning was clear but cold, and her breath swirled around her as she did some warm-up stretches on the porch. She was still debating which route to take when a familiar truck pulled up in front of her house. Her heart sped up in anticipation.

Joe stepped onto the sidewalk, dressed in black sweats and a gray sweatshirt. As he approached, she saw the dark stubble of beard on his jaw. He hadn't shaved yet, and he had that sexy just-rolled-out-of-bed look that she found way too appealing.

"What are you doing here?" she asked a little breathlessly.

"I need to show you something." He pulled an envelope out of the car as she moved closer. "I have some pictures of the catering staff. Two women seemed to fit your description of the woman you passed on the stairs. Maybe you can narrow it down."

She stared at the photographs. Both women appeared to be Hispanic, with dark hair and eyes and olive complexions, but one had long, thick hair that curled, and the other's was shorter and straight. "This one," she said, pointing to the girl with the straight hair. "That's who I saw on the stairs. Who is she?"

"Michaela Gomez. She's twenty-three years old. Her permanent address was San Diego. The catering company said she applied for a job about three weeks ago and said she was moving to Angel's Bay to be near family, but we haven't found any. Nor have we learned where she was staying."

"What about a phone number?"

"No longer in service, billing address also San Diego."

"And no one knew her? That seems so strange." She handed the photo back to him. "If she's still in town, it shouldn't be that difficult to find her if you show that picture around."

"If she's still in town," he agreed. He tossed the envelope back into his truck. "Where are we running?"

"We?" She narrowed her gaze. "You want to make sure I don't run by Sandstone Manor, don't you?"

He smiled. "That's a side benefit. I'm just looking for some exercise."

"I hope you are, because I'm taking a long run," she warned him.

"I can keep up."

"We'll see." She took off down the street at a quick pace that Joe had no trouble matching with his long, easy strides. It was kind of nice to have someone by her side. Of all of her friends, only Lauren was a runner, but lately, she'd been too busy with her bakery and her wedding.

As they ran, the silence between them was comfortable. It was a beautiful morning, the fog bank sitting well off the coast, the ocean sparkling in the dawn light. She loved mornings—there was so much potential for the coming day. Nothing was screwed up yet. Every moment was filled with possibility, and today those possibilities included Joe.

She took him through a thick forest of redwood trees that covered the hillsides, then across a meadow, finally ending up running along the bluffs that edged the sea. Angel's Bay was one of the prettiest places she'd ever lived, with a scenic view everywhere you looked.

The running path ended at a children's park that was just a couple of swings, a climbing structure, and a few picnic benches. She slowed her steps, giving him a smile. "Feel up to a little off-road run?"

"We're not done yet?" Joe asked breathlessly, beads of sweat on his forehead, his cheeks ruddy from the cold air.

"Not quite. I want to show you something. If you're up to it."

"Lead on."

She climbed over a waist-high wall on the other end of the playground and led Joe down a narrow dirt path that wound through a few more trees and then widened onto a flat patch of land that was barren except for a glorious cornucopia of colorful flowers in a six-by-six strip of ground along the edge of the cliff. She stopped in front of the wild garden and looked at Joe. "What do you think?" she asked. "Isn't it beautiful?"

His breath came fast as he used his sleeve to wipe the sweat from his face. "It's amazing," he agreed, looking around. "Strange place for a garden."

"I found it one day when I was a little girl. No one in town admits to taking care of it, but it's always like this, blooming with a dozen different kinds of flowers. The sea air doesn't seem to damage it. No weeds ever overtake the blooms. It's a little piece of heaven," she added, sudden emotion tightening her chest. "I haven't been here in a long time."

"Are you all right?" he asked, concern knitting his brows.

She hugged her arms around her waist, her mind floating back to the past.

"What's wrong?" he asked, moving to her side. "You're shaking."

"Am I?" she asked in bemusement.

He stepped in front of her and put his hands on her arms. "Charlotte, what's going on in your head?"

Gazing into his concerned brown eyes brought reality back. "I just remembered when I was here last. It was right after I lost the baby."

"I'm sorry," he said with compassion. "Should we go?"

She drew in a breath. "Not yet."

"Then talk to me," he said. "Tell me what you're thinking."

"If I start talking, I may not stop," she said, feeling a rush of words ready to flee the vault she'd kept them in for many years.

"You'll stop when you've said what you have to say."

"I've already told you what happened."

"The facts," he agreed. He gave her an encouraging smile. "But not all of the emotions. You buried those away."

She bit down on her bottom lip, trying to hold back. Finally, she said, "It was so long ago. Why does it still hurt?"

"Some pains go deep," he said simply. "And some never heal because they don't get sunlight or release. You couldn't let yours out back then, could you?"

She shook her head, her mouth tightening with the memory. "After I lost the baby, my mother told my father I had the flu and he shouldn't come near me, because I was really contagious and he had a wedding to do that weekend. She told Jamie and Doreen the same thing. She even moved Doreen out of our room and made her sleep on the pull-out couch for two days."

"And she left you alone?" Joe asked, outrage in his voice.

"She'd come in by herself. She thought bringing me ice cream and magazines would make it all go away, as if it was just the flu."

"What about your friends, Charlotte? Why didn't you confide in one of them?"

"I had strict orders from my mother, and aside from that, it was just too personal and shameful." She paused. "After I finally got out of bed, I came here. I couldn't cry at home, but no one could hear me out here except the wind and the sea and the flowers." She gave him a watery smile, tears threatening to fall. "The second I started crying, I felt guilty."

"Why?" he asked in surprise.

She met his questioning gaze. "Because I hadn't wanted the baby. I was seventeen; I thought my life was over when I got pregnant. I didn't think I'd make it to college, that I'd be a doctor. The miscarriage solved all of my problems." Her chest tightened, her throat clogging with emotion. "How could I miss something I didn't want? Why did it hurt so badly, when it was probably the best thing?"

His gaze was soft. "Because it was a life, Charlotte. It was a baby you lost, not a thing, and you have a big heart. You care about people. I'm not surprised it devastated you. I'd be surprised if it didn't."

"I remember thinking how strange it was that there was nothing to mark her or him as ever being alive. There was no grave, no headstone—it was like it never happened. I went back to school, and everyone was talking about prom dresses and SAT scores and college. All I could think about was that I'd lost a baby. It was surreal. Like I was living in two worlds."

"Your mother never should have made you keep it a secret. At the very least, your family should have known."

"It would only have upset my father unnecessarily," she said, quoting her mother word for word.

Joe's frown deepened. "I had no idea she was so cruel."

"She thought she was being a good mother, being realistic, making the best of a bad situation."

"That's why you don't get along."

"The biggest reason but not the only one. Actually, we're doing better now. We hadn't talked about the baby in a very long time, but when Annie disappeared a few months ago, we bonded over her child. While my mother didn't admit to any wrongdoing, at least we got it out in the open. I got to tell her how I feel, instead of saying it over and over again in my head."

"That's good."

"I just wish I'd had that opportunity with my dad. I delayed coming back when he was sick. Part of me was worried that I'd spill the beans after all this time, and what good would that have done? It might have helped me, but it wouldn't have helped him."

"It's too bad you couldn't tell him a long time ago."

"He would have been ashamed of me," she said quietly.

"Then he wouldn't have been the man everyone claims he was," Joe said.

"He was a good man. And he was proud of me. At my high school graduation, he told me I was going to do amazing things. Do you think he would have said that if he'd known how close I came to screwing it all up?"

Joe shrugged. "You'll never know."

"No, I won't. It's done." She drew in a breath and let it out, finally feeling free. "So, this is the garden that soaked up my tears and kept my secrets. I'm glad it's still here. I bet it's heard a lot of sad stories over the years."

"Maybe some happy ones, too," Joe suggested. He wrapped his arms around her and held her tight. "You're going to be okay."

She smiled up at him. "You're a good listener. I'm sorry I dumped all that on you. I can't imagine what you must think."

His smile reassured her. "I'm happy that you confided in me. I want to know you, Charlotte—all of you. The good, the bad, the ugly, the whatever . . ."

"Then maybe you should know something else." She bit her lip, debating, then the words spilled out. "I'm not sure I want to have children. I can't imagine going through that kind of pain again."

His gaze was more somber now. "Are you asking me if that's a deal breaker?"

"Is it?"

"I'd like to have a child," he said slowly. "And I think that you'd be an incredible mother."

Her heart swelled with his words. "Really?"

"Of course. But you're the one who has to believe that." He gave her a thoughtful look. "Did you go into obstetrics because of the baby you lost?"

"I always knew I wanted to be in medicine, but that did influence my choice of specialty."

"And since you became a doctor, you've delivered

hundreds of healthy babies. A lot of good came from your loss, Charlotte. Do you ever think of it that way?"

"I try to. Especially when I'm in church, and my father's voice rings through my head, telling me that God has a plan for me. But when I lost that child, I lost a lot of faith." Something flashed in Joe's eyes. "What?"

He shook his head. "Fiona mentioned to me yesterday that people come to Angel's Bay to find their faith, not just in God but in themselves or in the people around them, and that the angels help."

"I came back because my father died, and my mother needed me."

"And I came here because my uncle died and left me his house."

They stared at each other for a long moment, knowing there were a lot of emotional underpinnings to both of those choices.

"You don't believe in angels," she said.

"Neither do you," he reminded her.

"I used to. I used to have an imaginary friend. We came here to play."

"A lot of kids have imaginary friends."

"But I think mine might have been an angel."

"Of course," he said with a wry smile. "We are in Angel's Bay, after all."

"Yes, we are." She walked around the border of the garden, the colorful flowers making her feel alive, happy, complete—as if by coming here, she'd truly come home. She'd faced her past and her pain was fading. Looking at the garden now, she could see past the tears and anguish of her last visit. Instead, she remembered all the times before when she'd come with friends. Even when she'd come by herself, she'd never really been alone. Mary Katherine had always seemed to show up, laughing and smiling, encouraging her to put flowers in her hair and twirl around, dancing to the sounds of the waves crashing on the rocks below. She'd been so young and carefree then, looking toward a life with infinite possibilities, and suddenly the girl she'd once been didn't seem so hard to reach. She'd locked her away along with all the other bad stuff, but today she'd let her out.

As she glanced across the garden, her gaze met Joe's, and she smiled. He was partly responsible for her newfound sense of freedom. He'd given her the strength to look back, and he'd listened without judgment.

"Thank you," she said. "For letting me talk it out."

"Anytime."

"One of these days, I hope I can return the favor."

"I'll keep that in mind," he said with a smile.

Whatever secrets Joe had were buried deep. She drew in a breath of fresh sea air, feeling better than she had in a long time. Things could change now. She was ready to move on.

"You know, Charlotte, you're like this garden," he said.

"What do you mean?"

"You bloom beautifully all by yourself, without anyone taking care of you. Lovely and resilient, just like these flowers."

She was moved by his words, by the way he saw her. "You seem to get me like no one else. Or maybe I'm just very easy to read."

"I wouldn't say that," he said dryly. "Come here."

His smile took the edge off his command, and she walked back to him.

He pulled her against his chest. "I missed you last night."

Her heart skipped a beat. "I had to go to the quilting party."

"You should have come by afterward."

"I was trying to stay away from you." Here in his arms, that idea seemed ludicrous now. "That doesn't seem to be working."

"No," he agreed. "I've been trying to stay away from you for months, Charlotte, and I don't want to do it anymore. I like being with you. I like holding you. I like . . ."

His gaze settled on her mouth, and her nerve endings tingled with anticipation. "What else?" she whispered.

"This . . ." His kiss was warm and tender, filled with something that felt a lot like love.

Her heart sped up. Her defenses screamed at her to stop, that kissing him was dangerous. But how could she when she wanted him so much, when every touch made her want more?

She jerked away, her survival instincts overriding her desire.

Joe stared at her, his breath coming hard and fast, his eyes dilated to dark pools of disappointment and frustration, the things she was feeling. She wasn't being fair to him. She knew that.

"You need to stop being scared," he told her forcefully.

"I don't know how," she said.

"What are you afraid of?"

"I'm afraid of us. Of what could happen. Of what might *not* happen," she added in confusion. "We're good friends, and we could ruin that. We could end up hating each other."

"Or we could be great together," he countered.

"It's a huge risk. I'm not like you. I don't race down steep hills and fly into the wind."

"It's a hell of a ride."

"Or a hell of a crash. You should know that, after what happened with Rachel."

His jaw clenched, and the air between them crackled with tension and conflicting desires. Loving him could hurt, but not being with him was painful, too. They'd gone too far, yet not far enough.

"We should go," she said finally.

"Yeah," he bit out. He took off on a sprint, as if he didn't trust himself to stay with her one second longer.

She'd hurt him with the Rachel reference, but it was a fact. His marriage had ended, just like all of her relationships. It wasn't easy to believe in happy-ever-after.

She glanced at the garden one last time and then jogged back up the path.

As they ran through the playground, she saw a wispy figure sitting on the swing. The girl smiled, her voice carrying on the wind. *"I'm so glad you're back, Charlie, that you can see me again. I've missed you. Come back, and we'll swing the way we used to."*

She stumbled as she stopped in front of the swings. "You're not real," she whispered.

"I am if you believe in me."

"I don't."

"You want to—because then you can believe in him."

Charlotte blinked rapidly as a gust of wind blew sand in her eyes. When it was gone, so was the girl.

THIRTEEN

Just past one, Charlotte headed to Dina's Café to meet Fiona. The last thing she wanted to do was talk about angels, but she'd promised to meet the older woman, and no one stood up Fiona. Maybe it was a good thing. She might learn enough about Mary Katherine to convince herself that she wasn't having conversations with an angel.

Fiona was seated at a booth in the busy café, sipping a cup of tea. Charlotte's muscles protested as she slid onto the bench seat. She'd pushed her run way too hard that morning; now she was paying for it.

"Sorry I'm a little late," she told Fiona.

"It's not a problem. I know how busy you are. I ordered you the chef's salad with some iced tea. Kara told me that's what you always order."

"I guess I'm pretty predictable," she said with a smile.

"That's the last thing I would call you, Charlotte."

Fiona's sharp tone made Charlotte wonder if that was a compliment. She'd always found Kara's grandmother intimidating, and the woman often treated her like an errant schoolgirl. But Fiona was on a mission, and for some reason, Charlotte had been selected to join in.

"I've been thinking about your angel," Fiona said. "They usually show themselves for a reason. When did you last see her?"

Charlotte wanted to look away from Fiona's inquisitive gaze, but she couldn't. "This morning," she admitted.

Fiona gave her a knowing look. "I suspected as much. What did she say?"

"That she was glad I could finally see her again. Whatever that means."

"It means that she has something to teach you. Angels are messengers. They bring love, hope, faith—all of the intangibles that make life worth living." Fiona opened an envelope that was on the table next to her and pulled out a very old photograph. There were four people in the black-and-white picture, a man, a woman, a boy about ten, and a girl about twelve.

Charlotte caught her breath as her gaze came to rest on the little girl's face. She was surprised and yet not. "Is this the Worthington family?"

"Yes. It was taken just before they boarded the ship."

"Where did you get this?"

"After George Worthington and his son settled here, some of their other relatives came to live in

Angel's Bay. They brought family items with them, and one of them was this picture. It was donated to the Historical Society a very long time ago. I borrowed it so I could show it to you."

"If it's part of the Angel's Bay collection, I might have seen it at the museum on one of our school field trips. Maybe that's why I imagined this girl's face, why I knew her name." She felt better, having come up with a logical solution.

Disappointment filled Fiona's eyes. "Sometimes you have to believe with your heart, not with your mind."

"My heart has gotten me into trouble."

"Your heart is who you are, Charlotte. It always has been. Stop fighting your instincts. They're better than you think."

Charlotte sat back as the waitress brought over their order, thinking about Fiona's words. When they were alone again, she said, "While we're on the subject of the Worthingtons, I was wondering what you can tell me about Constance Garcia, the housekeeper at Sandstone Manor."

"She's come into the shop a few times to pick up some material. I don't know her well."

"Did you ever speak to her about the legend of missing gold?"

"No, until recently, Edward Worthington was alive and, as far as I knew, in full possession of whatever treasure the family owned. Mr. Worthington refused to participate in any of our Founders Day functions. And the few attempts I made to have a

conversation with him about family were quite un-
successful. He was not an outgoing man, even before
his wife died."

"But Mrs. Garcia must have known him pretty
well."

"I believe she did."

"And *someone* in this town must know her."
Charlotte leaned forward. "I need to find that someone. I believe Constance knows more than she's saying about the robbery, but she wasn't willing to talk
to me. I need some insight into her life—who she
is, who her friends are, what motivates her, who she
might be trying to protect at my expense."

Fiona's gaze sharpened. "I'm sure the police have
spoken to her."

"Yes, they have, but I need more information."

"Are you sure you want to get involved in this,
Charlotte?"

"I'm already involved, because I was upstairs the
night of the robbery."

"You should talk to Lottie at Delilah's Hair
Salon. You know her, don't you? She's Andrew Schilling's aunt."

"Yes, Lottie cut my hair a few times back in high
school. Why would she have information on the
Worthingtons?"

"She used to go up to the manor to cut Edward
Worthington's hair. Lottie thought the man had a
crush on her—but then, she has a big imagination,
almost as big as her mouth. If you need someone to
talk to, she's probably your best bet."

Charlotte smiled, excited about the new lead. "I'll go over there later this afternoon. Thank you."

"No problem." Fiona pushed an old journal across the table. "This diary belonged to Rosalyn Murray. You should read it. Sometimes the past holds more answers than we realize."

Joe had questioned many witnesses over the years of his career, and he'd learned how to read between the lines and pick up on nonverbal tells. Constance Garcia was one big mass of quivering nervous tension, from her eyes constantly darting to the door behind him, as if seeking escape or rescue, to her fingers sliding a cross along a gold chain hanging around her neck, to her shifting feet. There was no reason for her to be nervous of him, which meant he was missing something. She was afraid, and he needed to find out why.

"I have nothing more to say," she told him, not inviting him inside the manor.

"Well, I have something to say," he continued. "We went over the list of people who were working here the night of the party." He held up the photograph. "This woman, Michaela Gomez, was seen running down the stairs minutes before you screamed for help. Do you know her?"

She glanced at the photograph. "She was working here that night."

"We can't locate her. Any idea where she might be?"

Constance shook her head.

"Did you speak to her the night of the party?"

"I spoke to everyone," she said. "It was busy. We were working hard. She was serving the guests and cleaning up the used glasses and plates. Maybe she went upstairs to see if there were any up there."

He found it curious that she was making up an excuse for a woman she claimed not to know. "Anything else?"

"Why don't you ask the caterer about her? He hired her."

"He said she was a recent addition to their serving staff."

When Mrs. Garcia didn't comment, he changed course. "What can you tell me about the necklace that was stolen? I understand it belonged to the previous owner?"

"*Sí.* Yes," she said with a nod.

"Were there other pieces of jewelry that Mrs. Monroe acquired with the estate?"

"Señor Worthington kept many things in a safe. After he died, the lawyer came and locked up the house until he could sell it."

"Where did you go during that time?" he asked curiously.

"I stayed with my cousin Rita in Monterey, until I knew if the new owner would want to hire me back on." She shifted her feet again. "I think it was the doctor who did it. I told her I was sorry, but I had to say the truth. She was upstairs. It had to be her."

His gut tightened. "When did you tell Dr. Adams you were sorry?"

"Yesterday."

"Where did you have this conversation?" he asked, wondering why Charlotte hadn't told him about it.

"In her office. She came in while I was waiting for Dr. Shaw. I don't want to talk to her again," she added worriedly.

"I'll make sure that doesn't happen," he assured her.

"I have to go to work now."

"One second. You've obviously heard stories about gold being buried somewhere in this house. Did Mr. Worthington ever talk to you about that?"

She immediately shook her head. "There's no gold here. I've cleaned every inch of this place."

He paused. "Mrs. Monroe had several private sessions with a fitness trainer here at the house. Did you meet him?"

"Yes."

"Do you think they were having a more personal relationship?"

Her eyes widened, and she started shaking her head again. "I don't see anything. I just do my work. That's all. Please, no more questions."

As Joe headed to his car, he had a feeling that Constance made it a habit not to see anything. He couldn't blame her for being loyal to her employer. But was there more than just loyalty involved? It bothered him that so many people were unreachable: Michaela, the trainer's girlfriend, and Peter Lawson. The three people had no connection to one another, but he couldn't shake the feeling that one of them was involved.

After lunch with Fiona, Charlotte finished up work earlier than expected, since two of her appointments called to reschedule. She debated diving into Rosalyn Murray's diary but didn't feel quite ready to deal with the distant past. Instead, she decided to go to Delilah's Hair Salon; maybe Lottie could tell her something new about Constance Garcia or Edward Worthington.

Turning the corner by Lauren's bakery, she saw a crowd of people inside. Good—she wouldn't be tempted to get a sweet treat. Moving on, she checked out the window displays at the local antique shops, thinking how fun it would be to decorate her own house someday. Another decision she needed to make soon, but not today.

Then Joe called her name. She stopped as he got out of the dark police sedan and walked briskly toward her. Her heart skipped a beat at his approach, but the expression on his face said that he was in chief-of-police mode.

"What did I do now?" she asked warily.

"Mrs. Garcia," he bit out. He cast a quick glance around, then pulled her toward the wall of the bank so they weren't standing in the middle of the sidewalk. "You forgot to mention that you spoke to her yesterday."

"Right," she said, giving him an apologetic smile.

"I had a brief conversation with her while she was waiting for my partner to do her examination."

"Did you threaten her?"

"Of course not," she said, surprised by his question. "How could you ask me that?"

"Because she asked me to make sure you didn't try to talk to her again. Do you realize that your brief conversation could be seen as intimidation of a witness against you?"

She was blown away by the spin. "It wasn't like that. It was a simple five-minute conversation. She said I seemed nice. She wasn't at all scared of me, Joe."

"That's not the story she's telling now." He planted his hands on his hips. "I told you to stay out of this."

"It was a spur-of-the-moment thing. I saw an opportunity, and I took it."

His jaw tightened. "It was a mistake."

"Well, then it was a mistake," she said, unwilling to give in completely. "I can't stand by and do nothing. And if you weren't a cop, you'd do the same thing in my situation. You know you would."

He ran a frustrated hand through his hair. "But I am a cop, and we're working this case. Your getting in the middle of things doesn't help."

"Are you sure?" she challenged. "Maybe my talking to Constance shook her up a little, made her doubt what she saw. Because you know what? I'm not convinced she saw me at all. In fact, I'm wondering if she might be involved. And there's another thing. She said that *'they told her not to talk to me.'* Who do you think she was referring to?"

He frowned. "I don't know."

"I think she slipped up, Joe."

"Charlotte—"

"And what about the fact that she knows the house better than anyone? She'd know how to cut the lights. And she'd be able to move quickly through the house in the dark. Maybe she's the one who brushed by me in the hallway."

"Why would she wait until the middle of a party to steal Theresa's jewelry when she probably had access to it anytime?" he countered.

"Perhaps Theresa kept it in a safe."

"There wasn't a safe at the house. They had an alarm system, but it was turned off for the party."

"What about the other maid, the one you showed me a picture of? She was upstairs. Have you found her yet?"

"No. Look, I know you're frustrated, but you need to back off."

"I'll try to stay out of things, but I won't promise not to follow leads that come my way."

His gaze narrowed suspiciously. "What lead has come your way that hasn't come mine?" He looked around. "In fact, what are you doing right now?"

"Talking to you," she prevaricated.

"Where are you going? Why aren't you at work?"

"I had a short day, and I'm going to Delilah's Hair Salon."

"Really? What are you having done?"

"Do you care?"

"I care about everything that concerns you. I like your hair long. You're not cutting it, are you?"

"No, not today."

He glanced down the street. "I'll walk with you. Maybe wait until you're done, and then I'll buy you a coffee—latte with hazelnut sprinkles, right?"

She was impressed that he knew her favorite coffee but not excited about him hanging around the salon while she talked to Lottie. "I don't have an appointment. I'm just stopping in to say hello to Lottie."

"I hear she's a character. I didn't realize you were friends."

"She's Andrew's aunt."

"No kidding? I'll be glad to meet her."

He wasn't giving an inch. "You're determined to come along, aren't you?"

"You bet. Because you're up to something, and I want to know what it is."

Their gazes clashed and held for a moment. "Fine. Lottie used to cut Edward Worthington's hair. Fiona suggested she might be a good person to talk to. Now you know."

"I'm going with you."

"You'll scare Lottie with your official presence, and she won't tell me a thing."

"From what I know of Lottie, she doesn't scare easily."

Charlotte headed down the street, Joe dogging her steps. When she opened the door to the salon, she saw Lottie behind the counter. The big-haired blonde with the long fake eyelashes and overdone makeup was nothing like Andrew's mother, Gwen, who had always struck Charlotte as a prissy, uptight woman.

"Charlotte Adams," Lottie said in a loud, cheery voice. "I wondered when you'd finally come in and say hello." She moved around the counter and gave Charlotte a bear hug. "How are you?"

"I'm good. I'm sorry I haven't come by until now."

"Well, you've been busy, from what I hear. What can I do for you today? Your hair is too pretty to cut."

"No, I don't need a cut."

"Then it's you that needs a cut," Lottie said, turning to Joe. "I've been wanting to get my hands on that thick head of hair of yours. I can do a much better job than Bernie at the barbershop."

"I don't need a cut, either," Joe said quickly.

"No, he just wants a trim," Charlotte said, deciding to make Joe pay for hounding her steps. "He's a little nervous about having it done in a women's salon, so I said I'd come with him."

"Don't worry, I don't bite," Lottie said. "Well, only sometimes," she added with a laugh. "But not when I'm cutting hair."

Joe turned red.

"Don't be shy," Charlotte said, putting a hand on his back and nudging him forward. "Lottie is great."

Lottie led him over to her chair. There was one

other stylist sweeping up hair, but there were no other customers. "You're lucky. You hit us at a slow time," she said. "How about a shampoo?"

"No thanks," Joe said, sitting in the chair. He glared at Charlotte in the mirror as Lottie draped a plastic cover over him and spritzed his hair with water. "And don't cut very much off."

"Men are always afraid to lose their hair," Lottie told Charlotte. "But this one doesn't look like he's in any danger of that."

Joe's hair was thick, wavy, and a rich shade of brown. Charlotte had loved the feel of it in her fingers. "Don't cut too much off," she echoed. "I like his hair a little on the long side."

"And is it important what *she* likes?" Lottie asked Joe with a mischievous twinkle. "Funny, I haven't heard any gossip about you two. I hope I'm the first. I love to break news in this town." She glanced back at Charlotte as she reached for her comb. "I thought you and Andrew were getting together."

Charlotte should have seen that coming. She quickly changed the subject. "I wanted to talk to you about Edward Worthington. Fiona told me you used to go to Sandstone Manor to cut his hair."

"I did. We had some interesting conversations. But if you're asking if he told me where the gold was hidden, I'd have to say no," she said with a wink. "Don't look so surprised, honey. Everyone in town is wondering if that's what the thief was really looking for. Edward told me if there was any gold, he sure couldn't find it. He was a hard man—cynical, bitter, and quiet. It was tough to get much out of him. The only person he seemed to warm to was his house-keeper."

"Constance?" Charlotte asked, anticipation snaking down her spine. "Did they have a more personal relationship than employer-employee?"

"I never caught them doing anything personal, but she mothered him. She was always bringing him tea, checking up to make sure I wasn't bothering him. She was protective, and he seemed to like that." Lottie paused. "He mentioned that it was the curse of the Worthington men to lose the women and children who loved them. He'd decided to live the rest of his life alone, so as not to put anyone else in danger." Lottie pulled a comb through Joe's hair and snipped off the ends. "I was a little surprised that he didn't leave Constance anything in his will. Everything from his estate went to charity. Rich people may get close to their servants, but they don't usually forget that that's exactly what they are—servants."

Which gave Constance a good motive to try to get something from the estate for herself. "Do you know anything about the necklace that was stolen?"

"I heard it belonged to the Worthington woman who died on the ship. But who knows if that's true? Lots of rumors going around, including you being near Theresa's room when she got knocked out. Such nonsense, and that's what I tell everyone. You were always a good girl. I knew you'd do well for yourself, and here you are, a doctor. It's very impressive. My nephew never should have let you slip through his fingers."

"That was a long time ago, Lottie."

"Kid stuff, I know," she said with a wave of her hand. "But you two made a cute couple. I remember one time sitting on Gwen's porch, and you both came back from the beach, all golden blond, sunburned, and wind in your hair. You looked happy, the picture of young love. Then you whistled, and this scraggy, muddy mutt came running. You said your mother wouldn't let you bring home any more strays, so you needed someone to take the dog until you could find the owner."

"Andrew's mother was horrified," Charlotte said, smiling at Lottie.

"Which is why she made me take the dog. He was my loyal companion for seven years. I called him Bartholomew. He needed a royal name to make up for his not-so-royal lineage."

"I'm glad he had a good home." She cleared her throat, realizing that Joe was watching her in the mirror with a thoughtful look.

"Anyway," Lottie said, "I know love doesn't always last. Lord knows I've fallen in love a dozen times—and I enjoy it every single time." She gave Charlotte a mischievous grin. "Nothing wrong with being single. You can do whatever you want whenever you want, although it can be a little lonely, too. But there's always some bad that comes with the good."

"Yes." They'd drifted way off track. "Lottie, I need to clear my name. If you can think of anything else that might help me find the thief, I'd appreciate it."

"Isn't finding the thief *your* job?" Lottie asked Joe.

"I like to think so," he said dryly.

Lottie nodded. "Charlotte always had a mind of her own. Did she tell you about the time she organized a strike against Buck's Burgers?"

He raised an eyebrow. "No, she didn't. What did you do, Norma Rae?"

"You don't want to hear that story," Charlotte replied quickly, but there was no stopping Lottie when she was on a roll.

"One summer, old Buck decided to hire nothing but busty girls to wait tables. Well, one of Charlotte's friends couldn't get hired because she didn't have a lot in that department. So Charlotte organized a strike. She got all the pretty girls in town to picket, and none of their boyfriends would cross the line. Buck lost money and finally had to cave in."

"He really went in the other direction," Joe said. "The last time I was in his place, there wasn't a waitress under forty."

"Besides being a chauvinist, Buck is also cheap. There are far better gigs in town for good-looking young girls." Lottie measured the ends of his hair, then looked in the mirror. "What do you think, Chief? Short enough?"

"It's good," he said. "Charlotte?" He met her gaze in the mirror.

Sexy as hell, she thought. But Lottie had big ears and no censor on her mouth. "Not bad."

"Not bad." Lottie sniffed. "Own up, girl, he looks hot."

She gave up. "Okay, he looks hot."

"That's right. You've been a good sport, Chief. I know you didn't really want a haircut. You wanted information. But we all got something out of it, didn't we?" Lottie said cheerfully.

Joe got up and dug out his wallet, then handed Lottie two twenties. "Will this cover it?"

"I barely did anything. I'll get you some change."

"Keep it," he said. "You've been a good sport, too."

"Thanks, Lottie," Charlotte added.

"Anytime. Don't be a stranger, now."

"I won't." She followed Joe out the door and onto the sidewalk. "So what do you think about Constance being left out of the will? It would give her a motive. And she had the opportunity."

"But we don't have evidence, Charlotte."

"What do we do?"

"We get some coffee. Our time with Lottie wasn't a complete waste," Joe said as they started down the street. "We didn't learn a lot about Edward Worthington, but I know more about you now. Rescuing dogs, leading strikes . . . I'm wondering why the hell Andrew ever cheated on you."

She hesitated for a moment, but she might as well tell him. "I told Andrew that I loved him after we had sex for the first time. I didn't know it was a surefire way to get rid of a guy."

"Teenage boys scare easily where love is concerned," he said.

"Yeah, I learned my lesson. No more declarations of love."

"Not ever?" he asked, shooting her a sideways glance.

"Well, those words aren't really date one through three material, and most of my relationships haven't lasted much longer than that."

Joe opened the door to the Java Hut. Inside, they gave their orders, then took a table by the front window. Joe winced a little as he sat down.

"Sore?" she asked.

"A little. Tell me I'm not alone."

"That run *was* longer than usual. I wanted to see what kind of shape you were in."

"How did I do?"

"You looked pretty good to me."

He grinned. "Right back at you."

Her cheeks warmed under his gaze. "You really have to stop looking at me like that, Joe. Especially out in public. Lottie is probably already on the phone about us, and I don't think you're going to like the gossip."

He smiled. "Being coupled with you isn't all that bad. And I'm sure it will annoy the good reverend. You haven't talked to him yet, have you?"

"Andrew and I have been trading phone calls. But what I talk to him about is my business, not yours."

"Fine."

She let out a breath as Joe got up to get their coffees. She really did need to speak to Andrew. Maybe later tonight.

Joe slid her coffee across the table to her. She took a sip, delighted with the sweetness on her tongue.

"This is good, thanks. What did you get?"

"Chai tea."

"Another one of my favorites. It tastes like Christmas."

He took a sip. "I never thought of it that way, but it does."

She smiled at him. "Speaking of Christmas, did Santa bring you anything good this year?"

"Izzy gave me a fishing rod."

"I didn't know you fished."

"I've only been out a few times, but now that I'm living here, I'll probably have more opportunities. Do you like fishing?"

"I find it a little slow. I love to sail, though. I haven't done much of it since I came back, but maybe in the spring."

"Sounds like you're thinking of staying."

"I haven't made any plans to leave, but I also haven't made any plans to stay."

"You like to keep your options open," he commented, his smile losing a bit of its warmth.

"I suppose. But the way you said it sounded a little like a criticism."

"Just an observation. You're good at putting things off until tomorrow."

"Very good," she agreed. "You should see how many times I reschedule every dental appointment until I finally have to go. I hate getting my teeth cleaned. Mostly, I hate getting lectured by the hygienist about not flossing enough."

"Really? What else do you hate?" he asked with amusement.

"Waiters who won't write things down, as if they're trying to prove some sort of memory challenge."

"I don't like restaurants where there are six empty tables but still a wait list."

She nodded. "That *is* annoying. How about people who obviously have more than twelve items in the express line?"

"We should arrest them. Along with anyone who starts a sentence with 'No offense,' when obviously, whatever they have to say is going to be offensive."

"And what about the person who needs to control the remote and flip through all of the channels every five minutes?"

"Uh-oh," he said with a grin.

She sighed. "I should have guessed. You do like to control things."

"So do you."

"I can give up the remote. But if anyone touches my special stash of Ghirardelli dark, melt-in-your-mouth chocolate, there's war."

"I'm not big on chocolate, so your stash would be safe with me."

"If we spend enough time together, maybe my

bad habits would drive you crazy, and you wouldn't like me anymore," she suggested.

He shook his head. "Charlotte, if we spend time together, I'm only going to like you more," he said.

She tingled under his gaze. "We'll see." Had she finally met a man she couldn't run off?

FOURTEEN

His tea was hot and sweet—just like Charlotte, Joe thought. She was telling a story about something that had happened to her in high school, but he'd gotten distracted by the freckle over her top lip and the sweep of her dark lashes over her blue eyes and the way her hair glowed in the late-afternoon light. He couldn't remember ever being so aware of a woman, so turned on by the melody of her voice, the warmth of her laugh, the curve of her lips, the softness of her skin.

"Joe?"

Her voice brought him back to reality.

"I'm boring you," she said.

"Not at all." He tried to remember what she'd been talking about.

"Nice try. You went somewhere in your head."

He glanced around, but there was no one within

earshot. "I did go somewhere, but I wasn't alone. You were with me."

Her cheeks turned a rosy red. "You're so bad."

"You have no idea." His phone rang, the station number flashing across the screen, reminding him that he'd been gone longer than he'd expected. "Sorry, I need to take this."

"No problem."

"Sheila, what's up?" he asked briskly.

"The mayor has called three times. He wants to speak to you. He said either call or come by the hospital."

"All right. I'll stop by there in a few minutes."

"Detective Marlow said to tell you he spoke to Peter Lawson and his daughter, and it's a dead end. He'll catch you up when you get back."

"Thanks." He hung up the phone. "I have to go. The mayor wants to talk to me. And apparently, your mother's boyfriend is in the clear."

"That's good news."

"Yeah." He found himself reluctant to say goodbye to her. "Why don't you let me make you dinner tonight?"

"It's probably not a good idea," she said slowly.

"It's an excellent idea. How about seven-thirty?"

"But—"

"It's just dinner, Charlotte." He got to his feet. "You won't be disappointed."

"Maybe we should put it off until tomorrow."

"There you go again—putting things off until

tomorrow." He leaned over and whispered, "Jump, Charlotte. I'll catch you." Then he left, feeling damn good. Everything would be perfect—as long as Charlotte showed up.

Joe's good vibe ended at the hospital. Theresa had been moved out of ICU and into a private room. She was sitting up in bed, wearing a silk robe, looking a lot better than the last time he'd seen her. There was a bandage around her head, and her bones stuck out in her thin face, but her color was good. That was a great sign.

The mayor jumped up from the chair next to the bed. "What the hell is going on? Why haven't you arrested anyone yet?" Robert demanded.

"We're making progress," Joe said evenly. "Investigations take time. Our team is diligently following up every lead. How are you feeling, Mrs. Monroe?"

"I'm better," she said shortly. "But very concerned that I'll be going home tomorrow and the person who tried to kill me is still free."

"Have you been able to recall any other details from your attack?" he asked.

Her lips turned down in a frown. "It was a woman—I know that."

He stiffened. "How exactly do you know that?"

"Perfume. Whenever I close my eyes, I smell perfume. I can't place the scent. It's something cheap."

"And you smelled the perfume that night in your room?"

"Yes."

"You're sure the scent was in your room and not just lingering in your mind from the party? A lot of women were wearing perfume that night."

"You're trying to confuse me," she said, her brows knitting together.

"Not at all. Just asking questions. That's my job."

"Your job is to arrest the person who did this, not have a romance with her," Robert interjected. "It's all over town about you and Charlotte Adams."

Joe's jaw clenched as he looked at the mayor. "I am doing my job. We have no evidence or cause to arrest anyone."

"Charlotte Adams is playing you. I didn't think you were stupid, Silveira."

"He's just a man," Theresa put in cynically. "Not that hard to distract."

"I'm not being distracted," he said, although deep down, his conscience suggested that wasn't entirely true. "I'm also not going to jeopardize the case by arresting someone prematurely."

"Constance said she saw Charlotte outside my room," Theresa said. "What more evidence do you need?"

"There were several people outside your room, including Constance," he pointed out. "The lights were also out for several minutes, providing a cover of darkness for anyone to escape without being seen."

"Charlotte doesn't like me. She was always jealous of Pamela and me. I never should have invited her to the party."

"It's strange to me that you invited Charlotte to the party but not Pamela."

"Pamela doesn't live in town," Theresa said quickly.

"Where is she now?" he asked. "Has she gone back to L.A.?"

"No. She's just out somewhere."

"Look, Silveira," the mayor interrupted. "I've given you and Marlow plenty of time. I want justice, and if you can't give me any, I'll find someone who can. No one attacks my wife in my town and gets away with it."

A decade of training in being polite to unreasonable people kept Joe in check. Instead of saying what he really wanted to say, he replied, "I understand. I'll be in touch. Mrs. Monroe," he said, tipping his head. "If any other memories come back, please let us know."

As he left the room, he blew out a breath, and he walked out of the hospital feeling as frustrated as the Monroes. Not just because he didn't have a lead but because he needed to cancel dinner with Charlotte.

Their professional reputations were on the line now, and he couldn't allow his desire for her to get in the way of his judgment. They needed to put the brakes on until this case was solved.

As he reached the parking lot, he pulled out his cell phone. When Charlotte's voice came on the line, he almost changed his mind, but he forced himself to go through with it. "I'm sorry," he said. "Something has come up. Can I make dinner for you another night?"

"Oh," she said in surprise. "Sure, of course," she added in a breezy tone.

He'd thought he was getting past the pretense she put up for everyone else. She'd given him a glimpse past her walls, and he wanted all the way in, but that wasn't happening tonight.

"I am sorry," he repeated.

"I understand, Joe. You have a demanding job. Sometimes things come up."

"Well, great. I'm glad you're not upset about it," he said, feeling ridiculously annoyed that she wasn't more disappointed.

"Did something happen with the mayor? You seem tense."

She had no idea how tense he was, but that had more to do with her than with the mayor. "Theresa is going home tomorrow."

"That's good news." She paused for a moment. "The mayor said something to you about me, didn't he?"

"You were part of his overall theme of requiring justice," he said carefully.

"He wants my head," she said bluntly.

"I won't let him near your pretty head. I'll call you tomorrow, Charlotte."

"Good night, Joe."

He slipped his phone into his pocket, wondering why the right decision felt so wrong.

*   *   *

Charlotte stared into the mirror at her freshly made-up face and sighed. Here she was, all dressed up and no place to go. Her mother was out with friends. Even Annie had plans, having gone to a barbecue at her friend Diana's house.

Maybe she'd just get into her car and see where she ended up.

Twenty minutes later, she ended up at the church. Andrew had told her he had a Bible group meeting, but when she arrived at the auditorium, she found a basketball game in progress. It was a mix of teenage girls and boys, with Andrew in the middle of the action.

She watched from the doorway as he dribbled down court, making one agile move after the next, until he cleanly swished the ball through the net. High fives and celebration followed, along with the sound of a buzzer.

"That's it," Andrew said. "See you all next week."

The kids broke up, grabbing backpacks and Bibles off the benches.

Surprise spread across Andrew's face when he saw her. As he strode across the auditorium with a basketball in his hands, wearing black sweats and a T-shirt, he reminded her of the boy she'd first fallen in love with. Only then she'd been watching him on the baseball field, waiting for the end of the game, when her hero would look at her—only her. What a head rush that had been. The most popular guy in school had wanted her.

"Charlie," he said. "I wasn't expecting you."

"Spur-of-the-moment decision. I thought you had Bible group."

"This is Bible group," he said, stopping to say good-bye to the last of the stragglers. "We mix discussion in with a little basketball. Anyone who misses a shot has to recite at least one verse from the Bible."

"Sounds more fun than the Bible groups my father used to run. I always counted the minutes until those were over."

"That's exactly what these guys were doing until I brought in a ball. Then everyone woke up. So, what are you doing here?"

"I thought I'd see if you wanted to get something to eat."

"What did you have in mind?"

"Pizza at Rusty's?"

"Sounds like a plan. Why don't you come next door, and I'll take a quick shower first?"

"All right." She walked out of the auditorium with him, waiting as he turned out the lights and locked up. Then they walked through the trees to her old house.

It felt odd to be climbing her old front stairs with Andrew, to wait for him to unlock the door for her. She'd been in the house a few times since he'd moved in, but it still felt as if it belonged to her family.

"Help yourself to something to drink," he told her as he headed up the stairs.

She wandered down the hall into the kitchen. Except for a cereal bowl in the sink, it was very clean. She opened the fridge and took a can of raspberry tea, noting the shelves filled with casseroles, fruits, and cheeses. It looked as if Andrew was reaping the benefits of being a single minister in a congregation of single women.

As she popped the lid and took a drink, she glanced around the kitchen. There was nothing on the walls and very little on the counters. In her mind, she could see her family's kitchen: the colorful dish towels, the potted plants by the window that changed with the seasons, the huge calendar by the door that had maintained the schedule of their lives. She imagined her mother bustling around the kitchen and saw not Andrew's small round table but the big rectangular one where she sat to do her homework or make some art project with her sister or brother. A wave of nostalgia hit her and a little sadness for a time that could never be recaptured.

She glanced toward the door as Andrew walked in, dressed in jeans and a T-shirt, his hair damp. "That was fast," she said.

"I didn't want to take a chance on you leaving. You've been hard to pin down these last few weeks."

"Sorry about that. But we can catch up tonight." She paused. "We can skip Rusty's if you'd rather eat one of the casseroles in your fridge."

He shook his head. "Please, I'm casseroled out. I never thought I would grow tired of lasagna."

"Yeah, it really sucks that you're so popular and never have to cook for yourself," she teased.

"I doubt you cook for yourself, either, with your mother around."

"Okay, we're both spoiled in that area." She finished her tea and set the can down on the counter. "It would be a little weird to eat here, anyway. It's both familiar and strange." She gave him a smile. "I always thought of this house as mine, but I'm just one of the many people who lived in it and will live in it."

"You could live in it again, if you give me a second chance." He held up a hand as she opened her mouth. "Don't worry. I know tonight you're just giving me pizza."

"Did I say I was paying?"

"You invited me," he said with a grin. "But I'll drive."

Rusty's was busy with kids and families. When they finally made their way through the line and ordered, Andrew said, "Looks like our booth is open."

She smiled as they took the corner booth. "I wonder how many couples think this is their booth. It's the best one in the place."

"Tonight it's ours." He waved her in first, then slid in next to her. "I'm glad we could finally make this happen, Charlie."

"Me, too," she said, feeling a little guilty. If Joe hadn't bailed on her, it wouldn't have happened. And now that she was here, she wasn't quite sure what she wanted to say.

"Did you happen to notice the redhaired kid in the Bible group?" Andrew asked.

"No, why?"

"He's Randy Mitchelson's kid. Remember him?"

"The funniest guy in our class? Sure."

"He married Melanie Robinson right after high school. They divorced last year, and Billy is having a tough time."

"I'm sorry they didn't make it." She rested her arms on the table. "You must hear a lot of people's secrets."

"A fair amount. You, too, right?"

"Yes, and some I'd rather not know, but it's the job."

He nodded. "I know exactly what you mean. Other people's secrets can weigh you down if you let them."

Something in his words gave her pause. "Is something weighing you down, Andrew?"

"Not anything I can talk about," he said slowly. "There's a fine line between keeping a confidence and saving someone from trouble. And I don't always know when it's appropriate to cross the line."

"I think if anyone is in danger, then you have to cross the line. If not, you have to stay silent." The waitress set their pizza down in front of them. "This looks good." Charlotte grabbed a piece and picked off some of the black olives, catching Andrew's smile. "What?"

"We didn't have to order olives. I forgot you didn't like them."

"And I remembered how much you do."

"So you haven't forgotten everything?"

"Just eat," she ordered.

They avoided personal subjects, talking about the church fund-raiser, the new Thai restaurant in town, the condos being constructed on the northernmost beach. Being with Andrew was easy and comfortable.

"I'm stuffed," Andrew finally said, sitting back in the booth. "I shouldn't have had that last piece."

"Better you than me." She wiped her hands and mouth on a napkin.

"I'll have to join you on one of your runs."

"You hate to jog. If there's not a ball to chase, you're not interested, remember?"

He grinned. "Good point. Maybe I'll find a pickup basketball game at the gym tomorrow. Then I can run *and* score points."

Charlotte shook her head. "What is it with men and always needing to keep score? Some things you just do for the pleasure of doing them—like running."

"I can think of other things I'd rather do for pleasure." He leaned across the table and stole a quick kiss. "Like that."

She felt surprised and a little guilty. She didn't want to make more of it than it was, but inside she was reeling.

What was she doing? She couldn't juggle two

men. It wasn't in her. She'd been foolish to think she could.

"Charlotte, you okay?" Andrew asked, concern in his eyes.

"I'm fine." She glanced down at her watch. "I should go. I have to get to work early tomorrow."

"I blew it."

"You didn't blow it. I just realized what time it was." She grabbed her bag and slid out of the booth while Andrew tossed the tip onto the table.

As they walked out of the restaurant and down the street, the silence between them was no longer comfortable. Andrew pressed the button for the light, then said abruptly. "You didn't like me kissing you. Eveything was fine until then. But I don't get it. We were always good at kissing."

"The kiss was good. I didn't mind."

He dug his hands into his pockets as he gazed at her. "Didn't mind—wow, that's quite a declaration. Tell me the truth, Charlotte. You're not taking me back, are you?"

She drew in a deep breath. "I care for you, Andrew. But I'm interested in someone else."

His jaw tightened. "Do you really want to be with someone who's just getting out of a long relationship? Who failed at his first marriage? Don't you want to be special?"

His words hurt because they mirrored her own doubts. "Joe is a good man," she protested.

"He's cocky and controlling and moody."

"He's not a big fan of yours, either," she returned.

Andrew's gaze turned flinty. "I could make you happy, Charlotte. And unlike Silveira, you're the first and only girl I've ever loved."

"Is that really true?"

"Do you think I would lie to you?" he asked in amazement.

"A lot of years have passed. I'm sure there were other women in your life."

"And other men in yours. I understand that. But I knew what I lost with you, the second I lost it. And I've wanted to get it back ever since."

"You didn't try to get it back. You went to college, and I never heard from you."

"I didn't think you wanted to hear from me. And those were bad years for me—I barely remember some of them. But this isn't about the past; it's about now. We get along. We're good together."

"As friends, yes. I've been trying to think of our relationship as more, but I can't, Andrew. I'm sorry. I wasn't trying deliberately to string you along. I wanted to take my time and see what happened." She started to cross the street, but he caught her by the arm.

"Then keep taking your time, Charlotte. You don't have to decide this now."

"I can't pretend that I'm not attracted to Joe."

"That's not a crime. Have you slept with him?"

"That's not your business." She slipped out of his grip. "Andrew, part of me will always love you. But to be honest, I think I mostly miss the girl I was with you. The one who hadn't been hurt, who wasn't scared of being in love, the one who thought dreams could really come true. I thought if I got you back, maybe I'd feel that way again."

"But I'm the one who took away your dreams," he said heavily.

"I know why you cheated. I told you I loved you, and you didn't feel the same."

"I was afraid you'd want more than I could give. I was a coward."

"And I became one after that. I've never told another man I loved him. I've never let anyone get close enough."

"Because you thought they would run, like I did? I had no idea I messed you up like that."

"It wasn't all you. It was also losing the baby. It was my mother's betrayal, the secret she made me carry. It was the other guy I was with, the fact that I'd used sex as revenge and maybe made a baby out of it. I screwed up, and I've spent a lot of years with regrets. But no more. Our past is a piece of who we are, but it's not the whole story. We had our time, Andrew. It's over."

"There's always a second chance."

"Not always," she said with a definitive shake of her head. "Sometimes you don't get a do-over. You just have to live with it."

As the light turned green, she started across the street, her vision blurred by tears. She felt ruthless and a little cruel but also free for the first time in a very long time.

Caught up in thought, she didn't see the car

speeding around the corner until the headlights blinded her. She froze, not sure which way to go. Then someone grabbed her and shoved her across the street. She landed on her knees, the weight of a male body pressing her into the ground.

For several seconds, she didn't move, her heart pounding, her breath coming hard and fast. In the distance, she heard people talking; someone was calling 911.

"Are you all right?" Andrew asked.

She stared at him in a daze, seeing blood on his forehead. "You're bleeding."

He put a hand to his head. "Just a scratch."

He got to his feet and extended a hand. She stood up, her legs shaky, as adrenaline raced through her body, making her feel light-headed and sweaty. She clung to his hand for a moment to get her balance. She heard people asking if they were all right and Andrew replying that everything was fine.

There was chatter about the car that had run the light. No one knew what color it was, just that it was dark. All she could think about was how close she'd come to being run over.

"Charlotte?" Andrew squeezed her hand, drawing her attention to his worried face. "Are you sure you're not hurt? You're not talking, and that's not like you."

"I just can't believe what almost happened. No one drives that fast around here."

"Maybe they were drunk."

A moment later, a police car pulled up next to

them, and Charlotte was surprised to see Colin and
Joe get out of the car. Joe didn't answer routine traf-
fic calls.

"What's going on?" Joe's gaze zoomed in on their
joined hands.

She would have pulled away from Andrew, but
he was holding on tight.

"A car ran the light and almost hit Charlotte,"
Andrew said shortly.

"Andrew pushed me out of the way. He saved my
life, and he's the one who's bleeding. I'm fine."

"Do you need to go to the hospital?" Colin asked
Andrew.

"No, it's nothing," Andrew said.

"You might want to get checked out," Colin said.
"Head injuries can be tricky."

"It's just a scratch. I'm fine."

"If you're sure. I'll see what information our witnesses have." Colin moved toward the group gathered behind them.

"Did either of you notice any details about the
car or the driver?" Joe asked.

"All I saw was headlights," Charlotte answered,
pulling her hand out of Andrew's grip. Both men
seemed very aware of her action, and the tension between them was palpable. "Andrew was behind me.
Maybe he got a better look."

"It looked like a compact car, dark green maybe,"
Andrew said. "It came around the corner really fast.
Charlotte was ahead of me. I shoved her out of the
way, and the next thing I knew, my head was hitting

the pavement. I didn't see where the car went after that. I hope someone else did."

"Where were you coming from?"

"We just finished dinner at Rusty's," Andrew replied.

Charlotte shivered, chilled by the cool night and the near miss.

"You're cold. Why don't you get into my car?" Andrew suggested.

"You don't have your car, Charlotte?" Joe asked.

Every question seemed to carry a silent accusation, as if she'd been caught cheating on him. But he'd called off their plans. She had every right to go out to dinner with whomever she chose. If he was angry about it, that was his problem.

"It's at Andrew's house," she said. "He drove us here."

He nodded, his lips drawing into a tight, hard line. "Then by all means, get into his car."

"Why are you here, Joe?" she couldn't help asking. "You don't usually go out on these calls."

"The woman who called dispatch said it was you and the reverend. I wanted to make sure you were all right. Colin was on his way out, so I jumped in the car."

"Can we go?" Andrew asked.

"Yeah, sure. We'll let you know if we come up with anything."

"Great," Charlotte said, glad to get away. Turning on her heel, she walked down the street, Andrew following close behind.

He opened the car door for her and then slid behind the wheel. "He's pissed that you were with me."

"He doesn't have any right to be," she snapped.

They drove in silence. When they arrived at Andrew's house, he asked if she wanted to come in.

"No, I'm going home," she said, getting out of the car. "Thank you for saving my life."

He followed her to her car. "Charlotte, wait."

She sighed. "What, Andrew?"

"If you change your mind about Silveira, you know where to find me."

"And if I don't?"

"You still know where to find me," he said. "Friends forever, Charlie. I'd like a lot more, but I won't give that up."

FIFTEEN

Joe couldn't believe that Charlotte had gone out to dinner with Andrew. And she'd driven to his house, which implied that she'd initiated the night out. Had she gone after Andrew the second he'd called off their plans? *Shit!*

He had no right to be angry; he was the one who'd bailed on her. But dammit, did she have to run straight into the arms of her old boyfriend?

Now Andrew had quite literally saved her life. He hadn't missed the way she'd clung to Andrew's hand. It had taken her a long time to let go.

And what were they doing now? He envisioned them together in Charlotte's old house, reliving the past, maybe deciding to start things up again—if they weren't already started. He'd been feeling confident that Charlotte was over Andrew, but he wasn't so sure now.

"I've got nothing," Colin told him, returning to

his side. "No one got the license plate. Although Mrs. Kierney thinks it started with a J."

"That's not enough. Are we living in a town where everyone commits the perfect crime?" Joe fumed. "Someone saw something. Canvass the businesses on this block and around the corner."

Colin gave him a speculative gaze. "Because Charlotte almost got hurt or because you're concerned that this was more than just a red-light runner?"

He didn't want to believe that someone had gone after Charlotte on purpose, but he couldn't discount it. "That's what we need to find out. I'll take this side of the street, you take the other. I want to see who else was in Rusty's while they were there."

"No problem." Colin added, "She's all right, Chief."

"I know. The good reverend saved her life. How do you think she's going to thank him?"

"So it's like that," Colin said.

He sighed, realizing that he was giving too much away. "It's tough to compete with first love."

"Charlotte may feel the same," Colin said pointedly. He paused. "Kara tells me I'm very bad at advice, so take this for what it's worth—but if Charlotte wanted Andrew, she'd already be with him."

Joe thought about that as Colin walked away. The only problem was that Charlotte *had* been with Andrew tonight. Now he had to figure out what to do about it.

* * *

After Charlotte arrived home, she talked to Annie for a while, played with the baby while Annie went to make his bottle, checked her e-mail, and flipped through the television channels, but nothing held her attention. She felt restless. Partly from the close call but also because of Joe. He'd looked at her as if she'd betrayed him, and she'd felt a little as if she had—which was ridiculous. They weren't a couple. They weren't together.

She paced around the living room, a reckless idea taking hold in her head. Finally, she gave into it. Telling Annie that she was going out for a while, she grabbed her car keys and headed out the door.

Joe probably wasn't at home; he'd obviously been working when the 911 call had come in. But that was two hours ago.

When she pulled up in front of his house, his truck was in the driveway, and the lights were on. Drawing a deep breath, she walked up to the front door and gave a firm knock.

He answered a moment later. He'd changed out of his suit into worn jeans and a T-shirt, and the fact that he looked even sexier now just made her more annoyed with him. She brushed past him. "Is Isabella here?"

"She's at Nick's. What do you want?" His voice was no more welcoming than the cold, flinty look in his dark eyes.

"First of all, you have no right to be angry at me. You broke our date, not me."

"Well, you obviously found a substitute. What were you doing with him?"

"Eating pizza."

"Are you two together now?"

"Andrew isn't here, is he?"

Joe's eyes glittered with a mix of emotions she couldn't begin to interpret. She was having trouble just thinking, with her heart pounding and her palms sweating and her fingers itching to run along the hard, flat planes of his chest. Fortunately, she was distracted by Rufus, who awoke from a nap to greet her with happy kisses.

"That's enough," Joe scolded the dog.

Rufus whimpered.

"You don't have to yell at the dog."

"Do you want me to yell at you?"

"Maybe you should," she said, folding her arms across her chest. "You're obviously itching for a fight."

Rufus slunk away as Joe moved closer to her.

"What do you want, Charlotte?" he repeated.

"Why did you cancel our date?" she countered. "One minute you're planning to make dinner for me, and then it's over. What happened?"

After a momentary hesitation, he said, "The mayor thought I was crossing a line with you. He was worried that our relationship might influence the investigation."

"So you were concerned about your job?" she asked, disappointed in his answer.

"I was worried about your reputation, Charlotte. He accused you of playing me. And he threatened to bring in someone from outside the department if he didn't feel we could be objective. I don't want that to happen—not because I'm afraid I'll lose my job but because I don't want someone going after you at his order."

It made sense, but she didn't completely buy it. "Are you sure you didn't use what the mayor said as an excuse? Maybe you had second thoughts about us having dinner together."

"Maybe I *should* have had second thoughts, considering you went running to Andrew two seconds after I canceled our date," he retorted.

"I owed him a phone call."

"And that turned into dinner together?"

"Yes, and I didn't do anything wrong. I have nothing to feel guilty about."

"So why do you feel guilty?"

"Because you're making me feel that way!" she shouted in frustration.

"I haven't said anything."

"Exactly. But the way you looked at me tonight—"

"Andrew was holding your hand," he bit out.

"I was almost *killed*. I was shaky, and Andrew saved my life."

"I know. And I should be damn glad he was there. But seeing you two together . . . I didn't like it."

His possessive tone should have made her angrier. Instead, it was making her hot.

They stared at each other for a long, tense moment. She'd said what she'd come to say. She should go. But her feet wouldn't move.

"Why did you come here, Charlotte?" Joe asked again.

She gazed into his dark eyes and gave in to the recklessness that had driven her across town. "I want you, Joe."

He sucked in a sharp breath.

"I don't want to wait. I don't want to think logically or act reasonably or worry about what's going to happen tomorrow." She closed the distance between them, putting her hands on his face, her thumbs tracing over the dark stubble on his cheeks. She looked into his eyes. "I want to jump."

His hands slipped around her waist, and he pulled her against him with rough impatience. "Then jump."

She put her arms around his neck and pressed her mouth to his, giving in to the need that had been building inside her for weeks. Relief, exhilaration, anticipation took her from one kiss to the next.

Joe slid his tongue into her mouth, taking over with a cocky possessiveness that made her shiver. He would have her tonight, and she would have him. The thought sent another wave of desire to every nerve ending in her body. Her senses were filled with Joe, his taste, his scent, the strength of his hands, the power of his kiss, the hardness of his body against hers.

She slipped her hands under his shirt, delighting

in the warm, hard planes of his abs and chest. A moment later, she was helping him pull the shirt over his head. He tossed it onto the ground and groaned as she ran her fingers through the dark hair on his chest. And then his hands were stripping off her coat, her sweater, her camisole, his fingers finally finding the front clasp of her bra.

She was awash with sensation, his mouth on hers, his fingers sliding along the edges of her bra in a teasing way that tightened her nipples and sent a shock wave of heat down her body. Finally, he opened the clasp, his palm cupping her breast. And then, his mouth was sliding down the curve of her neck, leaving a trail of heat.

"So beautiful," he whispered as his mouth took her breast.

She ran her fingers through his hair, drawing in a deep breath as he ran his tongue around her nipple. Her legs felt weak. "God, Joe," she murmured.

He lifted his head and smiled. "Let's take this into the bedroom."

He led her down the dark hallway into his room, kicking the door shut behind him. Moonlight streamed through the parted curtains, illuminating the king-size bed. Then Joe was kissing her again, his fingers pulling at the zipper on her jeans.

His hand slipped inside her panties, making her even hotter. She kicked off her jeans, impatient to be rid of her clothes and his. She pushed his jeans down over his hips and caught her breath at the sight of his beautifully rugged body. Then she was falling backward onto the bed, onto a soft, pillowy comforter that contrasted with the hard male body that came down over her.

Joe kissed her again, his hands roaming over her naked curves with impatience. "God, Charlotte, I want to go slow, but . . ."

"Next time," she said, needing him now.

He grabbed a condom out of the drawer in the bedside table and quickly rolled it on. Then they reached for each other again, mouth to mouth, hip to hip, toe to toe. They moved in perfect unison, as if their bodies had been made for each other, as if they'd been waiting a lifetime for this moment, this intense, incredible connection. She loved his weight on top of her, the hairs of his chest rubbing against her breasts, his mouth seeking hers over and over again as he filled her body and her heart. She ran her hands down his back, his buttocks, her nails digging into his skin as the tension built between them. Her world was him. There was nothing else, no one else. A flash of fear that she was giving away too much was chased away by the way he said her name—with tenderness and with need and finally with fulfillment.

Loving his weight on her, she tightened her arms around him, her eyes closed as she just breathed in and out.

When he finally rolled over onto his back, he pulled her next to him. She rested her cheek on his chest, hearing the rapid beat of his heart. He stroked her back with a tenderness that made her feel cherished and protected. It felt so good—maybe too good. Nothing this amazing had ever lasted for her.

"You're tensing up on me, Charlotte."

He was right. She was letting her thoughts get too far ahead of the moment. She lifted her head, meeting his gaze. She wanted to say something light, like what she usually said after sex, but this didn't feel like sex. It felt like more.

Joe played with her hair. "So silky," he murmured. "Like sunlight. That's the way I think of you."

Her eyes grew moist. "Joe—"

"Shh," he said, putting a finger to her lips as he gazed into her eyes. "It's okay. It doesn't have to mean any more than you want it to."

What if I want it to mean everything?

She drew in a deep breath and put her head back down on his chest. Closing her eyes, she told herself to enjoy being close to him and worry about meanings tomorrow.

Joe woke up naked and alone in the early dawn. It was six-thirty, and Charlotte was gone. Rolling over, he pulled her pillow close. It smelled like her—like warm, flowering sunlight. His body tightened as memories of their night together flashed through his head.

His only regret was that he'd fallen asleep. He'd wanted to make love to her again, to take his time, to taste her, tease her, torment her. But that would have to wait for another time.

And there *would* be another time. He shoved away a niggling doubt. What they had together was fantastic, and Charlotte had been right there with him. God, he loved seeing her so passionate, so caught up in the moment, caught up in him. She hadn't held back, and neither had he.

Rufus meandered into the room and nuzzled his hand. "You could have barked when she left," he said.

Rufus woofed in response.

"A little late. Some watchdog you are."

Rufus hung his head, and Joe scratched him behind the ears. "It's okay, buddy. We'll get her back."

He just had to get to her before she had too much time to think. He threw on running clothes and shoes, grabbed his keys, and headed out the door.

At Charlotte's house, her car was there, but all was quiet. She could be inside . . . in which case, he was about to get a lot of exercise for nothing. But he had to take the chance, so he headed down the same route they'd run the day before.

Charlotte's legs were aching by the time she hit the bluff. She'd pushed the last mile as hard as she could, needing to burn off the worry that had hit as soon as she'd woken up in Joe's bed. She'd wanted to stay curled up next to his warm body, his arm around her shoulders, but she wasn't ready for a morning-after conversation. So she'd run—literally.

Slowing down, she walked the last few yards to the beautiful wild garden by the sea. Looking at the colorful flowers sparkling in the dawn light, she felt the same peace that the garden always brought her. She sank onto the ground and stretched out her legs, gazing at the sea. The nearby cliffs were steep and rocky, jutting in and out along the coastline. Fifty yards below, the ocean surged against large boulders, only a narrow strip of beach visible a few hours of the day.

About half a mile down the coast was a much wider beach, with gentler waves. Her generation had called it Bonfire Beach because they went there in the spring and summer to build bonfires and drink and swim. It was far enough out of town and a little hard to reach by foot, making it a great place to get into trouble. She wondered if the kids still went there, or if they'd found some other place to call their own.

With a sigh, she stretched forward, touching her toes with her fingers, feeling the stretch in her hamstrings. Her muscles ached, but she felt invigorated, too. Not just from the run but from Joe. Making love to him had changed her in a way she couldn't define, but she felt different—more alive, more in tune with her senses.

But she wasn't falling in love, she told herself firmly. Sex was about lust, not love. They were two separate things and she had to keep them apart.

As she looked at the garden again, a flash of white caught her gaze. "Mary Katherine," she breathed.

The figure seemed to take a more solid shape the longer she looked at her. Mary Katherine was blond, with freckles and wide-set brown eyes. Her dress was old-fashioned and rather dirty, especially where it touched the ground.

"I hoped you'd come back here."

"You're not real," Charlotte said, still trying to convince herself.

"And you're not a kid like me anymore. But you still remember me, don't you?"

"I made you up. You were my imaginary friend."

"I was sad the day you came here and cried about your baby."

"How do you know about that?"

"Because I was here. Only you couldn't see me anymore, because you stopped believing in love."

"Are you really an angel?" She couldn't believe she was asking the question.

Mary Katherine nodded. *"My mom and I died when our ship got caught in a horrible storm. It was so frightening. The waves were like huge monsters."*

"Your father and brother didn't die. Why did you? The women and children were supposed to go first."

"I didn't want to leave without my dad, so I ran to find him. My mother came after me. She should have gotten on the boat, but she loved me too much to leave without me." A shadow crossed her eyes. *"I couldn't find my father or my brother. My mother grabbed my hand when the ship broke apart. The water was so cold."* She shivered with the memory. *"And then there was*

nothing. My father found my mother's body on the beach right there," she said, pointing below. *"He carried her up here and laid her down, and he cried over her body, saying he was so sorry. Later he buried her in the cemetery with the others. But he came back here and planted flowers for her. I make sure they never die."*

"Your mother died here, but what happened to you?"

"They never found my body."

"So are you a ghost or something?"

Mary Katherine smiled. *"I'm not haunting anyone. I help people."*

"How do you do that?"

"If they can believe in me, they can believe in magic, and magic is love. Do you love him, the man you were with yesterday?"

"I'm afraid to," she admitted.

"So you still need me," Mary Katherine said.

"I guess I do."

"Some things you have to do yourself, Charlie. He's coming now. Don't run away from him."

"Charlotte!" Joe's voice drew her head around, he was running toward her.

Glancing back at Mary Katherine, she saw that her angelic friend was gone . . . if she'd been there at all.

She got to her feet as Joe drew closer.

"I had a feeling you'd be out here," he said.

"You seem to know me pretty well." Her heart took a tumble as she gazed into his eyes and remembered everything they'd done together.

"I wish you'd woken me up before you left."

"You were sleeping so peacefully. I didn't want to disturb you."

"I would have made you breakfast." He paused, searching her face. "Regrets, Charlotte?"

She shook her head. "No. I'm just not very good at the morning-after stuff, so I try to avoid it. No one quite knows what to say or do. Kind of like now."

"I know what to do." He took her hands and pulled her close to him. He gave her plenty of time to move away, but she stayed and watched the slow descent of his mouth with complete and utter delight. And when his lips touched hers tenderly, all she wanted to do was kiss him back hard and deep, long and slow. And when they parted, she let out a long sigh.

"You *do* know what to do," she said, tightening her arms around his neck.

He smiled. "That was the easy part."

She nodded. "Words are harder."

"We don't need any words right now." He turned her around to face the sea. "Look at this view. We live in one of the best places on earth. We should appreciate it."

"I do," she said, soaking in the sight. But it wasn't the view that was making her so happy; it was Joe. She stayed in his arms a few minutes more, then finally glanced at her watch. "I hate to say it . . ."

"But you need to get back. So do I, unfortunately." He took a breath. "Charlotte, I want to apologize. I shouldn't have behaved the way I did last night when I saw you and Andrew together. I acted like an ass. It was uncalled for."

She put her hands on his face. "Joe, I came to you last night. Doesn't that tell you anything?"

"I'm afraid to guess."

"I told Andrew that I was interested in you."

Surprise flared in his eyes. "You did?"

"Yes."

He let out a breath. "Okay, then."

"Okay." She dropped her hands and stepped back. "Let's go." She took off at a medium pace, with Joe alongside her. She'd spent most of her life as a solo jogger, but it was nice to have company. They didn't talk, but there was no tension, just a mutual enjoyment of the quiet morning.

When they reached city streets again, she slowed down as a For Sale sign on an old car caught her attention. She crossed the street. "Isn't this a Mustang?" she asked Joe.

"Looks like it's from the seventies."

"It's for sale."

"I can see that."

"Well . . ." she prodded.

"What? You want to buy it?"

"I was thinking *you* should buy it and fix it up, like you used to do with your dad. Maybe you could even invite him up to work on it together."

"I haven't worked on a car in years," he protested.

But she could see the interest growing in his eyes as he walked around the car, checking it out, and she wished she had a pen to write down the telephone number.

"This car would take a lot of work, a lot of time," he said.

"And you don't have time? You don't like work? Why are you hesitating?"

"I let this hobby go. It got in the way of my life."

"Your old life," she said.

He met her gaze. "In my experience, women don't like to come in second to an old car. I saw it with Rachel and with my mother."

"Well, if I was with a guy who wanted to work on a car, maybe I'd work on it with him."

He grinned. "You'd be bored in two minutes."

"Quite possibly, but it might be fun. However, this car is for you—not me. Everyone should have something they like to do besides work. Think about it, Joe. You don't have to answer to anyone but yourself."

"That's a strange thought."

"And while you're thinking about buying this car, you might want to consider looking into some furniture for your house that doesn't look like it belongs to an eighty-year-old man."

"Now you want to redecorate my home?"

"You moved here, but you didn't really move in. A few things in your house are yours, but most of them were your uncle's, right? It's time to make the place your own."

"Look who's talking. You live with your mother." He tilted his head, and his gaze narrowed thoughtfully. "Where's your furniture? You must have had an apartment."

"It's in storage," she said. "And I am not planning to live with my mother for very much longer."

"Where are you going to go?"

"Still to be decided."

"Tomorrow," he said with a laugh. "Your favorite phrase."

Joe gave the car's hood a loving pat as they jogged past it down the street. Charlotte hoped he'd call and find out the price. She had a feeling he needed that car as much as it needed a new owner.

"I assume you parked at my house," she said as they turned the corner.

"I did."

"So much for not adding to the gossip about us."

"Yeah, I should have thought about that," he said with an apologetic look. "Sorry."

"Maybe no one will be up yet."

Her hope went by the wayside as they turned the corner. In fact, there was a small crowd gathered in front of her house—Annie, her mother, and a couple of neighbors.

"What's going on?" she wondered. As she drew closer, the pack of people shifted, revealing two men in uniform, one on crutches. "Oh, my God—it's Jamie! My brother—he's home!" She sprinted the rest of the way. "Jamie!" she called out.

Her brother turned his head and gave her a big grin.

"I can't believe it," she said, coming to a breathless halt in front of him. She wanted to hug him, but he was leaning on his crutches, a cast on one leg, and there were bruises and cuts on his face. "You're hurt."

"It's nothing, Charlie."

He was lying. She could see the pain in his eyes and the weary lines of his face. "It doesn't look like nothing."

"Let's get you into the house, Jamie," her mother said quickly. "Everyone can come by later," she told the neighbors. "He needs to rest."

As the crowd dispersed, Charlotte's gaze moved to the man standing next to her brother. He was well over six feet tall, with a strong, powerful build and light brown hair that was longer than the usual military cut. He was older than Jamie, maybe early thirties, with green eyes that looked as weary as her brother's.

"Lieutenant Gabe Ryder," her brother said, catching her curious look. "My sister Charlotte."

"Nice to meet you," Gabe said.

"You, too."

"The lieutenant saved my life," Jamie added.

Gabe shrugged. "You're delirious, Adams. Must be the painkillers."

"And you hate to be the hero," Jamie said.

"I'll feel more like a hero if you let me help you into the house," Gabe said.

Jamie nodded, his lips drawing tight as he

handed one crutch to Charlotte, then put his arm around Gabe's shoulders. Gabe took the brunt of his weight as they made their way to the house, Annie and her mother following close behind.

"So that's your brother," Joe said.

Startled, she'd forgotten he was there. "Yes. I'm sorry, I should have introduced you."

"I'll meet him later."

"I didn't know he was hurt. Or that he was coming home. We haven't heard from him in more than a week; I guess this is why. He looks so much older. He was nineteen when I saw him last, and that was four years ago, right before he shipped out."

"Call me later." Joe gave her a quick kiss. "I'm glad he's home."

"Me, too. This is turning out to be a great day."

Sixteen

Jamie was sitting on the living-room couch, his leg propped up on an ottoman, when Charlotte entered the house. His friend Gabe was in the armchair, and she could hear her mother and Annie in the kitchen.

"Mom's making breakfast," Jamie said with the crookedly endearing smile that usually got him whatever he wanted.

"I hope you're hungry, because I'm sure it's going to be extra special."

"I could eat."

She sat down on the couch next to him. "We were getting worried because we hadn't heard from you in a few days."

"I couldn't get to a computer for a while, and then I figured I'd be coming home."

"For good?" she asked hopefully.

He shook his head. "Just until I'm well enough to go back."

She hated his response. "Haven't you done your duty? You're hurt."

"I'll get better. But let's not talk about that. What about you? What's going on? Who was that dude you were with?"

"Joe Silveira. He's the chief of police," she said.

"Something going on with you two? I thought Mom said you were hooking up with Andrew again."

"She's caught up in the dream of me following in her footsteps, but I'm not going to be with Andrew."

Jaimie nodded. "He was never good enough for you."

She smiled. "Can I get you anything? What about you, Lieutenant?"

"It's Gabe," he said. "And I'm good, thanks."

"Me, too," Jamie added.

"So you're the sister who was always getting into trouble and taking the heat off Adams here," Gabe drawled.

She shot her brother a dark look. "Thanks for sharing."

Jamie gave a weary laugh. "I wasn't lying."

"Yes, that's me," she told Gabe. "And my little brother was the spoiled brat of the family."

"She adored me," Jamie interjected.

"Mother adored you," she countered. "I kept you humble."

"Yeah, you did," Jamie said, his eyelids fluttering, then finally closing.

"He's had a rough couple of days," Gabe told her.

She moved to the chair next to his. "Can you tell me what happened?"

He met her gaze. "I could, but it's his story to tell. I just wanted to make sure he got home. I promised him I'd do that."

She respected his loyalty. "What happens to you now? Do you go back?"

"No, I'm done."

"Then you'll stay here for a while?"

He shook his head. "I'll leave tomorrow. I have another promise I need to keep." His voice drifted away, as he stared at her brother. "He's a good kid," he added a moment later. "He taught me a few things."

"Really?" She was surprised that her kid brother could have taught this world-weary warrior anything. "What did he teach you?"

Gabe didn't say anything for a long moment, then he slowly smiled. "How to believe in the impossible."

"He got that from our father."

"Jamie said your father was a hard man to live up to."

His words took her by surprise. "I didn't realize he felt that way. He's quite a bit younger than me, so he did a lot of his growing up while I was away at school."

"I understand you're a doctor."

"Ob/gyn," she said. "It's one of the happier parts of medicine."

"I'll bet. Can you tell me where the restroom is?"

"It's down the hall, first door on your left."

"Thanks."

As Gabe left, she got up and headed into the kitchen. Her mother looked happier than she'd been in a long time. Her skin was glowing, her eyes sparkling, as she scrambled eggs, made toast, and flipped pancakes.

As she passed by with a pitcher of orange juice, Annie gave Charlotte a smile. "Can you believe he's home?"

"No, I can't," she replied. "Now, what can I do to help?"

"Maybe you could shower," her mother said. "You smell a little ripe."

"Good idea." As she passed by her mother, she gave her a hug, ignoring her mother's squeal of displeasure. "Jamie's home," she said, meeting her mom's eyes. "Everything is right with the world."

Her mother's eyes glistened with tears. "Yes, it is." She snapped her kitchen towel at Charlotte. "Go change. We're going to have a big family breakfast."

Over breakfast, Charlotte learned a little more about the firefight that had injured her brother and killed one of his friends. Jamie told them again that the lieutenant had saved his life, which made Gabe more uncomfortable. It was clear that the two men had become close and that Gabe was somewhat of

a big-brother figure. Charlotte was glad Jamie had
had someone he could trust to watch his back and to
bring him home.

Neither man was inclined to talk about what had
happened in any detail. Jamie was more interested in
what was happening at home, and soon her mother
was regaling him with stories, including details of
the New Year's Eve robbery.

"Figures you'd wind up in the middle of it, Charlie," Jamie said.

"I just was in the wrong place at the wrong time,"
she said with a shrug.

He smiled. "That doesn't sound like you."

"Ha-ha."

"I can't believe you're still here. I didn't think
you'd ever make a permanent home in Angel's Bay."

"Well, I haven't said it's permanent," she hedged,
avoiding her mother's suddenly questioning gaze.

"This house is nice," Jamie said. "I kind of miss
the old one, though. I heard that your old boyfriend
got our house. Weird."

"He wants to be her current boyfriend," her
mother put in.

"She can do better than him."

"He's a minister now," her mother said sharply.
"He's grown up, changed. Andrew is a very eligible
man. If Charlotte knew what was good for her, she'd
accept his invitations and stop flirting with the chief
of police."

Charlotte cleared her throat. "Let's talk about
something else."

"Everyone in town is talking about you, Charlotte," her mother said. "What were you doing together this morning?"

"We went running," she said shortly. "Who needs more pancakes?"

"I do," Jamie said, even though his plate was still half-full.

"Great." She took his plate to the kitchen and piled on another stack.

"So I guess I have a little sister now," Jamie added, looking at Annie. "And an honorary nephew."

"I'd be honored if you'd consider us that way," Annie said a bit shyly.

"You're even prettier than I thought. The videos didn't do you justice."

Annie flushed a little at his compliment. "You're so nice. No wonder your mother loves you so much."

"He's not *that* nice," Charlotte teased as she set his plate down. "He used to dress my Barbies in his GI Joe combat fatigues and send them to war."

"Hey, you should be happy I included the girls in the war games," he protested.

"I was, until you put black-out under their eyes and gave them military haircuts."

He laughed. "I forgot about that."

Charlotte sat back in her chair, listening as Jamie and her mother told more stories. "Oh, my God," she said suddenly. "We need to call Doreen."

"I already did," her mother said. "She's going to come down on Sunday with the kids. We'll have the whole family back together." She drew in a deep breath. "Well, almost the whole family. I wish your father could be here." She blinked quickly and then set down her napkin. "I'll get us all some more coffee."

Charlotte turned to Gabe. "Where are you headed after you leave here?"

"A town called River Rock. It's up north of San Francisco about an hour."

"Is that where you're from?"

"It's where I'm going," he said.

"You should call first," Jamie interjected, the men exchanging a look.

"I'll call when I get there," Gabe replied. "That will be soon enough."

"Well, tonight you'll stay here," her mother said, refilling coffee cups.

"I don't want to put you out," Gabe said.

"You won't be. You can have Charlotte's room. She can stay with one of her friends."

"Yes, I can," she said quickly, seeing the hesitation on Gabe's face. "We would love to have you stay here."

"Do I have a room in this place?" Jamie asked.

"Of course you do," Monica said sharply.

"Do you really think Mom would buy a house without a room for you? It has all your old things in it," Charlotte added.

"Maybe one of you could show me. I'm kind of tired."

"Of course," Charlotte said. Gabe helped her get Jamie into his bedroom. Her brother collapsed onto the bed with a groan. She helped him off with his shoes, and by the time she was done, he was asleep again.

Gabe looked beat, too. She wondered again what the men had been through, but it was clear she wasn't getting any answers anytime soon.

"My room is up the stairs," she told him. "I'm going to work, so it's all yours."

"I don't want to put you out, Charlotte. I can take the couch."

"You're not putting me out. I'll be gone all day, and I have lots of friends in town I can stay with tonight. You've done a lot for my brother. Please take me up on the offer; it's the least I can do."

"I would appreciate a bed. I haven't had much sleep the last few days."

"Then let me show you to your room." She led him down the hall and up the stairs. Grabbing some of her clothes off the bed, she tossed them into the hamper in the closet. "I'll change the sheets for you."

"Don't bother. It's fine."

"Is there anything else you need?"

"I'm good."

"Okay." She drew in a deep breath. "Thanks for seeing Jamie home."

"Your brother is a brave man," Gabe said. "It was my honor."

"I can't understand why he would want to go back."

Gabe gave her a small smile. "No, you can't. Not if you haven't walked in his shoes."

"So what will you do next?"

"It depends on what I find when I get to River Rock."

"You're looking for someone?" she asked, remembering her brother's words.

"Yeah—someone," he said cryptically.

When he didn't explain, she said, "I'll see you later, then."

She walked into the hall, turned to shut the door, and saw Gabe take a photo out of his wallet. He gave it a long stare and then put it back. Then he tossed his wallet onto the table and dropped onto the bed.

She quietly closed the door and went downstairs, telling herself it was none of her business who he was looking for. He'd be gone in the morning.

Smiling, she headed off to work. And at the thought of spending the night with Joe, she smiled even wider.

Joe took the chair by Jason's desk late Friday morning. "Give me some good news."

Jason sat back in his chair and ran a hand through his hair. "I might actually be able to do that. We've cleared the trainer and his girlfriend. Both have alibis for New Year's Eve."

"What else?"

"Got some information on Michaela Gomez, the woman Charlotte saw on the stairs. She was born at the hospital in Montgomery and given up for private adoption at birth. She was raised by a family in San Diego. Those parents were killed in a car crash last year. She worked at a restaurant until a month ago, when she quit. Her manager said she told him she had some family issues to address."

"Where are you going with this?" Joe asked, seeing the gleam in Jason's eyes.

"You'll see."

"Get there faster," he said impatiently.

"Constance Garcia gave birth to a child in Montgomery on the same day that Michaela was born, and she gave her baby up for adoption."

"Now you have my attention."

"Put the two together. Constance is Michaela's mother. I suspect Michaela came here looking for her biological parents after her adoptive parents were killed. She took a job with the catering company a couple of days after she arrived in town. The caterer thought she was staying at the Windmill Motel. I checked the motel, and she spent five days there and left. No one seems to know where she went after that."

"I wonder if Constance and Michaela connected with each other or if Michaela was just checking out her mother before announcing who she was."

"Well, Constance certainly never told us she had a daughter working the party." Jason paused. "In looking into Constance's background, I learned that she was working at the manor during her pregnancy. And I have to wonder if the biological father was also there—either as another employee or as the owner."

"That's a big leap to make."

"Agreed. But think about it, Chief. Constance has a relationship with her boss, gets pregnant. He doesn't want the baby. She gives it up and continues to live with him for the next twenty-something years. He dies, and what does he do? He leaves all his money to charity, not one penny to his trusted and loyal housekeeper. Now the daughter shows up, looking for her mother. The two of them think, why shouldn't they take something for themselves? Something they're both owed." Jason looked extremely proud of his theory.

"Not bad," Joe said. "Now comes the part where you find some proof. Get Constance down here. She was extremely nervous when I talked to her yesterday, especially when Michaela's name came up. I want her questioned on our turf."

"Will do."

Joe returned to his office just in time to pick up a call from Charlotte.

"How's your brother?" he asked.

"He's okay. Exhausted and obviously in pain, but he's home for a while, and that's really all that matters. As you can imagine, my mother is over the moon. Annie is thrilled, too. I thought she might be nervous, since her father was mentally disabled by his military experiences, but she seems to be okay around my brother. Anyway, I know you're busy, but

Jamie's friend Gabe needs a place to stay tonight, and my mother offered him my room. She was sure I could find a bed somewhere."

He smiled. "I'm more than happy to share mine. Is that what your mother had in mind?"

"I doubt it, but it's what I had in mind. What about Isabella?"

"She comes and goes. I have no idea what she's doing, but it's not a problem. She's had Nick here many times."

"Okay. Well, I want to have dinner at home with Jamie, so I'm not sure what time I'll be there."

"Come anytime you want. Just save some room for dessert."

"I can always eat dessert. Before I go, Joe, I drove by that old car and got the owner's phone number. Is it too pushy to give it to you?"

He smiled to himself. "If I said yes, would that stop you?"

"No, because I really think you should look at that car."

Laughing, he said, "Give it to me."

After he hung up, he stared at the number. It wouldn't hurt to find out how much they were asking. The idea of restoring a car was appealing. Charlotte was right: he had moved to Angel's Bay, but he hadn't moved all the way in, and he wanted to. He wanted to stop putting things off and start living his life.

Maybe Charlotte would realize that was exactly what she needed to do, too.

* * *

Andrew entered the back of the church around five o'clock, surprised to hear someone singing. Choir practice didn't start until five-thirty. As he moved down the aisle, he was even more surprised to see Tory at the piano, singing one of his favorite hymns with a voice so beautiful and pure it made his breath catch in his chest. But she wasn't in the choir. At least, she hadn't been before now.

As soon as she saw him, she stopped, giving him an embarrassed smile as she got to her feet. "How long have you been standing there?"

"Long enough to know you have an incredible voice. Why haven't I heard it before?"

"It's the acoustics in here. They make me sound better than I am."

"I hope you're joining our choir."

"I'm just subbing in for Joan Schumacher while she has her tonsils removed. I'll step out when she comes back."

"No need to do that. We can always use more singers."

"I'll think about it. It depends on my schedule at the theater." She smiled. "I wanted to find out what happened with Charlotte after she saw us together the other night. Did she take the bait?"

"She was curious, but we went out for pizza last night, and she made it clear that she's interested in Joe Silveira."

"Oh, I'm sorry," she said with sympathy.

He shrugged. "I'm not throwing in the towel yet. I don't think Charlotte should be with someone coming off a long marriage. She should be someone's first love."

Tory flinched a little, and he realized his mistake. "I—uh, that didn't come out the right way."

"Didn't it?" she asked a little sadly. "I can understand where you're coming from. I'm sure I'll have the same problem as Joe when I start thinking about dating again. Who wants to be second?"

He frowned, realizing he'd let his own jealousy hurt someone he was beginning to care about. "No, Tory, don't pay any attention to me. I don't know what I'm talking about."

"You're talking about not wanting Charlotte to be with someone who vowed to be with someone else until death do them part."

"It was more about not wanting Charlotte to be with anyone but me."

"Why do you love her, Andrew?"

He caught his breath at the question. "All the usual reasons. She's beautiful, kind, generous, smart. She's my girl. The first one I fell in love with. I was just too scared to commit to what I felt back then. I didn't treat her well."

"I find that difficult to believe."

"I didn't give much to any relationship I was in. I was a taker. Whatever they were giving, I took, but I didn't give anything in return. I cheated on Charlotte, and as she told me quite bluntly, not everyone gets a second chance."

"Steve wants a second chance, too."

"Well, he doesn't deserve one."

She raised an eyebrow. "Really?"

It wasn't his place to give an opinion, but he couldn't help himself. "He did more than cheat on you. He rejected his own child for months, and even now, all he does is send Annie a monthly check. He doesn't see the kid. He needs to change his life, and until he does, he probably needs to be on his own." He let out a breath. "And that wasn't my professional opinion; it was a personal one. Because I consider you a friend."

She smiled. "I think of you that way, too. So I have to ask a harder question. Do you ever consider the fact that you and Charlotte might not have lasted, even if you hadn't cheated on her? Some relationships just have their moment in time, you know? And that's okay. You love, and you live, and you move on." She tilted her head, giving him a thoughtful look. "When I asked you why you loved her, you didn't tell me one thing that was unique to her."

"So it was a trick question?" he asked.

She shook her head. "When I fell in love with Steve, I loved the way he held me at night, like a teddy bear he couldn't let go of. I loved the way he sang in the shower and the way he cut the crusts off my toast when I was sick. Love is in the details, Andrew. And you don't seem to have any details about Charlotte. Maybe you don't know her as well as you think you do."

"Because she's not letting me back into her life," he said, feeling defensive.

"Have you let Charlotte in?"

"Of course."

"Are you sure?" she persisted.

"Do you think I'm holding back some deep, dark secret?"

She considered that for a moment. "Sometimes when I look at you, I see shadows in your eyes, as if you're somewhere else, someplace that doesn't make you happy. But as soon as you realize I'm looking, you cover up."

Her words were a little more insightful than he liked.

"There are things I haven't told Charlotte— things I'm ashamed of. It's all in the past now, but our relationship has been so tenuous, I haven't wanted to rock the boat. Now I'm a little worried that my secrecy could hurt the one person I'm trying to protect."

"Then you should tell Charlotte."

He nodded. "I know. I'm going to do that."

"Now?" she pressed.

"I doubt she'll answer her phone."

"Well, you can try." She paused as several other members of the choir entered the back of the church. "Looks like it's time for practice."

He was sorry to have their conversation end. Tory challenged him in a way that no one else did. And talking to her helped cut through the confusion in his brain. "What are you doing after this?" he asked.

"Going home, making dinner, and taking a bath."

"Feel like some company?"

"Well, my tub isn't that big."

He grinned. "How about the dinner part?"

"Sure. I feel like some company. How about seven-thirty?"

"It's perfect," he said.

"But Andrew, if you get hold of Charlotte and want to break the date, I totally understand."

He shook his head. "Steve was an ass to cheat on you."

"Yes, he was. I'm amazing," she said lightly.

She was only kidding, but a part of him wanted to convince her she was exactly that.

SEVENTEEN

After work, Charlotte entered the kitchen and found Jamie inhaling a bowl of cereal. He'd changed out of his uniform and was wearing a T-shirt and baggy gray sweats that hid his cast. "I'm glad to see you haven't outgrown your love of Cocoa Puffs," she teased. "Did Mom make a special trip to the market for you?"

He gave her a slightly crooked grin and said, "You bet she did. She got all my favorites."

"Because you're her favorite. She can't wait to spoil you. Not that you don't deserve it." Her smile faded as her gaze drifted to his injured leg.

"Don't think about it, Charlie," he advised. "There's no point."

"I can't stop thinking about it. I want to see your X-rays. I want to talk to your doctor. And I want to take you to one of the orthopedists in town."

"Stop," he said, putting up his hand. "I've had my

fill of doctors. I'm healing. There's nothing else to be done."

"Are you sure?"

"Positive. I don't need you to be a doctor, just a sister."

She sat back in her chair. "I can do that. I talked to Gabe a little earlier. I told him that I couldn't imagine what you'd been through, and he said I was right, I couldn't. He's a very cryptic guy."

"He doesn't have a lot to say, but when he talks, it's usually important. He carried me on his back for six hours, Charlotte, and he promised me he'd get me home." Jamie's mouth tightened. "That's exactly what he did."

"It sounds horrible."

Jamie shrugged, shaking off the emotion he'd just revealed. "There's bad and good in every job."

"Most jobs don't put you in danger of bullets or landmines."

He grinned. "Yeah, most jobs are boring."

She gave a helpless shake of her head. "How can you love what you do?"

"Because I'm proud to serve my country."

"I'm proud of you, too."

He gave her a smile. "How are you and Mom getting along?"

"The usual. She criticizes. I try harder. She criticizes. I don't try at all. She criticizes, and we start all over again."

"Being critical is the way she loves you."

"Well, I'd like her to find a different way."

"Why are you still here if things are that bad?" he asked.

"I brought Annie into the family, so I couldn't leave her with Mom. Although they get along better than Mom and I do."

"Mom likes to be needed, and Annie needs her—you don't. Your independence has always made her feel a little unimportant, so she overcompensates."

"What do you think I should do—move out, break the ties?"

He spooned more cereal into his mouth. "I think your duty is done. You came to Mom in her hour of need; you saved Annie. Now it's your turn. What do *you* want to do?"

"I have a few ideas," she admitted.

"Any of them have to do with the guy you were with yesterday?"

"Some." She took a breath. "I might be falling in love with him, Jamie. But don't tell Mom."

He laughed. "I'm not a snitch anymore."

"I hope not. You used to get me into all kinds of trouble."

"I'm glad you finally found someone."

"It's still early and a little complicated, and I don't know exactly where it's going. He was married, and I've never been good at relationships."

"Don't start thinking of reasons it can't work," he said, shaking his head. "You always do that."

"I do *not* always do that, and how would you know, anyway?"

"Doreen writes to me a lot, and she always tells me about the latest guy you've dumped. It makes for entertaining reading."

"I'm happy to help you pass the time," she said dryly.

"What on earth is going on in here?" her mother interrupted as she entered with bags of groceries in her hands. "I'm about to make you a lovely dinner, and you're eating cereal?" She shot Charlotte a scolding look. "Couldn't you at least make him a sandwich if he was hungry?"

"He was already eating the cereal when I got here," she protested.

"Well, don't eat anything else," Monica said. "I'm making beef stroganoff with a big salad and fresh fruit. I bet you haven't eaten anything fresh in weeks."

"It sounds great, Mom," Jamie replied.

"I just need to make one phone call, and then I'll get it started. Charlotte, if you want to chop some vegetables, that would be lovely. One thing you were always good with was a knife."

Charlotte exchanged a look with her brother as her mother left the room. "At least there's one thing I'm good at."

Jamie lifted the box of Cocoa Puffs to refill his bowl.

"Stop with the cereal. You're going to ruin your appetite, and I'm sure I'll be blamed for it," Charlotte warned.

"Believe me, I'm going to eat every last bite of

Mom's cooking. I used to dream about her beef stroganoff."

"Yet you still want to go back? Can't you get out on a medical disability?"

"I'm going to get better," he said. "As soon as I'm fit, I'll return to my unit. It's what I do, Charlotte. It's who I am."

"Don't you want to get married, have a family?"

"I can do that and still be a Marine."

"Not if you're on the other side of the world."

He grinned. "I'm not as old as you are. I've got plenty of time to find someone."

She crinkled up a napkin and tossed it at him. Then she got to her feet and grabbed a bag of cucumbers to wash and peel.

Joe was heating up a frozen pizza when Isabella walked into the kitchen Friday evening. She gave an appreciative sniff. "Pepperoni and mushrooms?"

"Only big enough for one," he said. "I haven't seen much of you this week. What's been going on?"

"Nick had to go down to Los Angeles, so I'm hanging out with Megan. He'll he back tomorrow. I just came home to grab some clothes." She sniffed again. "Are you wearing cologne?"

"I took a shower."

"And shaved," she said speculatively. "Do you have a date? It can't be dinner, unless that pizza is just an appetizer."

"Charlotte is going to come by later," he admitted.

"I like Charlotte. She's real, down-to-earth, very warm and open. She brings out a different side in you. It's nice." She paused as he pulled the pizza out of the oven. "I guess you didn't invite her for dinner?"

"She's having dinner with her family. Her brother came home this morning."

"The one who's in the Marines?"

"Yes, and he had a cast on his leg. It looked like he'd seen some action, but he survived."

"That's good. Well, I'd better get my things. Megan and I are going to Dina's for dinner."

As Isabella disappeared down the hall, Joe pulled out a plate for his pizza, interrupted by the ring of his cell phone.

"We finally got a break," Jason said with excitement. "As you suggested, I got Mrs. Garcia down to the station. She was extremely nervous, and it didn't take long for her to admit that Michaela is her daughter."

"Nice job."

"Apparently, Michaela tracked her down about a month ago. Mrs. Garcia said it was the first time she'd seen her since she'd given her up for adoption. She told Michaela about the party, and Michaela applied for the catering job so she could earn some money to rent an apartment."

"Where is Michaela now?"

"Mrs. Garcia says she doesn't know. She thinks Michaela got scared after the robbery, because she went upstairs to collect glasses and plates right around the time Mrs. Monroe was attacked. She didn't tell us about Michaela earlier because she wanted to protect her daughter."

"What about the biological father? Is it Worthington?"

"That's when she clammed up. She said she wouldn't say any more without a lawyer."

"Okay, good. We're getting somewhere. Stay on it."

"I will."

As Joe hung up the phone, he felt a wave of relief. Poking holes in Constance's story would be to Charlotte's benefit. They were still a ways off from solving the crime but much closer to getting Charlotte in the clear.

Andrew was finishing up some paperwork when Pamela strolled through the door of his office. He hadn't seen her in two days and had hoped she'd gone home. Apparently not.

"What do you want?" he asked, getting to his feet, because where Pamela was concerned, he always felt he needed an advantage, even if it was only height.

"You're never happy to see me," she said with a pout. "I don't understand why."

"We've said all we had to say."

"That's true." She walked to the front of his desk, a sly gleam in her eyes.

Pamela had always been easy to look at. She had a great body, nice hair, and a way of looking at a man that made him think she'd do anything he wanted.

And most of the time, she did. But now, he couldn't remember why he'd ever wanted her. Because underneath her pretty exterior was a selfish, calculating, ruthless woman who loved to manipulate and destroy people's lives, including her own.

"Like what you see?" she drawled.

"Just thinking about how far we've come."

"I'm glad you're thinking about the past, because you owe me, Andrew. And I'm here to collect. I need help."

Is this about money?

"I could use some cash, but that's not what I meant." Her mouth tightened. "I'm in trouble."

He sat down in his chair, his stomach turning over. "What kind of trouble?"

She hesitated. "What if I said that Mitch was involved in the robbery at my sister's house? What would you do?"

"Go to the police."

"Just like that? He was your friend, too, once."

"A long time ago. I certainly don't feel any need to protect him." He stared back at her. "Mitch couldn't have done it alone. If he got into the house, you helped him. One of you cut the lights. The other one stole the jewelry." As he said the words, he was almost positive he was right. "Did you almost kill your sister?"

Pamela paled. "Do you think I'm that much of a cold-hearted bitch?"

"It could have been an accident. Then maybe you decided you might as well grab her jewelry on your way out." He tilted his head. "Have you been waiting around to see if she remembers?"

"I never said I did any of that."

"But you're hiding something. I knew it from the beginning. I just didn't want to believe it."

"Or maybe you didn't want to get involved because I might tell everyone about your past?"

"I might have hesitated when I shouldn't have," he admitted. "But I won't be blackmailed or held hostage by my past. You should come clean, Pamela. Whatever you're hiding, it's only going to wreck your life."

"My life is already wrecked," she said flatly.

"Not true. You have a lot of years ahead of you. Find a way to make something good out of them. I know where you've been; I was there, too. But I got out. I changed. You can do the same thing."

"You had God on your side."

"So do you."

"He gave up on me a long time ago." She paused. "Is your life now really what you want it to be? Or did you just settle? Because I remember when your dreams were big."

"I didn't settle. I like what I do. I'm happy now; I feel like I'm where I'm supposed to be."

"Like you finally found the right pair of shoes," she said with a sigh.

"Exactly."

"I tried so hard to corrupt you, Andrew, but the good in you came back. You need to be with someone good, don't you?"

"I need to be with the right person."

"Are you avoiding me now because you're afraid you'll want me again, and history will repeat itself?"

"I don't want you, Pamela. I don't think I can be more clear about it." She flinched, but he couldn't take the words back. Pamela only saw what she wanted to see, but he needed her to see the truth. "If you're in trouble, I'll try to help. But I won't break the law for you."

She got up and walked toward the door. "I wonder if one day you'll regret that."

EIGHTEEN

Joe tried to catch up on paperwork while waiting for Charlotte to arrive at his house, but his mind kept wandering. He hadn't felt so distracted by a woman in a very long time. He couldn't get Charlotte out of his mind, couldn't stay away from her. Every time she left, he started thinking about when she'd be back. Maybe it was crazy to move so fast into another intense relationship, but it also seemed crazy to spend any more time apart. Since the first time he'd seen Charlotte, he'd been fighting an attraction to her.

He was relieved when the doorbell rang just before ten. Rufus immediately jumped to his feet and started to bark, and Joe smiled. Old Rufus was falling for Charlotte, too.

"Sorry I'm here so late," she said when he opened the door.

"It's fine." His gaze swept across her pretty face, her sparkling blue eyes, her long golden hair, and his gut clenched in a familiar ache of desire.

She set a small overnight bag on the floor. "Change of clothes," she said. "I hope this is all right."

"Of course. I wanted you to stay last night."

"I know, but now I'm coming with a bag. It feels a little awkward."

"The last thing you need to feel with me is awkward. How about some wine?"

"Sure," she said with a smile.

"I'll meet you in the living room."

He retrieved wine and glasses from the kitchen, then settled in on the couch next to her. Rufus had taken up residence at her feet.

After pouring her a glass, he said, "How's your brother doing?"

"Really well. I'd forgotten how funny he is. And how easily he could wrap my mother around his little finger with his crooked smile and his silly jokes."

"He's a lot younger than you, isn't he?"

"Eight years. I sometimes wondered if he was planned or an accident, but asking my mother about her sex life was *not* something I wanted to do. When he was first born, I followed my mother around, begging her to let me change him, hold him, rock him. Doreen was just the same, so he had three mothers for a while. Of course, then he grew up and became kind of a pest, and by the time I hit my teens, we were leading separate lives. But Jamie was always good about keeping in touch. Better than me, in fact." She sipped her wine.

"How bad is his injury?"

"He doesn't want to say. I'll press him a little harder in a few days. Maybe he'll be more willing to talk then."

"Or not," Joe said. "Sometimes talking about it makes it worse."

She gave him a curious look. "You sound like you have some experience."

"I wasn't in the military, but I've seen some things I wish I hadn't seen. And I certainly didn't want to talk about them."

"You don't think it would have helped to get it out?"

"No, I don't."

She smiled. "You didn't even hesitate. You're not big on sharing."

"Not things like that. Sometimes you have to compartmentalize to survive. And we're talking about Jamie, not me."

"Well, I hope he doesn't suffer posttraumatic stress, but I know it's hard to avoid. I just don't want him to cover up his pain with so many jokes that we miss the fact that he's really hurting."

"You won't let that happen, Charlotte. Your brother is in good hands."

"So what went on with you today? Any updates on the case?"

"I do have a little news. Michaela Gomez is Constance's biological daughter, given up for adoption at birth."

Charlotte's eyes widened. "Wow! I knew there was something between those two, but I didn't suspect that. How did you figure it out?"

"Jason did most of the work. It doesn't mean that Michaela was responsible for the theft or Theresa's attack, but it certainly creates doubt about Constance's account of what happened that night. And if there's some possibility that Michaela is the daughter of Edward Worthington as well, then—"

"You're going there?" she asked.

"You're the one who suggested there was something between Edward and Constance. Michaela was born about two years after Worthington's wife died and Constance started working for him. We don't have anything more than pure speculation at this point, however. Constance has lawyered up, and Michaela has disappeared."

"If Constance has a lawyer, she must have something to protect." Charlotte blew out a huge breath of relief. "This is great—the break we've been waiting for!"

Joe hated to burst her bubble. "Don't get too excited. By your own admission, you were upstairs at the time Theresa was attacked. Even without Constance's testimony, you're a suspect."

"But Michaela is, too. She passed me on the stairs when I went up." She paused. "I wish I could remember if she was carrying anything, but it's just a blur. Why did Constance try to hide the fact that she and Michaela were related?"

"She was nervous because their relationship was recent. Apparently, Michaela had shown up just a few weeks earlier."

"Have you told the mayor?"

"Not yet. I'd like to get a few more facts lined up first. However, it's possible that Constance will tell him. Theresa went home today."

"I'm happy that she's going to recover." Charlotte glanced around. "Isabella isn't here tonight?"

"She's having dinner with Megan and spending the night with her. Nick is away on business. So it's just you and me."

She set her wineglass on the table and then slid a little closer. "You promised me dessert," she said with a seductive smile.

Joe swallowed hard. His brain tended to stop working when she was within reach. "I have lemon bars in the kitchen, courtesy of Lauren's bakery."

"I had something else in mind." She whispered in his ear, "You."

His heart jumped. Then her lips were moving along his jawline, her tongue sliding between his lips. He put his hand through her hair so she couldn't escape—not that she seemed to be interested in that. She was fumbling with the buttons on his shirt, her fingers slipping inside, her nails grazing his chest.

He threw off his shirt and pushed her back against the sofa cushions. He liked her under him, on top of him, surrounding him in every possible way. He cupped her face and took one kiss after another, never getting enough, and then he licked his way down her neck, across her collarbone, around the low vee neck of her T-shirt. She was soft and curvy and hot in all the right places, and he wanted to take his time to explore, but impatience was building inside him.

"We should go to bed," he said with a groan.

"Too far away," she said breathlessly.

"I—I . . ." He stuttered as she pulled her top up over her head and shook out her hair. Her bra was black and lacy, barely covering her tantalizing breasts. He pulled the edge of one cup down and tongued her nipple, delighting in the way it peaked for him, loving the way she pulled his head back down for more. He wanted to give her more. He wanted to give her everything.

"Don't stop," she said as he lifted his head.

"Condoms. Bedroom."

"My purse," she said.

He grabbed her bag and handed it to her. "Thank God."

He shoved off the rest of his clothes as she shimmied out of her jeans, happy beyond belief when they were skin to skin, no barriers to his hands or his mouth—or to hers. Because Charlotte was as spontaneous and generous in sex as she was in every other part of her life. He liked the way she moved, the way she wrapped her legs around his back, the soft sounds that came out of her mouth as he loved her, the way she loved him back.

It took a while to come down from the high. An hour later, they were still wrapped up in each other's arms on the couch.

"Dessert?" Joe suggested.

She gave him a happy, satisfied smile. "Again, already? I'm flattered."

He grinned. "I'm always ready where you're concerned, but I was talking about food this time. Are you hungry?"

She stretched in his arms. "We did work up an appetite, and I do love lemon bars."

"Meet me in the bedroom, and I'll bring you some. Do you want anything else—coffee, tea, water?"

"Some water would be good." She stood up.

"I'm going to watch you so don't go too fast," Joe said.

"How's this?" she said with a deliberately sexy sway of her hips.

"Nice ass," he called as she sauntered down the hall. He grabbed his boxers off the floor and put them on, then went into the kitchen.

When he got to the bedroom with lemon bars and water, Charlotte was under the covers. He sat on the other side of the bed, putting the plate of lemon bars between them."

"Yummy," Charlotte said between mouthfuls.

He smiled at her sugar-sprinkled lips. "I'm glad I didn't bring any napkins. I'm going to enjoy helping you clean up."

She smiled. "I didn't realize you had such a playful side. You were so serious when I first met you, and you're still that way at times, but it's nice to see this other side."

"I deliberately put up some walls when I first moved here, especially where you were concerned. I was way too attracted to you, and I knew that could be dangerous."

She stared at him, all humor gone. "I didn't break your marriage up, did I, Joe?"

"No, Charlotte. I had plenty of reasons to end my marriage that didn't involve you, and so did Rachel. That's why I moved here and took the job. I wanted to force a change in my life. I had gone along with Rachel's plans for most of our marriage. I moved into the house her parents bought for us, even though I wanted something different. I gave up some of my old neighborhood friends to hang out with the people at her tennis club. I tried to make her happy. I even sold my Mustang. Somewhere along the way, I lost myself. But I didn't want to acknowledge the problems, because I didn't want to fail." He drew in a breath. "And I really think that's all I have to say on the subject. Probably more than you wanted to know."

"I want to know whatever you want to tell me." She gave him a compassionate smile. "For what it's worth, I know you tried to make it work. Because you don't quit on people. And you loved Rachel."

"At one time. I know you see yourself as being second, Charlotte, but that's not the way I see you."

"How do you see me?"

"As a beautiful woman who wants to trust, to fall in love, to give her heart, but doesn't quite know how."

She drew in a sharp breath. "That's good. But I'm not the only one who's wary. This is moving kind of fast, and neither of us knows where it's going to end."

"Maybe it won't end."

"Do you still really believe in happily ever after?"

He thought for a long moment, realizing the seriousness of her question. "I want to."

"I do, too. I just don't know if it's possible."

"Well, you have two choices. Never give your heart and never get it broken, or go all in and risk everything."

"I want a third choice."

He smiled. "That's all I've got at the moment."

She lay back against the pillows. "Changing the subject, what about your old friends? You never talk about the people you left behind in L.A., and no one comes to visit. Why is that?"

"Most of my friends were the guys I worked with on the LAPD. I had to make a break with that world. That might sound ruthless, but it was a survival instinct. I didn't want to get pulled back in."

"Now you have a new life here; you could reconnect. Invite someone to come up and go fishing."

"I might do that. I would like you to meet Sonny. He and I met back in the police academy. He's married with triplets now, and I'm the godfather to the oldest one."

"I'd like to meet him sometime."

"What about your friends?"

"The ones from college and medical school are

scattered about. I never let anyone get that close to me, though. I was busy with school, then there was internship and residency and tons of pressure and competition. Friendships, relationships, they all suffered. When I came back here and caught up with Kara and Lauren again, I realized how much I'd missed having really close girlfriends. And I realized that my work can't be my whole life."

"So here we are," he said softly. "A new chapter for both of us."

"Yes," she agreed, meeting his gaze. "Are you going to kiss me again anytime soon?"

"How about now?" He set the plate on the table and slid under the covers.

She rolled into his arms and pushed him onto his back. "My turn to be on top."

"Honey, you can be wherever you want to be—as long as it's with me."

When Charlotte woke up just after ten on Saturday morning, Joe was in the shower. She stared up at the ceiling and sighed with pleasure. Joe had shown her a new way to greet the day that didn't involve running five miles in a cold wind.

Each time with Joe was better than the last and not at all predictable. Sometimes he was impatient and rough, then sensitive and tender, then playful and teasing. She liked all of his sides, and she was teetering on the precipice of falling totally in love with him. Protecting herself had become a hard habit to break. Risking it all seemed both exhilarating and terrifying. But maybe she didn't have to choose quite yet.

Sliding out of bed, she grabbed a T-shirt out of Joe's drawer and pulled it on, then went into the kitchen to make some coffee. After getting the pot started, she gave Rufus a good scratch and walked out onto the deck. It was cold, with dark clouds hovering on the horizon. She shivered and quickly retreated into the warm house. She didn't have much on her schedule today. She could go home, spend time with Jamie, and maybe take a nap before Lauren's bachelorette party.

In the kitchen, Joe's cell phone began to vibrate. She took a mug out of the cupboard, surprised when his house phone rang a moment later. Someone was eager to get in touch with him, but it wasn't really her place to answer his phone.

Then the answering machine picked up.

"Joe, it's Rachel."

Charlotte froze.

"I have to see you. I have to talk to you. This can't be over. I still love you. I was looking through our photo albums last night, thinking about how happy we were. I was wrong to throw it away. I miss you. I think we could still have what we wanted— a marriage and children. You know how much you wanted to have a child. I want to give you one now. Please, call me back, or come home. It's not too late. Call me."

Charlotte stared at the machine. There was such

pain in Rachel's voice. Would Joe one day realize he'd made a mistake? That he'd acted in haste? Would he want the children Rachel was promising to give him?

Joe had assured her that he was emotionally past his marriage, and she wanted to believe him. But Rachel's voice ran around in her head, pleading for Joe to call her back. She'd almost been begging and Rachel had never struck her as a woman who would like to beg. She was sophisticated and opinionated and strong, but on this message she hadn't been any of those things.

Charlotte licked her lips, wondering if she was the reason Joe hadn't called Rachel back. Maybe they would reconnect if she wasn't in the picture. Should she give them that opportunity?

She grabbed the clothes that were strewn all over the living room and quickly dressed. She'd just finished when Joe walked into the room, his hair damp, his cheeks shaven, looking heartbreakingly handsome, which challenged her desire to get away from him before she lost the will to leave.

"You're not running out on me again," he protested.

"I got coffee started. But I have to go to the hospital."

"Someone is in labor?"

"Maybe, not sure. I'll talk to you later."

"What about tonight?"

"It's Lauren's bachelorette party. You're going to Shane's, right?"

"Right." His eyes darkened. "What's going on, Charlotte?"

"Nothing."

"You're running scared again."

"I'm not running. I'm just leaving." She kissed his mouth, then hurried to the front door. "You should check your messages, Joe."

As the door shut behind Charlotte, Joe walked over to his answering machine with an uneasy feeling. The red light was blinking. A moment later, Rachel's voice came over the line, and his heart sank. Charlotte had obviously heard every word. And the part about kids—*damn*. Charlotte wasn't even sure she wanted kids, and now Rachel was offering to get pregnant to win him back.

But he knew what Rachel's promises were worth.

This had to stop. Rachel always wanted what she couldn't have. And as soon as someone else wanted something, she wanted it, too. He'd seen it happen a hundred times. Her desperation would turn into obsession. In the past, he'd try to help her get what she wanted or get back what she'd lost. He'd encouraged her to make up with friends she'd dumped in a moment of pique or because they weren't important to her at that moment. Because sooner or later, she always wanted them back. And sooner or later, most of them came back.

But he wasn't going back.

With shocking clarity, he realized that he really *was* done with her. The love was gone. He would always care about her and want the best for her, but he no longer wanted to be with her.

He needed to make sure Charlotte understood that he was fully committed to her. She might still have doubts, but he didn't.

But first he had to call Rachel back. Avoiding her was only making things worse.

Her voice came over the phone a second later. "Joe," she said. "Thank God, you finally realize that we need to talk."

"Rachel, I'm done," he told her.

"You don't mean that," she said in disbelief. "I'll do whatever you want. I'll even move to Angel's Bay. That's how much I love you."

"It won't work, Rachel. And you don't love me. You just hate being alone."

"I made a mistake. I pushed you away, and I didn't mean to."

"You outgrew me. We outgrew each other. You fell for Mark Devlin."

"Mark isn't with me anymore, Joe."

"That's too bad. I want you to be happy, Rachel—but it's not going to be with me."

Silence followed his words. Then, "You're really sure, Joe? We had a lot of good years."

"And those are the ones I'll always remember."

"I thought I could change your mind," she said sadly. "But there's someone else, isn't there?"

"Yes," he said honestly. "But our divorce has

never been about anyone but us. Devlin wasn't to blame. You wouldn't have gone after him if you'd been happy with me. And I wouldn't have stayed here in Angel's Bay if I'd really wanted to make things work with you."

"Thank you for admitting that," she said. "Okay, Joe. I'll let you go."

"Good-bye, Rachel," he said, snapping the phone shut with relief.

He'd finally convinced Rachel that they were over. Now he had to convince Charlotte.

NINETEEN

As Charlotte drove home, she wondered if she'd made the right decision. Joe thought she was running scared again, afraid to face what was happening between them, but that wasn't it. She wanted more. She just didn't know if she had the right.

Hearing Rachel's voice had shaken her. It was one thing to know a couple was getting divorced and another to be in the middle of it. And even though she truly believed in her heart that she wasn't responsible for their breakup, she was afraid that she could be responsible for Joe not giving Rachel a second chance.

But maybe Rachel didn't deserve one. Maybe Joe had truly had enough. And maybe it was all none of her business.

She stopped at a light and sighed, weary of the confusion muddying her mind. This was why she didn't do serious relationships.

How quickly things changed. Last night, she'd

been as happy as she'd ever been. They'd gotten so close, physically and emotionally. Now there was a huge wall between them named Rachel.

Her cell phone rang, and she glanced down at the number. It was Joe. She really didn't want to pick up. But . . . "Hello."

"I called her back," Joe said shortly. "Not because I wanted to but because I needed to. It's over with Rachel. I told her that there was no going back."

"Maybe you should think about it," she replied, feeling uncertain and a little scared.

"Don't do this, Charlotte. Don't use Rachel as a reason to back off."

She jumped as someone honked the horn behind her. She drove down the street and then pulled over.

"Charlotte?" Joe said again. "Are you still there?"

"Yes, I'm here. I just don't know what to say."

"Say you'll meet me and we'll talk about this."

"I need to think."

"That's the last thing you need to do," he said firmly. "You'll just talk yourself out of this. I know you're gun shy. I am, too. But last night was amazing. We're great together—and not just in bed."

"What happens in the dark doesn't always make it to daylight."

"I'm coming over."

"No," she said quickly. "I don't want to have this conversation in earshot of my mother. Plus, my brother is there, and Annie and the baby."

"Then I'll meet you somewhere else. You're not really going to the hospital, are you?"

"No."

"How about the bell tower?"

She hesitated again. "It's a busy day, Joe. We have the parties tonight; maybe we should just put this on hold."

"No way. Either agree to meet me, or I'm going to camp out on your mother's doorstep."

"Fine, I'll be at the tower in an hour. I need to go home and check in on my brother."

"I'll see you then," he promised.

She closed her phone and tossed it onto the seat, hoping she'd made the right decision. As she was thinking about it, her gaze caught on a couple standing by the front entrance to the Seagull Inn.

Although she couldn't hear what they were saying, it was clear that they were arguing. The man, who appeared to be in his thirties, wore a gray hooded sweatshirt and jeans. The woman was dressed in jeans and boots and a bright red jacket. From the back, she looked a lot like Pamela. The man grabbed her arm, and she yanked it away. Then he slapped the woman hard across the face.

"Oh, my God." Charlotte pulled her car keys out of the ignition and jumped out of the car just as the man shoved the woman up hard against the cement wall of the building. She stumbled and fell to the ground. "Stop!" Charlotte shouted, running down the street.

The man glanced at her and took off running in the opposite direction. Charlotte moved toward the woman. It was Pamela. Her temple was bleeding from a long cut over her eyebrow, and her eye was swelling up.

"Are you all right?" she asked, squatting down next to her.

Pamela stared at her in bemusement, her hands going up to her head, coming away with blood. She whitened at the sight. "I'm—I'm bleeding."

"Let me help you."

"Charlotte," Pamela said, recognition dawning in her eyes. Then she glanced past Charlotte. "Where did he go?"

"I don't know. We need to call the police."

"No police," Pamela said quickly. "I just need to go to my room."

"You're staying here?"

"Yes."

Charlotte helped her get to her feet and walked with her into the lobby of the inn. The desk clerk gave them a curious look, but Pamela didn't give her a chance to ask questions, walking quickly to the elevator, head down. The doors opened right away, and Charlotte followed her inside.

"Who was that guy?" she asked as they rode up to the second floor.

"Nobody." Pamela stepped off the elevator and walked down the hall to her room. Her hand shook as she foraged around in her bag for her key. Finally, she found it and opened the door.

The room hadn't been made up yet, Charlotte noted, following Pamela into the messy bathroom.

"You might need stitches," she said as she ran a

washcloth under the water, then gently wiped away some of the blood. "Let me take you to the hospital."

"I'm fine," Pamela said. But she didn't seem fine when she sank onto the edge of the tub.

Charlotte knelt down in front of her. "At least let me call the police."

"No hospital. No police," Pamela said. "What are you even doing here? You don't like me. You don't care what happens to me."

"I care about anyone who is hurt," she said. "You need some ice."

"I'll get it myself. You can go."

"Who was that guy?"

Pamela stared back at her. "You didn't recognize him?"

"No. Is he your boyfriend?"

Pamela shook her head. "He's nobody."

"Has he hit you before?"

"A lot of people have hit me," she said wearily. "Believe me, this is nothing."

"Why would you let anyone treat you like that?"

"You think I have a choice? I didn't grow up the princess of Angel's Bay, like you did. I had to fight for everything I got. And I'm still fighting."

"You weren't fighting him."

"It would have only made him hit me harder. I know when to pick my battles." She took the towel from Charlotte's hands. "I'm fine. You need to go."

Charlotte hesitated. "What about Andrew? Do you want to call him?"

"Get out, Charlotte, before I throw you out."

Pamela didn't look as if she could even stand up, much less throw Charlotte out, but it was clear she wanted her to leave. So Charlotte got to her feet and walked through the bedroom and out the door. She went straight to her car, muttering about how ungrateful Pamela was. If she hadn't stepped in, the guy might have hit her again. Pamela should have thanked her instead of telling her to get out.

But as she sat in her car, she started thinking about the nasty cut on Pamela's head. And how she really should take care of it. Another few minutes of debate had her grabbing her medical bag out of her backseat and digging through it for first-aid supplies. She took what she needed and then headed back down the street. There was no one at the front desk when she walked in, so she went straight to the elevator. When she got off on the second floor and approached Pamela's room, she saw that the door was slightly ajar. Maybe Pamela had gone to get some ice.

She pushed open the door, saying, "Pamela, I brought you some antiseptic ointment and a bandage. That cut really needs—"

Her mouth dropped open in shock. Pamela was standing by the desk, and the man who'd hit her was right behind her. And next to them on the table were two pieces of glittering jewelry. Her heart skipped a beat.

The necklace. The ring. Pamela had had them all along.

"You really shouldn't have come back," Pamela said.

"*You* stole the jewelry from your sister? You're the one who almost killed her?"

Pamela glanced nervously over her shoulder, and that's when Charlotte saw the gun in the man's hand.

He raised it, aiming it straight at her. "Looks like we're going to have some company on our trip."

She didn't know what to do, what to say.

He walked slowly toward her. "We're going to go down the back stairs and through the alley, and you're going to keep your mouth shut. Understand?"

"Just leave her here," Pamela said. "She's not going to cause any trouble."

"If we leave her here, they'll be on us too fast. Put the jewels in the bag, and let's go."

Pamela shoved the ring and the necklace into a plastic baggie and then thrust it into her shoulder bag. "Just do what he says, Charlotte, and you won't get hurt."

She didn't believe that for a second; there was an air of violence about this man. There was also a certain familiarity to his features, although it was difficult to get a good look with his hood over his head. Still . . .

"Who are you?" she asked.

"No questions." He waved the gun at her. "Walk."

She turned slowly around, her mind racing with the possibilities as he urged her out the door and into the hallway. There was no way she wanted to get into a car with these two. She had the terrible feeling that if she left the inn with them, she was never going to get away. She opened her mouth to scream, just as something hard came down on the back of her head. And everything went black.

Charlotte wasn't at the bell tower when Joe arrived. He was a little early, but as each minute passed, his stress level increased. Maybe she wasn't coming. Perhaps Rachel had scared her away for good. Or maybe her own worries about commitment, about children, were keeping her away. He never should have given her the hour she'd asked for.

Another ten minutes passed, and he was starting to feel like a fool. What if Charlotte just didn't feel about him the same way he felt about her? He had a lot of baggage. He had already failed at one marriage. Maybe she wasn't being scared, she was being smart.

He gave her another five minutes, then went down the stairs and drove to her mother's house. Her car wasn't in the driveway. He tried her cell phone, which went to voice-mail. Had he missed her?

He got out of his car and went up the front walk.

Annie opened the door, giving him a welcoming smile. "Hello, Chief."

"Annie. How are you doing?"

"Good. Come in."

As he walked into the living room, he saw Charlotte's brother on the couch, his leg propped up on the ottoman. He gave him a nod.

"Joe Silveira, right?" Jamie asked.

"Right, and you're Jamie."

"Only Charlotte and my mother call me that. Everyone else calls me James. I'd get up, but . . ."

"No problem," Joe said, walking over to the couch to shake his hand. "That looks nasty."

"I'll survive," he said with a shrug.

"I'm looking for Charlotte. Is she here?"

"I haven't seen her since yesterday."

Joe looked over at Annie, who was now perched on the edge of the couch. "She was on her way over here when I talked to her about an hour ago."

"She hasn't been home," Annie said. "Maybe she went to the hospital."

His uneasiness deepened. Charlotte had said she was going home.

"Is something wrong?" Annie asked.

The last thing he wanted to do was worry Charlotte's family. "No, I just wanted to talk to her. Tell her I stopped by, will you?"

"Of course," she said.

He looked at Jamie. "I'll see you around."

"I have a feeling you will," Jamie said with a smile. "Charlotte's got a thing for you."

"Not so sure about that," he said, feeling a little grim about his prospects in that department.

"She's a tough nut to crack but worth the effort."

"I'm trying, believe me."

He drove back to the church, but there was no sign of her car in the parking lot. It was starting to rain and it was now almost thirty minutes past their meeting time. Maybe she'd changed her mind or had an unexpected emergency. He called the hospital and asked them to page her. A few minutes later, a nurse came on the line saying that Charlotte wasn't there. She wasn't at home, she wasn't here, she wasn't at the hospital. Where the hell *was* she?

Andrew's house?

His stomach turned over at that thought. No way was he going there. If she'd run to Andrew again, then maybe they were done.

He drove to the police station. He might as well check in at work. At least there he knew what he was doing.

When Joe arrived at the station, Andrew was in the lobby. He gave him a wary but determined look, and Joe's gut tightened.

"If this is about Charlotte . . ." he began.

"Only partially," Andrew said. "I was going to speak to Jason, but he's not in. Can we talk in your office?"

"All right." He ushered Andrew into his office and shut the door behind him. Andrew looked tired, with dark shadows under his eyes. Joe moved behind his desk and sat down. "What's on your mind?"

"Pamela may have been involved with the robbery at the manor," he said abruptly. "We had a disturbing conversation last night. She's been involved with a man who grew up here, Mitch Harding. He got out of jail a few months ago, and Pamela suggested to me that he might have had something to do with the robbery." Andrew paused. "If Mitch was involved, then Pamela was, too. Mitch couldn't have done it alone."

Joe sat up straighter. "Why would Pamela stick around Angel's Bay if she was responsible?"

"I think she came here so she wouldn't be a suspect. And she hung around because Theresa didn't remember anything, and she wanted to keep up with the investigation. Mitch Harding is bad news, and Pamela can't control him. That may be how Theresa got hurt."

Joe gave Andrew a speculative look. "And you would know all this . . ."

"Because I used to live with them," Andrew said tightly. "In our early twenties, we partied together a lot. In the beginning, it was fun. But Mitch got into more addictive drugs, and he needed money to support his habit. He started stealing. Petty stuff in the beginning. Then he kept increasing the stakes. Finally he ended up in jail. If you look up his record, you'll get the whole story."

"Why didn't you tell us this before?"

Andrew drew in a long breath. "I thought there was only a very slim possibility that Pamela had anything to do with what happened. When she told me about Mitch, I asked her to talk to you."

"Bullshit. You didn't come in because you didn't want us digging into your past." Joe looked him straight in the eye. "You didn't want Charlotte to know the kind of man you'd been."

"That was part of it, too," Andrew said with a nod.

Joe was surprised by Andrew's candor, but that didn't make up for his withholding information. "I need to talk to Pamela."

"I'd like to go with you. She might be more forthcoming if she feels she has some support."

"And you want to support her? Why?"

"Because I know where she's been. Because I found my way out, but I didn't try to take anyone else with me."

"So you want to save her soul?"

"That *is* my business," Andrew said, getting to his feet. "She's at the Seagull Inn."

"Let's go." On his way out, Joe asked one of his officers to run a background check on Mitch Harding.

They didn't speak on the short drive to the inn. When Joe pulled into a parking spot down the street, he was surprised to see Charlotte's car. Had she gone to the inn to see Pamela?

The hotel clerk gave them a nervous smile. She was a young woman, barely out of her twenties. "Can I help you?"

"We need Pamela Baines's room number." Joe flashed his badge in case she had any doubts.

"Two-twelve," she said. "Is this about what happened earlier?"

"What happened earlier?"

"I saw Ms. Baines going upstairs with some

blood on her face. There was another woman with her, a blonde."

Dammit! Without another word, he bypassed the elevator and ran up the stairs.

"You think she was with Charlotte?" Andrew asked, right on his heels.

"Her car is right down the street."

"I noticed that, too, but they hate each other. Why would they be together?"

Joe pushed open the stairwell door to the second floor and rapped sharply on two-twelve. The door wasn't latched and swung right open. As he walked inside, fear began to take root. There was a bloody towel in the bathroom and more blood on the rug. But there was no one in sight.

"Maybe Charlotte took Pamela to the hospital," Andrew said. "The clerk said she was injured."

Joe took out his phone and called the ER. Pamela Baines had not been admitted, and no one had seen Dr. Adams. "Not there," he said tersely, pacing around the room, looking for some clue. "When's the last time you talked to Pamela?"

"Last night about six."

"What were her plans?"

"She didn't say. I didn't ask."

Joe's next call was to the mayor, on the off chance that Pamela had gone there. Robert told him that he hadn't seen Pamela since yesterday, and Theresa was sleeping.

"What's next?" Andrew asked, concern in his eyes.

He *should* be concerned. He should have come forward a hell of a lot earlier. But now wasn't the time for that conversation.

"We'll go back to the station. I want to get some officers looking for the two of them."

They stopped at the front desk on the way down. "Did you see anyone else come into the inn this morning who didn't belong here?" he asked the desk clerk.

She shook her head. "We had another couple check in, but other than that, it's been quiet."

"Do you know if Ms. Baines has had any visitors since she arrived?"

"There was a guy here the other day who came down the elevator with her."

"Could you identify him if you saw him again?"

"I don't know. He had on a baseball hat and baggy clothes. I didn't really see his face."

"All right. Make sure that no one enters that room until one of my officers has gone through it."

"Did something bad happen?"

"We're not sure yet."

As they walked down the street, Joe paused by Charlotte's car. The doors were unlocked, and her cell phone was lying on the passenger seat. His stomach flipped over. "Why would she leave her phone?" he muttered. He picked it up and looked at the last call. It was from him. She hadn't called or received a call from anyone since then, more than two hours ago now.

He turned to Andrew, who had paled considerably.

Andrew immediately shook his head as if trying to convince himself everything was all right. "She just forgot her phone. Charlotte does that sometimes. She's always hard to get hold of."

"She picks up when I call," he said.

Andrew gave him an irritated look. "What now?"

"We find them."

When they arrived at the station, Andrew took off to look for Charlotte. As much as Joe wanted to do that himself, he needed to get hold of Jason and get a search under way for Pamela and Mitch. He didn't know if they were guilty of anything, but blood in the hotel room and Charlotte's unreachability had him very concerned. He prayed that Charlotte was okay. She was a strong, brave woman, but something had happened suddenly. What?

Charlotte felt a throbbing pain in the back of her head. She wanted to move, but it hurt so much she was afraid to try. Voices made their way through the thick fog in her brain. A man and a woman— Pamela and the man who'd pointed a gun at her and ordered her to move. He'd hit her and knocked her out, she realized.

Where was she? There wasn't any movement, so they weren't in a car. She wanted to open her eyes, but instinct told her it would be better if she pretended to be unconscious.

"We shouldn't have brought her with us," Pamela said.

"We didn't have a choice. She knows too much."

"What are you going to do?" There was fear in Pamela's voice.

"Make it look like an accident."

Charlotte's heart began to pound. She told herself to breathe, to stay calm. She had to think—not act impulsively for once in her life.

"You can't kill her. This isn't what I agreed to," Pamela complained. "Stealing the jewelry is one thing. Murder is another."

"Shit happens," he said coldly. "This is your fault. I told you to come back to L.A. But you had to hang around, catch up with the old boyfriend, make nice with your sister and pretend you care about her."

"I do care about her. I didn't want Theresa to get hurt. I just wanted some of what she had. The rest was an accident."

"I'm sure the cops will believe you."

"Mitch, this is wrong. This is going too far."

Mitch? There had been a Mitch in their class. Mitch Harding. Was it the same guy? He had looked a little familiar—what on earth had happened to him? And to Pamela, too? She'd never imagined that Pamela was capable of robbing her own sister or being involved with a kidnapping, maybe murder.

She didn't want to think about that. Maybe Pamela could get through to Mitch.

"There is no 'too far,'" Mitch said with deadly intent. "And there's no other way out."

"People saw Charlotte with me. The clerk in the inn, probably some other people. It's going to point to me. And a lot of people in this town know we don't get along."

"Better you than me."

"We have to find another way out," Pamela said desperately. "We'll go to Andrew—he'll help us. As long as we don't kill Charlotte, we can get out. We can give the jewelry back. My sister won't press charges. And Andrew will get Charlotte to keep quiet."

"You're dreaming, babe. Your sister isn't going to forgive you for almost killing her. And Andrew doesn't give a shit about you. He never did."

"I thought *you* did," Pamela said. "I thought you loved me, Mitch. Now you want me to go down for murder?"

"No one is going down. We'll make it look like an accident. She got lost and fell off a cliff."

"That won't work."

"We won't stick around long enough to find out. This is just to buy us some time. When we're in Mexico with our money, life will be sweet. Just think about that."

There was a pause, and then Pamela said, "Where are you going?"

"I'll be back in a few minutes. I need to get some stuff out of the car."

Charlotte heard a door open, and a cold damp

wind hit her face. She could smell salt air—they were close to the beach. Then the door slammed shut.

If she was going to do anything, she needed to do it while Mitch was gone. Fighting the pain in her head, she opened her eyes. She was lying on a hard wooden floor, her hands tied behind her back. They were in a cabin. One of the summer rentals, judging by the sparse decor and cheap furniture. As she tried to lift her aching head, Pamela came into view.

"Help me," she said, her voice thick.

Pamela stared at her in shock. "There's nothing I can do, Charlotte. I was hoping you wouldn't wake up, wouldn't know what was about to happen to you. Maybe I should knock you out again. At least then you won't suffer."

Charlotte rolled onto her knees, sending waves of pain through her head, but she fought past them. "You can help me get away."

"He'll find you," Pamela said dully, as if she'd lost her will to fight.

"Not if the police find him first. Untie my hands."

"It's duct tape."

She looked wildly around the room. There were two doors, one off the living room, another off the small kitchen. An upstairs loft and a bathroom were the only other rooms. "Which way did he go?"

"Out the front to the car."

She stumbled to her feet. "Come with me."

Pamela stared at her in shock. "Why?"

"Because neither one of us wants to die."

"I'll go to prison."

"But you won't be dead. Please help me." She moved toward the back door. She stared at the doorknob in dismay. Such a simple thing but such a huge barrier to her escape.

Then Pamela pulled out a knife, grabbed her arms, and sliced through the duct tape. They exchanged a quick look as Charlotte opened the door.

As they left the cabin, thunder shook the earth, lightning lit up the sky, and rain poured down on them. The storm had arrived. It was black as night, and the area surrounding the cabin was thickly wooded.

"Where are we?" Charlotte asked as they ran for the trees.

"Near Bonfire Beach."

Of course they were, she thought ironically. She'd run through these woods the night she'd seen Andrew and Pamela hook up. Ending up here seemed only fitting.

Then a man's voice rang through the air; Mitch was coming after them. Charlotte ran faster, praying for escape, or at least somewhere to hide.

"I can't find Charlotte," Andrew said as he reentered Joe's office. "I've been everywhere. No one at her house has seen her. She hasn't been in touch with Kara or Lauren. She hasn't been at the hospital. The only one who saw her today is the clerk at the inn."

"Then we have to assume that she's with Pamela, and probably Mitch." Joe's stomach turned over. While Andrew had been searching for Charlotte, he'd dug up a lot of information on Mitch Harding, and it was seriously bad. "I've got everyone out looking for them, but you know them the best. Where would they take her?"

"L.A.?"

"Too far. Too risky. If they've got Charlotte, they'll want to do something about her right away."

Andrew stared at him in shock. "How can you speak so calmly about it? I thought you cared about her. I thought she was important to you."

"She is very important to me, but I have to be calm. Thinking like a cop is the only way we're going to get her back safely." He forced his fear away; emotion would get in the way. "You need to think logically, too. You said you lived with Mitch and Pamela, so you know how they think."

Andrew ran a frustrated hand through his hair. "I don't know."

"Is there anyone else in Angel's Bay who would help them hide out somewhere?"

"Pamela doesn't have any family aside from Theresa. No friends that I'm aware of, and Mitch's parents left a decade ago."

"But they both grew up here. They know this town. They know where to hide. And so do you."

"There were a few places we always went in high school. Some of them are gone now or boarded up like the Ramsay House." Andrew paused, then a light came into his eyes, "The summer cabins. There are three of them out by Bonfire Beach. They're usually deserted in the winter."

"Charlotte mentioned that beach."

"The cabins are in the woods. I can show you where they are."

"I'm sure someone in the department can tell me."

"You just said they're all out looking for Charlotte. I'm your best bet, Chief. And I want to find Charlotte as much as you do."

As much as Joe hated to admit it, Andrew was right. And there was no time to waste arguing.

Charlotte was soaked and lost and terrified that every crash behind them was Mitch getting closer. Pamela was starting to tire, her breath coming hard. She stumbled and fell, and Charlotte stopped to help her up.

"I can't run anymore," she gasped.

"You have to. We're not far enough away. We have to get back to town, or at least somewhere more public than this."

"I'll be arrested."

"I don't know what's up ahead for you, but I know who's behind us. And he's not going to thank you for helping me escape."

"He'll probably kill me, too. Maybe that's the way it should be. I told Andrew yesterday that I was too far gone to be saved, but he wanted to try. After everything, he still had some hope that he could put me on the right path."

"Andrew knew you stole the jewelry?" she asked in shock. "I can't believe he didn't go to the police, that he would protect you."

"He didn't know for sure." Pamela paused. "I didn't think there was a line I wouldn't cross, but when Mitch told me he was going to kill you, I suddenly found one. I don't like you, but I don't want you dead."

"Likewise. We have to keep going," she said, looking behind Pamela, wishing there was more light to see through the trees.

"I'm just going to slow you down. Save yourself. And if you do, tell Andrew he can thank me sometime for getting his girl back to him."

"I'm not his girl, Pamela. Not anymore. Now get off your ass and start running, because I'm not going without you." She grabbed Pamela's hand and yanked her to her feet, dragging her along through the woods.

After a while, Pamela began to lag again, and she finally collapsed on the ground.

"My side is cramping. I can't go any farther."

A thunderous blast echoed through the woods, and Charlotte jumped back as the trees next to her exploded from a lightning strike. A branch hit her hard on the shoulder, knocking her to the ground, and it took her a minute to wrestle free of the branches. She looked over at Pamela, who was almost buried beneath the large branches of the tree. She moved as close as she could get. "Are you all right?"

"I can't get my foot out," Pamela said, struggling to free herself.

Charlotte grabbed the branches, trying to move them.

"It's no use. Just stop." Pamela said.

"Dammit, Pamela—"

"Take this." Pamela handed her the bag with the jewelry. "If I don't get out of here, give them to my sister and tell her I'm sorry."

"I'm not leaving you—"

"You don't have a choice. I'm stuck, and unless you have a chain saw, I'm not going anywhere. Cover me up with the branches. With any luck, if Mitch comes by, he won't see me, and he'll keep on running."

Charlotte quickly grabbed as much loose brush as she could find, covering Pamela as best she could. "I'll come back for you later." Then she raced through the woods.

A wisp of white caught her eye, and anticipation raced through her as Mary Katherine's ghostly figure took shape, beckoning her to follow. And she did. Because right now, she really needed a miracle—and who better than an angel to provide one?

"They're gone," Andrew said with disappointment as they searched the cabin.

"But they were here, and not long ago," Joe replied, having more trouble keeping the fear away now. "The car out front is still warm. Stay here. Backup is on the way." He headed out the kitchen door, pulling out his gun.

"I'm going with you," Andrew said, right on his heels.

"No, you're not. I can't guarantee your safety."

"Fuck my safety. I'm going after Charlotte. And you can't stop me."

"Then stay behind me." There was a rough path through the trees; maybe it would lead them to Charlotte.

They ran quickly and silently through the woods, listening acutely for any voices. But it was hard to hear anything over the roar of wind, the cracks of thunder and lightning.

Joe didn't know how long they'd been running, but they didn't seem to be getting anywhere. And there was no sign of anyone.

"We could be going the wrong way," Andrew said breathlessly. "Maybe they went in the other direction."

"You said the beach was this way."

"I thought it was, but we should have hit it by now."

Joe slowed down for a moment, scanning the woods, and flash of white caught his attention. "Over there," he said.

"What?" Andrew asked.

"I saw someone." He sped up, seeing another glimpse of light in the shadows.

"I don't see anything," Andrew said, running behind him.

"It's a woman, I think."

But as the figure appeared again, he thought it
looked more like a girl. He blinked rapidly, wondering if she was some sort of a mirage. "Do you see
her?" he asked.

"I don't see anything but trees."

"She's right up ahead."

The girl was motioning for him to follow her,
and as he ran, her words rang through his head.
Charlotte's in trouble. She needs you.

He was either having a hallucination, or he'd just
seen an angel. Either way, he was going to follow
her. She was the only lead he had.

She'd ended up near the garden, Charlotte saw with
amazement, the flowers the only color on the black,
stormy landscape. She was still yards away when she
glanced back and saw Mitch come out of the trees
after her. He raised his gun.

Oh, God! She ran as hard and as fast as she could,
zigzagging to the right and the left so he couldn't
take a clean shot at her, but any moment, she expected a bullet to take her down.

When she reached the garden, she panicked.
What to do now? Keep going? There was nothing
but open land for the next half mile. Try to get down
to the beach? There were plenty of boulders to hide

behind, but could she make it down the steep, slippery hillside?

Mary Katherine seemed to have disappeared, so she was going to have to save herself.

A blast went off, and she instinctively ducked. As she did so, she tripped, her stumbling feet ripping up the beautiful flowers. She felt a momentary regret as she scrambled over the edge of the bluff.

It was a terrible mistake. The hillside was steeper than she'd thought. The tide was coming in, so there was no beach. The waves were huge, hitting the coast with tremendous force, and the pounding was stripping away rocks and dirt from the surrounding cliffs. She'd gone only ten feet when a large chunk of ground a couple of yards ahead broke apart, the dirt and rocks sliding into the sea.

She froze, uncertain of the ground under her feet. If she went farther down, there was a good chance she would die in the turbulent sea and screaming whitecaps. But if she went back up to the bluff, where Mitch was looking for her, she could die as well. She was trapped

It didn't take him long to see her in her bright clothes. There was no escape. She was caught. Mitch lifted the gun, taking his time since she had nowhere to go.

Desperate, Charlotte pulled the baggie out of her pocket and held it up, the gold and diamond sparkling in the lightning flashes. "If you kill me, you won't get these back!" she shouted over the storm.

"We can work something out. I won't say anything. No one has to know."

"Where's Pamela?" he asked, looking around.

"Headed to the police department to turn you in," she lied. "You won't get away."

"Neither will you," he said, aiming the gun at her.

She instinctively dropped to the ground, making herself as small a target as possible. A blast filled the air. A gunshot? Lightning? She was too afraid to look. Holding her breath, she waited for the bullet to hit her.

Another blast followed, but there was still no pain. He'd missed her again.

Or was he even shooting?

The ground around her was shaking as lightning streaked across the sky like fireworks. Lifting her head, she saw the bluff splitting apart, huge chunks of ground falling down the hill in a torrent of mud and flowers. The garden was falling into the sea.

And along with it was Mitch.

She saw the stupefied expression on his face as he landed on his back, as he struggled to find something to hold on to against the pull of nature. But the elements were too strong for him. With a scream of fury, the sea roared up and swallowed everything within reach.

She was on an island now, and she clung to the sodden grass. There was at least five feet of nothingness between her and the remaining bluff. Down below, the waves were churning. She had to find a way out.

"Charlotte!" Joe yelled.

His voice shocked her to the core. How on earth had he found her? And Andrew was right behind him.

"Hold on!" Joe yelled, looking around for something to bridge the gap.

But she knew he would find nothing. There was no branch to hold out, no rope to toss.

Joe soon came to the same conclusion. "Go back to the cabin," he told Andrew. "Get rope, a pole, a board—something."

"Don't give up, Charlotte!" Andrew called to her. "It's going to be all right. Have faith."

She wanted to have faith, but the earth was falling all around her.

Joe moved to the very edge of the bluff and eyed the distance between them.

"I'm running out of time," she said. "I don't think this bit of ground I'm on is going to last."

Joe met her gaze, his jaw rock hard. "Don't give up, Charlotte."

"There's nothing we can do. If Andrew doesn't get back in time . . ."

He climbed a couple of feet down the hillside.

"What the hell are you doing?" she screamed in fear and anger. "Go back!"

He was at eye level now. "You're going to have to jump, Charlotte."

Was he out of his mind? "No way. I can't make it."

"You can. It's not that far."

It looked impossibly far, and down below, the angry sea waited.

"You have to trust me, Charlotte. I'll catch you."

He was asking the impossible. He wanted her to put her life on the line for him.

Isn't that what love is all about?

If she didn't go for it, there was a good chance she wouldn't make it, anyway. Her island was growing smaller with each slide of dirt and rocks, each waving hitting the bottom, the ocean taking back some of the earth. If she jumped, she had a chance—a small one.

"You can do it, Charlie. You just have to believe in him. Believe in love." Mary Katherine stood on the bluff, encouraging her.

"Jump, Charlotte," Joe urged.

She slowly stood up, hoping her shift of weight wouldn't take her choice away. It was only a few feet, she told herself. She could do it. She closed her eyes and pictured herself landing in Joe's arms. She could feel his strength, his purpose, his courage flooding through her.

Drawing on every last bit of strength she had, she jumped.

For a moment, she kicked at nothing but air, but Joe's powerful grip pulled her in tight. She couldn't breathe, afraid he'd lose his balance, lose her, but Joe wasn't letting go.

He dragged her up to the top of the bluff, not stopping until they were a few yards away from the edge. She fell to her knees on the solid ground, her hands still locked in his.

Joe knelt in front of her, his gaze searching hers. "I told you I'd catch you."

"I knew you would," she said, rain and tears streaming down her face as the adrenaline rush hit her hard.

He gathered her up, holding her close, pressing his lips against her forehead. "You're okay. You're safe now."

She breathed in and out, letting the storm swirl around them. It seemed less intense now, or maybe it was just because she was no longer in danger of falling into the sea. She pulled away slightly so she could look into Joe's eyes. "Thank you."

"God, Charlotte, don't ever scare me like that again."

"Mitch was going to shoot me."

"I saw," he said grimly. "I was about to shoot him, then suddenly he wasn't there anymore."

"He went into the sea. His face was shocked, and he reached out to me. I almost thought he'd take me with him." A flicker of white made her turn her head, and she saw Mary Katherine by what was left of their garden. The girl gave her a wave, then faded into the darkness. "She's gone," she murmured sadly. When she looked back at Joe, she saw an odd expression on his face. "Did you see her?"

He nodded slowly. "She came to me in the woods. She led me to you, Charlotte. And you're safe now. It's over."

"It *is* over." She dug into her pocket and pulled out the baggie with the jewelry. "Look what I have."

His eyes widened in amazement. "Where did you get those?"

"Pamela." She stopped. "I buried her underneath some tree branches! We have to go get her."

"You killed Pamela?" he asked in disbelief.

"No, I hid her. She helped me escape from the cabin, but when we were running through the woods, a tree came down, and her foot got stuck. I couldn't get her out, so I covered her up, hoping Mitch wouldn't find her."

"Clever."

"It was her idea. She gave me the jewelry and told me to give it back to her sister in case she didn't make it. If she hadn't helped me, Mitch would have killed me, Joe."

"How did you even get involved with them? I thought you were going home. I thought you were going to meet me. I went to the tower; I searched all over town for you."

"It was a complete accident. I pulled over to talk to you, then I saw Mitch hit Pamela. They were right in front of the inn. I got out of my car to help her."

"You jumped into the middle of their fight."

"He was beating her up."

"You don't even like her," he said in wonder.

"I wasn't thinking. I just acted. But Pamela didn't want my help. After I got her to her room, she told me to get out. I was about to drive away, but I thought I should at least give her a bandage; she was bleeding. When I went back to her room, Mitch was there with the jewelry. He hit me over the head, and the next thing I knew, I was waking up on the floor of the cabin." She put a hand to the back of her head and winced. "It hurts."

"You need to go to the hospital."

"It's not that bad—"

"Don't even try to persuade me otherwise," he said firmly, just as sirens split the air.

Charlotte slowly got to her feet. The rain had stopped, and the clouds were parting, allowing moonlight to shine down. Her gaze went to her garden.

It was almost completely destroyed, only a few flowers clinging to life. She carefully moved closer, Joe's arm still around her shoulders as if he was afraid to let go of her. "The garden is disappearing. It's sad."

"Maybe it was only meant to be here as long as you needed it." He leaned down to pick up a droopy rose. "For you."

She held the flower for a few moments, then laid it back down with the others. "It belongs here." She was about to stand up when her gaze caught a sparkle of gold. "What's this?" She dug her hand into the soft, muddy earth, touching something hard and rectangular. She pulled it out with some effort; it was heavier than she expected. Rocking back on her heels, she stared at it in amazement. "Oh, my God." She stood up, looking at Joe. The same shock was on his face, for in her hand was a solid bar of gold.

"It was here," she said in wonder. "Worthington buried the missing gold in the garden he planted for his wife and Mary Katherine. It was here all along."

Joe shook his head in disbelief. "It really exists. Who would have thought?"

She couldn't speak, too caught up in amazement. Had Mary Katherine known the gold was here? And would she ever see her angel again?

A clatter of shouts and footsteps distracted her. Cops, firemen, and paramedics were coming from two directions; Joe had called out the troops for her.

Then Andrew was back with rope and what looked like a shower rod. He ran over to her. "Thank God," he said, dropping his supplies so he could hug her. "I was so afraid that I'd never see you again."

"I'm okay," she reassured him.

He stepped back, looking at Joe. "How did you save her?"

"She saved herself. She jumped," Joe said with a proud smile. "*And* she found the missing gold."

Charlotte held up the gold bar in her hand. The crowd gasped, throwing out a dozen questions that would have to be answered, but not right that second.

Joe gave her a loving smile. "All in a day's work, right, Charlotte?"

She hugged him around the waist. "And just think, you didn't want me to get involved."

"Next time, I'll save my breath." Joe looked over at Jason and Andrew. "We need to find Pamela. She's trapped under a tree in the woods."

"I can show them," Charlotte offered.

"You're going to the hospital. We'll find her.

And then we'll take her to jail." He kissed her hard on the lips.

"That should give the town something to talk about," she said breathlessly, aware of a dozen pairs of eyes on them.

"I don't care," he said with a smile. "I'll see you later."

Charlotte spent the next hour in the ER. She was stripped of her clothes, wrapped in warm blankets, and examined by every doctor on duty, most of whom were her friends. They insisted on checking her into a room for the night, just in case her head injury was serious.

When they wheeled her up to her room, she found her mother ordering the nurses to bring her more pillows and blankets. As her mother shouted out commands, telling the nurses that they'd better get their act together, Charlotte's eyes filled with tears.

And then her mother was helping her into her bed. She couldn't remember the last time her mother's hands were on her. They never hugged. They never even touched. But her mom was supporting her weight, then pulling up the blankets around her and tucking them in at her sides, the way she'd done so many years ago.

A tear slipped down the side of her cheek. As she wiped it away, her mother sat down on the bed next to her with a frown. "Are you in pain? Do you need more medication? I'll get the nurse back in here."

"No, it's okay," she said, putting her hand on her mother's arm. "I'm all right."

Her mother's lips tightened, and there was fear behind the anger in her eyes. "What were you thinking, jumping into the middle of a domestic fight? You should have had more sense."

Charlotte let go of her mother's arm, wondering why she'd tried to stop her from leaving. She wasn't really in any state to hear a lecture. "I just wanted to help," she said wearily.

Her mother shook her head, biting down on her lip, and Charlotte was shocked to realize that her mother was about to cry. But she fought it back, and then she said, "Your father would have been so proud of you."

Charlotte's heart stopped. "Really?"

"You're so like him. You just do what needs to be done, no matter what the consequences."

Tears filled her eyes again.

Her mother drew in a big breath. "I'm proud of you, too, Charlotte."

Now the tears streamed down her face. She'd always felt like such a disappointment to her parents. It shouldn't matter anymore what they thought, but it did.

Her mother tucked her hair behind her ear in a loving gesture. "You need a haircut."

Charlotte smiled through her tears. "I know. Mom, would you stay with me for a while—until I fall asleep?"

"Of course," her mother said, blinking back a tear herself. "If I don't stay, Lord knows what kind of care these idiots will give you."

Charlotte closed her eyes, exhaustion finally overtaking her.

When she woke up, sunlight was streaming through the windows, and it wasn't her mother holding her hand anymore, it was Joe. He gave her a tired smile. "You're awake. My early riser. I knew you wouldn't sleep past dawn."

She smiled back at him as he raised her hand and kissed it. "I don't think I'll be running for a few days. I feel sore all over."

"You should stay in bed," he agreed. "Preferably mine."

"It is pretty comfortable." She drew in a breath. "So what's been happening? Did you find Pamela?"

"Yes. She's in a room down the hall with a broken ankle. She'll be going to jail later today."

"Theresa must be devastated."

"She actually didn't seem as shocked as I expected. Maybe down deep, she always suspected Pamela. Anyway, she has her jewelry back and is on the way to a full recovery."

"What's going to happen to Pamela?"

"That will be up to the DA and eventually a jury."

"She did save my life. And I don't know if it was Mitch or Pamela who masterminded the plan."

"She'll have a chance to tell her story. You don't need to worry about her."

"I guess Mrs. Garcia is off the hook now. We were on the wrong track there."

"Not completely. After she realized that both she and Michaela were in the clear, she told me that she'd been afraid that Michaela had done it. That's why she'd tried to protect her. She'd learned that Michaela didn't have the great life she'd imagined when she gave her up for adoption. And when she told Michaela that Edward Worthington was her father, Michaela was bitter that she'd never gotten anything from such a rich man."

"So maybe Pamela just beat Michaela to the goods."

"Maybe," he said with a nod.

"How did you figure out I was with Pamela?" she asked, curious about that piece of the puzzle.

"Andrew came to the station and told me what he knew about her and Mitch and that he suspected they'd had something to do with the robbery. He should have come forward right away. If he had, your life wouldn't have been in danger."

"I'm sure he never anticipated that it would be."

"He was worried that the car that almost ran you down belonged to Mitch. He didn't know if it was deliberate or just drunk driving, which Mitch has been known to do, but he finally stepped up. We went to the inn, saw your car, and the clerk told us she saw you with Pamela. It was Andrew who figured out that you might be at the summer cabins," he added grudgingly.

"I can't believe you worked together without killing each other," she teased.

"We had a more important goal: saving you. He does care about you."

"I know," she said, meeting his gaze. "And I care about him. But I'm in love with you, Joe."

His fingers tightened around her hand.

"I was hanging on to Andrew because he reminded me of the girl I used to be, before I lost the baby and locked away my heart. I thought maybe I could get myself back if I was with him again, but he's different now, and so am I. Actually, we're probably better versions of ourselves now. But Andrew doesn't push me the way you do. He doesn't make me ask more of myself. And I need that. I need you." She drew in a deep breath. "I love you, Joe. You taught me how to take a risk, how to have faith in myself and in others."

"I love you, too, Charlotte. You brought the light back into my life. You reminded me of who I used to be."

"Fearless guy on the skateboard?"

"Yeah, that one," he said tenderly. "I was afraid I'd lost you when Rachel called."

"I didn't want to be the reason you didn't give her another chance."

"I thought you left because she mentioned children," he said somberly.

She nodded. "That did shake me a little. It made me question if I could give you what you really wanted."

He gazed into her eyes. "Charlotte, I want *you*. If it's just you and me, I'm happy with that. If you want children one day, then I'm happy with that, too."

She smiled hesitantly. "I keep imagining having a little boy who looks like you."

"Funny, I keep seeing a little girl with blond hair and a stubborn streak who looks just like you."

"Who are you calling stubborn?" she demanded.

"You. And impulsive, beautiful, amazing, courageous—"

She put her hand over his mouth. "Just kiss me, already. And don't stop for a long, long time."

He smiled and pressed his lips against hers.

EPILOGUE

It was a beautiful day for a wedding, Charlotte thought as she hurried toward the church to make sure everything was in place for the ceremony. Gone was the horrific storm from a week ago. There were no clouds today, only sparkling sunshine. She was glad Lauren had chosen to have a morning wedding; everything was fresh and new and full of promise.

Andrew met her on the steps, wearing his officiating robe and a big smile. They'd had a heart-to-heart talk after she'd come home from the hospital. He had apologized over and over again for not telling her about his past and not going to the cops right away. He'd also come clean with the church board and given a sermon about accepting responsibility for past mistakes.

Charlotte had never been more proud of him. And as for forgiveness, she assured him that it had happened a long time ago. They were both ready now for the rest of their lives, as friends. And judging by how much time Andrew had been spending with Tory lately, she suspected he was already moving on.

"How's the bride?" Andrew asked.

"Nervous but ready. What about the groom?"

"I just told the guys to line up at the front. It's a packed house. Want to see?"

He opened the back door a crack, and she peeked in. She saw her mother, Jamie, and Annie and the baby toward the back. Jason's girlfriend, Brianna, was sitting with her in-laws and her son, Lucas. Isabella, Nick, and Megan were there, with the rest of the theatrical Hartleys. And her heart swelled as she saw Jenna and Riley and their daughter, Lexie. They'd come back to town just for the wedding, another couple who had found love in Angel's Bay.

Andrew shut the door. "I have to admit, I'm a little nervous myself. I've never married two people I've known my entire life."

She kissed him on the cheek. "Break a leg."

"Hey, are you kissing my girl again?" Joe demanded with a confident smile as he walked toward them.

"She kissed me," Andrew retorted, but there was no anger or bitterness in his voice. "I'll see you both inside."

"You weren't jealous, were you?" she asked Joe with a mischievous smile.

"No way. I know you love me."

"I do," she said, kissing him on the lips. "I have to go get the bride."

"I'll miss you."

"You'd better," she said with a laugh, then crossed the courtyard to the bridal dressing room.

The crowd had cleared out. Lauren's mother was seated in the church, leaving only Kara, Lauren, and her dad. He was dressed in a black tuxedo, and his eyes looked alert for the first time in a long time. His Alzheimer's had been stealing his mind away, but for today, he seemed to have won that battle.

"I know you girls want to have a toast," he said. "But my turn first."

Kara handed Charlotte a glass of champagne.

"To my beautiful daughter, Lauren," he said, saying her name with deliberate purpose. "Even when I forget you, I will always remember you here—in my heart." He pressed his palm against his chest. "That's where the memories are."

"Thanks, Daddy," Lauren said, taking a deep, shaky breath. "I wish Abby were here, too."

"Your sister is here, with the other angels. I see them all the time now." He kissed her on the cheek. "Be happy, Lauren."

Kara pulled out a tissue and handed it to Lauren as her father left.

"Okay?" Charlotte asked as Lauren dabbed at her tears.

"He's really with me today. I almost can't believe it."

"Believe it. This is your day," Kara said.

Charlotte lifted her glass. "To friendship and to love."

Lauren and Kara echoed her words, and they clinked their glasses together.

Then, in a swirl of dresses, they walked to the church. Lauren met her dad at the back, he took her arm, and they started down the aisle as the music began to play.

Charlotte gave Kara a hug as they watched. "We're really lucky to have each other."

"And our wonderful men," Kara said. "Colin looks so handsome up there."

"He does," Charlotte agreed, her gaze on Joe. He was sitting on the aisle a few rows up, looking only at her. One day soon, she would walk down the aisle to him.